The Eighth Plague

The Eighth Plague

A Novel

Kyle C. Fitzharris

iUniverse, Inc.
New York   Bloomington

The Eighth Plague

A Political Thriller

iUniverse books may be ordered through booksellers or by contacting:

iUniverse
1663 Liberty Drive
Bloomington, IN 47403
www.iuniverse.com
1-800-Authors (1-800-288-4677)

ISBN: 978-0-595-52404-4 (pbk)
ISBN: 978-0-595-51225-6 (cloth)
ISBN: 978-0-595-62457-7 (ebk)

Printed in the United States of America

iUniverse rev. date: 11/26/08

To Áine, who showed me my true strength.

Prologue

This is a good day to die.

The hallucinations came in waves as the man tossed and turned in the tattered cot. His body sank deep into the blood-stained canvas of the homemade stretcher that was now his bed, its support rods resting on piles of bricks that kept him just slightly above the dust-covered floor.

Sweat beaded on his forehead, first trickling then racing down his temples to make room for the next round as moisture percolated from every pore. His fever was high; his body dehydrated, broken, and limp. All the man could think of, while passing in and out of consciousness, was how he wished he were stronger.

He had prepared himself for the inevitability of death, but he wasn't prepared for the long, slow agony that added insult to fatal injury. He wasn't prepared to witness the soul-crushing spectacle of his fellow man suffering in this ramshackle hospital, with nothing more than shredded bedclothes for bandages and a few black iron kettles to boil water for sterilization.

This is a good day to die.

He must have whispered it as he went under again.

The phrase was haunting him now as he remembered lying flat on his back in the rust-rotted bed of an old pickup truck. The pitted desert roads hadn't helped his condition. Every pothole and bump caused him to recoil from the searing pain that coursed through his body. In his delirium, he envisioned a Great Plains Indian brave galloping full-speed into battle, bareback on his most prized pinto, its mane and his pigtail blown straight back by the wind. He could see the brave turn his face to the sun and with a guttural battle cry roar:

This is a good day to die.

But he was not given to such fits of bravado. He was no rollicking, fearless Indian brave. He could see this all too clearly now as his own garbled fever screams shocked him into moments of clarity.

Just before entering the hospital, his head hanging at an odd angle so that one eye was just able to see above the rocking stretcher, the man had taken in the sun-drenched town square he was being rushed across. With roiling mind and rolling eyes, he had just managed to capture a detailed snapshot of his surroundings, like a postcard from the 1800's: a Mexican village lost in time, a circle of white stucco and red clay hovels surrounding a dusty plaza whose centerpiece was an enormous, ornate fountain surmounted by an imposing statue. No pavement. No sidewalks. No theaters. No grocery stores. No cars or electrical wires. The brightness of the sun had made him blink. As the background had come into blurred focus, he could just make out stony-faced villagers hauling water in bloated goatskin bags, one dripping bladder on each end of the sticks they nimbly balanced across their shoulders. In the distance, children splashed, women washed clothes and old men bathed in the same aqueduct where the dark bladders were filled with the village's drinking water.

If he hadn't been delirious, he would have recognized this village—especially the looming old fountain in the center of the square, fed by its own underground spring, the only other source of water here in the desert besides the government-run canal system.

If he hadn't been delirious, he would have recognized this parched area of Mexico, locally known as the Badlands. He would have remembered that this part of the Chiapas state was unlike the often windy and moist jungle terrain that surrounded it. Here, the air was always thick and hot. Dry and still. Stifling. The slightest breeze like a god descending to earth.

But the man didn't know where he was. Or who he was, for that matter. Or even if he were alive or dead. Was he dreaming?

Inside now, golden slivers of sunlight streamed through the dusty slats of old wooden window shutters. Sometimes the air pooled and became surprisingly cool in the weird, forgotten corner his body now inhabited. Sometimes he could see shadows cast over the ridges of the aged stucco walls as they moved, strange and slow. Circular. Linear. Still. There was a muted sound of water dripping very slowly, far, far away, and it made him feel so lonely that he would swear the place was haunted. He was lucid only in sporadic spurts throughout the day and night, but when he was—in those seconds or fractions thereof—all his senses were severely heightened, straining to take in all they could before the curtain came inevitably crashing down again.

Even in his deepest torpor, the endless chorus of soft grunts and moans from those around him pierced the veil of fever and darted around his par-boiled brain like old, angry ghosts. He knew he could never truly rest here, never be sure if he were asleep or awake or perpetually imprisoned in a bad dream.

In an effort to take his mind off things, he fantasized, imagining what it would have been like in Auschwitz or on a slave ship. In those situations, would he have been man enough, just once, to have stood up and fought for his freedom?

"I am a fighter!" he screamed inside his head. But it did no good, seeing as he lay helpless on the tiny cot, sandwiched tightly between other tiny cots full of fellow rotting flesh sacks, riddled with intravenous tubes and completely unable to latch on to anything like a concrete fact.

Why was he here? How had he come to this godforsaken place?

The man wanted to ask someone these questions. There, that young woman over there. The one who always seemed to be staring at him during his moments of consciousness. For hours, it seemed, she had been standing there coddling and cooing at a baby in swaddling, her supple, tan skin glowing through her drab, starched uniform with the light of a million stars; staring at him and only him, and with such a magnificent glint of grace and goodness in her eyes. Surely she would tell him what he needed to know, if only he could…

Suddenly he shocked himself by shouting out loud, "Where am I? Somebody, where am I?"

His own voice sounded alien to him. The glowing woman laid the infant down in a makeshift crib and glided to the man's bedside. He now believed he was in heaven, and she was his own personal angel.

"You're safe," she said, with the kind of mellifluous voice he'd always imagined his guardian angel might have. "Please do not move."

She dipped a towel in the wash basin and wrung it out in one elegant move, then wiped the man's face to cool the fever. He slowly calmed, still delirious, but relaxed under the moist towel and the gentleness of her touch. She stared at the silver Saint Christopher's medallion still safe around his neck, then looked into his eyes as though they'd met before. Her touch stirred something oddly familiar within him, but he could not focus on her face.

"Sleep now," she said.

With that, she passed one perfectly sculpted hand over his eyes like a hypnotist, or like the angel she very well may have been. And before the man drifted off into a sweeter sleep than he had known in ages, he began to remember.

I

The windows at the *Washington Post* allowed us to see about anything that happened in D.C., and my desk commanded one of the best views. I calmly watched rush-hour traffic crawl across the Potomac Bridge and snake over the Beltway into the city while the other reporters in the newsroom hustled and bustled around like a bunch of idiot early birds all after the same worm. I used to have a corner office when I was a real hotshot, no-bullshit, stand-up journalist. It was private. Dignified. Since then, I haven't allowed myself to be that idealistic.

The day all this started was a particularly routine one. As usual, I was watching the miniature rat race in the newsroom with bemused detachment. I was the antithesis of the other *Post* reporters. Those clowns were already red in the face, yelling and cursing, furiously speed dialing and taking out their frustration on their handsets, headphones, speakers—whatever they could hit or throw. They pathetically begged sources to confirm their stories as they hunted down leads, desperate to secure all details before deadline. Every one of them wanted to be a star, but the only way to do that was to dazzle and amaze and always, always, meet the deadline. I refused to take part in this willful invocation of chaos.

It was about that time of the morning I'd always get my best shut-eye. If I didn't catch a wink or two before noon, my hangover could last well into the evening, which could really affect my regular drinking schedule. I had a way of folding my arms and propping my chin up that dependably led novices to believe I had been burning the midnight oil, when really I'd been up all night at Callahan's or Writer's Block, out on the piss.

Everything was going great. I was dreaming about some distant, exotic country ablaze with burning debris, where I frantically scribbled down notes while bullets whizzed past me from all sides. Ah, the good ol' days... Then, suddenly, some red-cheeked, ass-kissing newbie bumped my desk and tore me from dreamland.

"Mr. Riley, sorry to interrupt you, you were probably here all night working on yet another incredible story, but Kate Walker over there asked me to get your okay on this memo."

I looked up and sneered at the twenty-something intern, who was already shaking in his overpriced loafers and looking like he was about to take a dump for having to disturb me. Just to add to my reputation, I swiped the paper from him with a growl. I opened the memo and read its vital contents: *Wake your ass up and get to work.* I looked up at the intern and gave a single nod of approval. He quickly scampered from my sight. Without even looking across to the author, I put my head back down on my desk. I felt a slight tap on my head. Then another. Then two more. Shit. My day was, unfortunately, beginning. I ran my fingers through my hair and looked up just in time to see four or five spit-wads fall to the desk. I turned to give Walker a dirty look. She was happy enough with herself by now. "You're pathetic," she mouthed, unseen by anyone else.

Kate Walker was one of what I considered a "new breed" of women. She was too young to remember the struggles of the seventies, so she took sexual equality for granted—a first generation modern woman, with no ax to grind and no hang-ups about her own power or place in the world. Because of this, she wasn't a pain-in-the-ass feminist like I'd seen or interviewed or mistakenly slept with over the years. Yeah, she was independent and all that crap, but she was a real woman, too, when she wasn't breaking my balls.

She stood about five feet, seven inches tall; slender, with a nice pair of tits and an ass you could melt butter on. Of course, that's only what I'd heard everybody else say. I was always strictly professional with her. No office politics or sexual harassment here. No sir, it was all business. At least on my end.

She giggled like a schoolgirl and tossed her long brunette hair over her shoulder. Sitting on the edge of her desk with her legs entwined, she dug deep into a Chinese take-out box with a pair of chopsticks. Was it lunch time already? She never seemed to wear a dress, just slacks and durable sneakers. Cut from the Kate Hepburn pattern: cocky and acerbic but a helluva good writer, with great instinct to boot. She had a crush on me, but I was pretty sure she would die rather than admit it.

"Charlie's gonna can your ass if you don't shape up," she mumbled through a mouthful of noodles. "You know you should really…"

A hot, wet noodle slid onto her white blouse, splattering teriyaki sauce across her left breast. "Son of a bitch!" she shouted.

I never said she was a lady.

From three desks over, a shrill but familiar sound assaulted my ears: "Riley! Line one!" The placard on her desk read: *Jean Smiley - Associate Editor*. Next to it was a *No smoking* sign and an ashtray overflowing with smoldering butts. She was a veteran of the news game and she looked the part.

"Who is it?" I asked.

"Another death threat! This one's gonna blow up your car or your cat or something. You know I can't understand these psychos."

I smacked my lips. Man, did I need a drink. "Put him in my voice mail."

Thin, wrinkly lips stretched taut to expose repulsive yellow teeth as Jean snarled, "Just because I have a pair of tits doesn't mean I'm your damn secretary." To further illustrate her already obvious point, she grabbed her breasts and shook them at me in a burlesque parody. "Got it?!" Then she let out a violent huff of a sigh and buried her head back in a pile of copy.

"Jesus, you're sick." Kate didn't bother to look up as she dabbed at her blouse with a napkin drenched in club soda. "You know, one of these days, one of those sickos is gonna really come after you," she mumbled, her chin buried deep in her cleavage as she concentrated on cleansing the offending teriyaki stain.

I reached for the Styrofoam cup at the edge of my desk and scanned the room for any digestible liquid. Ah, coffee. "Would you rather get feedback from an eight-year-old kid in Bum-Fuck, Maryland or decent criticism from a stalker that has followed your career and could possibly have insight that the normal reading public doesn't?" I knew that was an unassailable justification for any real reporter.

Kate just looked at me, confused, with pity-filled eyes, and said, "Oh, Terry, you need professional help."

I took a swig of the coffee I'd found. Before I could swallow, I spit it out quickly into the trash. "Blah! I hate cold coffee!" I said as I wiped my tongue with a fast-food napkin. Kate pointed to the placard on my desk. It read: *Terry Riley - Senior Political Reporter*. Then she tapped her watch. "Aren't you forgetting something?" she said. I shrugged, trying to dismiss her without being too rude. Her eyes widened and she threw her chin towards me. "Senator Pritchard... in the square... today?" I looked at my watch. Damn, late again.

As if on cue, a large wooden door opened across the room. This was the office of Charlie Petersen, Editor-in-Chief. The shadow of his enormous belly preceded him into the bullpen. Charlie Petersen was the bane of my existence: obese, balding and always chomping a cigar. A cheap cigar, no less. It dangled from his lower lip as he bellowed, "Riley, goddamn it! If you miss another press conference you'll be writing copy for the Junior League by sundown, I shit you not!"

He hadn't yet seen me, so I had time to duck under my desk like a high school kid trying to avoid another visit to the principal's office. Pretty wimpy, I know, but I've never been brave unless I absolutely had to be. I began to make a dash for the door then realized I had forgotten the tools of my trade.

Kate always enjoyed my misery. It was her vicarious way of castigating me. As was usual in these cases, she supported me in a constructive fashion by shooting paper clips at my hand and spit-wads at my head. I reached up from under my desk and felt my way across the top: Let's see…note pad, good, microcassette tape recorder and, of course, the jewel of my kit, my gold pen.

I scrambled down an aisle, crab-legging it as quickly as I could, hoping I would pass Kate's desk without incident. *Wham!* She kicked me in the guts as I crawled by—not too hard, just a tough-love tap.

"Remember, deadline's at seven sharp! I'm not bailing you out this time." Again with the schoolgirl giggling. That was starting to get to me. It was no fair Kate being such a hard-ass and a shameless flirt at the same time.

II

The village with the huge, ornate fountain in its plaza was called San Cristobal. It was a backward, inhospitable, poverty-stricken place with little hope of advancement, and the hospice across the plaza from the fountain was just a crumbling, old adobe with little to no medicinal or technical resources—no reason to glamorize it. It couldn't be called a proper hospital with its makeshift appearance. It had been gutted to make a large hall capable of housing three or four dozen people, but not comfortably. Although the room was long, it was barely wide enough for two long rows of narrow cots crammed closely together, with a one-lane footpath down the center.

The only luxury in the whole place, provided you could stand squarely on your own bare feet, was the divinely cool floor—cooler than any other surface on the premises and kept that way by the thick hard-pack of clay that covered it. If walking was out of the question depending upon the advancement of your disease, you might be lucky enough to fall out of bed and land on your face on that soothingly cool floor. To feel the sensation of coolness against your skin, your cheeks, your mouth, just one more time: That was God. That was heaven. It was a final wish worth the selling of your soul.

Worn mattresses seemed to support the rusted rails of the beat-up frames beneath them, while atop, a threadbare blanket was the only source of privacy, warmth or possession most patients could claim. The older nuns allocated what little actual bedding there was to the worst cases near the end, like last meals. The formerly clean sheets had slowly turned from a pristine, sanitized white to their current iodized rust, the old weeping hue of blood, as patient after patient had struggled to survive, ultimately losing the battle.

The sour smells of bleach and antiseptic permeated the stagnant air, yet nothing ever seemed clean. Everything was bland and colorless, a grayish sepia tone, except, of course, the blood. There was always plenty of that. Red, red blood.

The lucky ones—the old, the newborn—bled from their rectums quickly, expiring within a couple days. They avoided the anguish of suffering for too long as their fluids poured out of their every orifice. Others languished slowly, blood weeping here and draining there, keeping them just alive enough to experience real agony, until this thing had finally gnawed away their very beings. Yet here, in the wizened heart of the Mexican Badlands, the uneducated villagers of San Cristobal were wrapped in the embrace of Christ himself. They believed that he and God and the Holy Spirit would band together in their support, always and forever. Or until they turned up one morning as withered, bloodless corpses.

Unlike the cholera that was common to this part of Mexico, this bug should've been classified a "super virus." Like Ebola or any of the old hemorrhagic fevers of the Congo, this outbreak literally bled people dry. It was a nasty little fucker. A vampire on a bender. Bloodletting as a sport. Waste it, who cares? There's another poor slob in the next bed to keep you amused.

A young nun walked the length of the hospice hall, her white linen headdress flapping on either side of her face like wings. It—the walking, the flapping—or perhaps she, Isabella, had a calming effect on the suffering patients. Passing in and out of the shadows, she would appear, disappear then reappear as she entered each section of the hospice. The patients stared at her, seemingly transfixed, as she approached, passed and disappeared into the distance. Sometimes one of them would reach up as if to receive some kind of salvation or benediction from her. It was a futile gesture, really. Where they were, at that point, there were no more bargains to be made with God, no way to somehow stave off the painfully inevitable. It was just death and dying: full stop. But Isabella's calm gait and warm smile and crisply starched habit placated them, and that was enough. Some of them swore she was an angel as they slipped away.

In her arms, Isabella carried a small bundle wrapped in a gray tattered blanket. It could've been a bundle of flowers or some groceries except for the fact that she held it so tightly to her breast, like a new mother, walking with a sense of urgency, just a bit quicker than normal. A look of concern stretched her usually pleasant features into an exaggerated grimace. She looked dog-tired. Not angelic at all. But no one was going to convince her many dying fans of that.

At the end of the large room, the soft, ambient light shone on a short, balding man: Father Pedro Gonzalez. In his crude burlap frock and rope belt, he looked more like a humble monk than the proper Catholic priest he was. Around his neck was a large, finely carved wood crucifix. It was obviously a valuable relic, and though it was simple, it looked almost garish on this simple, poverty-sworn man. It preceded him, swaying slightly, as he leaned over the unmoving body of a woman in one of the hospice cots. At first glance she might have seemed a normal, if pale, woman in her late thirties or early forties, her tan skin not yet ruined by the sun or thinned from age. But upon closer inspection, it was clear that this disease or malady or whatever it was had stolen all traces of her inner light and left an empty shell. Void. Gone.

At her side, an old, weathered man knelt and comforted her, holding her tiny hand as if it were as fragile as a hummingbird's egg. He had a kind look, a gentle look; not a look to be confused with weakness but a caring, truthful look. He was in his early sixties, but his strong, worn features made him appear older. His short, thick, farmer's fingers gently rubbed the woman's delicate hand in a circular motion, to calm her, to give her peace. It was a natural human gesture that offered little more than last-minute solace. There was no dramatic final gasp or tell-tale tensing of muscles; only a single tear that slowly ran down the woman's expressionless face as she expired.

Suddenly, Isabella appeared at the priest's side. She crossed herself, speaking Spanish in a soft, respectful tone: "*Padre! Madre de Dios,* please bless this poor child."

Without skipping a beat, Father Gonzalez passed his hand over the eyes of the dead woman and closed them. He mumbled a quick prayer, made the sign of the cross over her corpse then turned to the young nun. He left his hands in the air, ready to make a new blessing without hesitation.

Isabella unwrapped the bundle to reveal a small gray mass. It was a prematurely born infant that couldn't have weighed more than a few pounds. Pasty and blue, its eyes were sealed with a thin film of tissue, never having opened at birth, not even for a moment, not even for a tiny glimpse of the world they would never see. Isabella pressed her eyelids together tightly as a tear poured down her cheek. There were plenty of tears in this place now. Plenty of tragedies and paradoxes to cry over. Plenty of death.

Father Gonzalez took a small clay bowl from a nearby stool and dipped his thumb in, rubbing the bottom to get the tip of his finger wet. The holy water was nearly gone from all the blessings that day, but he proceeded out of repetition and duty. He placed his damp thumb on the child's head, and made a small *t*. With his other hand he did the same, but with a grandiose gesture in the air, covering double the length of the baby's body.

"In the name of the Father, and of the Son, and of the Holy Spirit, Amen," he muttered under his breath. He bent over the child and kissed it softly on the forehead.

Just then, the old man stood up and broke the silence. He reached over to a small nightstand and grabbed a worn and yellowed straw hat—the kind a farmer or gardener might wear. He glanced down at the dead woman in the bed, plucked the hat up and shoved it firmly onto his head. Then he sharply turned and walked past the priest, snapping, "It is time."

The old man was Doctor Alberto Ramos. He was *Jefe*. The Chief. This was his hospital, but you wouldn't know it by his humility. There were no signs on the doors or windows, no markings, no commercial endorsements whatsoever. This place had successfully avoided the trappings of capitalism and made a go of it anyway. As a not surprising result, it habitually suffered from a lack of funds—a lack of everything, for that matter.

Doctor Ramos never ruled with an iron fist, nor did he flaunt his power or station in the village hierarchy. He never stepped out of line and took fastidious care of the many nuns who were his life helpers, his nursing staff, cleaning crew, cooks and confidants. He had a capacity and a duty to accept anyone and everyone into his life and into his heart. He took everything that happened to someone else, anyone else, personally. Very personally. He was a man of uncompromising ethics and loyalty.

He was once a tall man once, but years of backbreaking work and osteoporosis had cut his frame down by thirty percent. Now he looked like a Mexican version of Quasimodo, complete with hunched shoulders, a shattered spine and bowed legs.

In order to carry on a conversation, Doctor Ramos would be forced to tilt his head to either side to look you directly in the eye. It wasn't hard to look back at this disfigured man. His eyes were soft within his mangled features, his smile infectious. Once you saw it, you saw that he was a kind man and a loyal man, a man that would go to the wall for you.

He was weary from months of non-stop death and blood, and his gait was slow, yet determined, as he hobbled toward the front of the building. It wasn't a matter of loving or hating his work. There was no choice for Doctor Ramos; he had to do the job. Period. People, his people, were dying all around him, and he had to save them, or at least do his best to try.

Father Gonzalez appeared next to him, walking quickly to catch up like an obsequious handmaiden, his crucifix swinging back and forth across his chest. He could have reached out and stopped Doctor Ramos with a simple tap on the shoulder, but instead placed his hands together as if to pray and shook them in desperation. "Please, Doctor, please, we need you here," the priest pleaded.

Doctor Ramos never broke stride. Blinding light and waves of dry heat scorched his eyes and poured into the darkened room as he opened the front door. Father Gonzalez was forced to cover his eyes momentarily, then noticed that the doctor looked distinctly angelic with his silhouette illuminated in the bright, open doorway. Maybe this was some kind of omen, the priest briefly thought, but before he could regain his faculties, another object crossed his field of vision. A young woman approached the doctor and handed him a black leather medical bag. She reached out and threw her arms around him in a tight embrace. "Oh, Papa," she said as her eyes welled and tears streamed down her face.

Maria Ramos was the doctor's only daughter. In her late twenties, her smooth brown facial features perfectly topped off her lean frame. Her figure would have been enviable to any woman, but it was her hair that was special. It flowed long and black down her back, no waves or curls—it was just naturally straight, and thick, with an iridescent sheen to it. Everything about Maria Ramos was natural, including her true, inner beauty, which outshone even her stunning good looks. She was a knockout with a heart of gold.

Her dress looked more like a nurse's uniform than a nun's habit. Plain, brown, simple in the lines, durable. The only distinction was a thin rope belt and a tiny gold crucifix pinned to her lapel. Maria was a novice, a nun who had not yet taken final vows. Whether by choice or because she was still studying, she had not yet totally committed her life to Christ.

In the doorway, Doctor Ramos took the medical bag and softly kissed Maria's cheek, wiping the tears from her face with his thumbs. Her eyes were big and brown but their whites were laced with bright red. She looked worn out to him: perhaps a bit anemic, perhaps worse. Had she been eating enough during this stressful time or was she, too, getting the sickness?

The dark circles under her eyes bespoke her tireless strength and resolution, but made him worry for her health. Yet he could not deny there was determination in that tired face of hers, and that was her driving force. As Doctor Ramos gazed deeply at her one last time, he realized he had never been so proud of his daughter than at that very minute. She could have stopped him easily with a tug of his sleeve like she had as a child, or made some dramatic gesture that would have torn at his heart, but she knew his dedication to helping others was greater than her love for him.

A small boy of about four slowly appeared from behind Maria's skirt, breaking the tension. He was called Pepe. With an innocent grin, he rolled his doe-like eyes and cocked his head to one side as though he had been playing hide-and-seek and was now revealing himself. Doctor Ramos looked down and smiled. Pepe slowly pulled a brown paper sack from behind his back and offered it to him. Curious, Doctor Ramos placed the black medical bag on the ground and took the sack from the boy. Opening it, he suspiciously spied its contents, then playfully raised an eyebrow as he reached in and pulled out a large yellow tortilla chip. After taking a bite, he winked at the boy and rolled the bag closed with one hand.

Doctor Ramos opened the medical bag to place the paper sack inside, but instead retrieved a large manila envelope that read: *East L.A. Mission, Alvarado Avenue, Los Angeles, California. Attention: Doctor Carlos Ramos.* He handed the envelope to Maria and squeezed her hand.

Just as he turned to exit, Father Gonzalez began to bargain with the old man: "Doctor Ramos, please stay. There is no moon tonight and the roads will be dark. The ancient ruins cast strange shadows over the weary traveler."

The doctor embraced the priest then leaned in to whisper, "I thought men of God weren't superstitious. Light a candle for me, old friend."

With that, Doctor Ramos turned and walked outside toward the center of the village. Father Gonzalez had to block Maria from following as tears welled again in her eyes. She shouted, "Papa!"

III

D.C. is a bland city, even when it's not raining. Oh sure, there's the wooded parks, the mall, and all the marble statues and monuments, but at street level it's kind of dingy like Manhattan or Cleveland—or even downtown L.A. Why couldn't the Capitol be in Billings, Montana? I ran just fast enough to not break a sweat. The other reporters were already at the steps of the Senate, ready for the assault.

I used to love press conferences. The energy. The fanfare. The pomp and circumstance. The reporters, the spectators, even the Secret Service agents buried in the crowd. A good press conference took on a life of its own. It surged like one being. You'd see dozens of reporters vying for position like stock car racers or marathon runners. Civilians, as I called them, regular folks just there to get a glimpse of their favorite political celebrity, would come out in droves. Ted Kennedy, Mike Huckabee, hell, even Chief Justice Scalia—all of them were more popular than any film actor in this town.

But the other reporters were the ones I really loved. They'd always be just this side of rude as they shoved and pushed their way into the fray for the ideal strategic position. Paparazzi? They're a bunch of pussies compared to an ambitious journalist with his eye on a byline.

It was all about position in Washington. If you weren't under a politician, you had to have something over him. News was the great equalizer and newsies were the enforcers. If a candidate or congressman pissed us off or didn't play ball, didn't shoot straight with us, we'd wipe them clean off the face of the political map. And that was death. Political suicide.

Deep down, everybody hates reporters, and why not? We pry and dig into the private lives of our quarry, splash their faces on the front page and smear their reputations if they don't please us. Of course, we exalt those who interest us for a time, then we send them into oblivion by keeping them out of the press or crucify them when they tire us. It's not just a job—it's an aberration.

I could see Pritchard as I hustled to get a better spot. The Senate has a lot of steps. Every reporter in D.C. learns that the hard way. Screw bounding up them just to suck wind and be out of breath right as your guy is coming out of the revolving doors. We let the bastards come to us now. Maybe it's a small concession to our true power, but maybe it's just more practical to place the podium halfway down the stairs.

Even the reporters were listening intently to the forked-tongue speechifying of Senator Daniel Pritchard, Democrat from the great state of Missouri. The "Show-Me State." Yeah, show me to a toilet.

It was no trade secret that Pritchard and I were sworn enemies. We didn't actually swear it, but the fact that my ex-wife, Marilyn, filed for divorce two months after becoming one of his "consultants"—after years of him hitting on her—was a clear enough pact of enmity for both of us.

He was in his early fifties by now, and he had this bullshit, down-home country drawl that would melt the panties off any post-teen coed. Interns like Monica Lewinski and Chandra Levy were prime targets for this letch. Sure, he was strong and poignant and dressed like an Italian suit designer, but I knew he was dirty. Filthy dirty. The problem was that I couldn't prove it.

Each time hands flew up in the air for another question, I pushed my way further into the fray. One question usually equaled two to three steps. I was on a roll, my timing impeccable.

"Ouch!" said a rookie from the *Herald* as I stepped on his cheap shoes in an attempt to advance my career. "Hey, what are you doing?"

I never broke stride as I laughed, "You gotta get up earlier than that, Kid, if you want to get a scoop." I could feel him gritting his teeth in frustration as I settled into a cushy spot just close enough to the podium to screw everything up. I'm a prick, I admit it.

"I'm tell'n y'all, I'm excited about this conference next week in Mexico City," Pritchard began. He animated each sentence like a marionette puppeteer. "This will be the first ever International Ecological Conference and the first time a real global commitment will be made to our future. A commitment to safeguard our fragile environment. A commitment to protect the citizens of this planet we call Earth." The crowd began to cheer as reporters furiously scribbled notes on their worn pads.

"Some of the brightest men and women from around the globe are gonna convene to discuss the major ecological problems that are plague'n our world today. We're gonna have us a serious pow-wow and get right down to solv'n these problems once and for all," Pritchard orated. A reporter salvoed back, "Senator Pritchard, what problems will you focus on?" Duh! What a lame question. A rookie question. I was just waiting for my cue.

"Well, Peter, we'll start with some of Global Warming's contributors and be discuss'n the worldwide impact of that terrible fire that swept through Mexico and destroyed over a million acres of virgin rainforest. We'll cover the updates issued by NAFTA to regulate pollution south of the border, as well as the depletion of our world's natural resources. Hell, Son, I'm gonna tire 'em out with everything I've got to say," Pritchard said smugly. Other reporters laughed in a disingenuous, kiss-ass manner. I couldn't help but roll my eyes at the cheese factor.

"But Senator, why have the conference in Mexico City?" inquired another journalist. "After all, it's notoriously the world's most overpopulated city, with the worst living conditions and pollution levels on earth. Not to mention the twentieth century's worst ecological disaster."

Not bad, I thought. This one's got potential. She tried to get him off balance, but she didn't ask the big question.

"That's just the point, Kathy. If there's one place on earth that can benefit from a summit of this kind, it's Mexico City." He segued into a new tack now that he had his audience riveted: "You know, Congress asked me that same question when we proposed our AMERIMEX Water Purification and Aqueduct Project. A few years ago those folks liv'n just outside Mexico City were bath'n and drink'n the same water that was being used for sewage. There were no treatment facilities, no purifiers to speak of. If you recall, I designed the AMERIMEX System, that clean-water project, with the help of my environmental task force and some buddies at the EPA." Pritchard half-turned as he said his last line and pointed to a tall, lean, African-American man in a smartly tailored blue suit. His hair was short and he had deep set eyes—the kind of eyes that made you unsure whether he was a nice guy or a real asshole.

Pritchard continued: "That's when I liberated my right-hand man, Dexter Grace. Hell, a biology lab is no place for a young politician." Waving Grace to his side, he added, "Yawl know my right-hand man, Dex, don't ya?" Pritchard plopped his hand down on Dexter's shoulder as he stepped up to take his place next to the senator.

I'd seen his Ivy League resumé in the updated press kit: Cornell grad in Medical Science turned senator's aide, Dexter Grace. Mid-thirties. Single—no surprise there. Ambitious. Tight-assed. I didn't know Dexter. Never met the man. But any ally of Pritchard's was an enemy of mine. And you can quote me on that!

Dexter Grace hesitantly leaned into the microphone and said, "How can you argue with a man like this?" The crowd of supporters roared.

Fuck! Why don't you just whip it out for the groupies? The only thing keeping me there at that point was the fantasy of somehow bringing down this guy's boss, the wolf in sheep's clothing. I was clearly in the minority.

Dexter stepped back as Pritchard returned to the mic. "With the help of scientists and engineers, we've built a revolutionary water treatment facility that allows clean, fresh water to flow throughout all of Mexico." His Senatorship seemed to be building to a crescendo. "We pushed it through Congress at the begin'n of my first term because it was that important!" He slammed his fist down hard in time with the last two words to drive his point home.

I started snickering again just as Dexter drew a bead on me with his shark-like eyes. There was no love lost between the two of us. He had his job to do and I had mine. He knew who I was: the enemy. But they needed me. Neither one of us would give up an inch. We played on opposite teams.

I decided to strike at that very moment. I sent my lucky gold pen straight into the air as the crowd was busy doting over Pritchard. "Senator Pritchard," I shouted over the din of blatant kiss-ass-ery, "this sounds more like a presidential campaign speech than a press conference. Rumors are floating around Washington that you plan on throwing your hat into the ring come next election. Care to comment?" Ha! I had him now. I'd picked my moment well. He had no choice but to answer yes or no, and he couldn't shy away from it at the risk of embarrassment in the press. He wouldn't be able to finish the press conference and get all his policy out there now because all focus would be on my question. Will he or won't he? I was able to steal that prime moment of glory from him by announcing it before he could. For one second, I was very pleased with myself. Sleep with my wife, will you?

He tried the old "laugh it off so no one notices" technique. "Well, now, now, Mr. Riley, you oughtta know better than to be listening to D.C. scuttlebutt. You shoulda double-checked your sources before go'n off half-cocked with a question like that." He gave a quick, stern leer at Dexter then faked a martyred look to the audience. Talk about bad acting. "My supporters know my only agenda is to manage the programs we've designed in order to stabilize a world on the brink of ecological Armageddon." That was his answer? I wasn't going to let him off the hook that easily.

"But Senator, what about those hidden agendas of yours? Public records and the Freedom of Information Act show you're directly linked to numerous politicians at home and abroad who are unscrupulous, to say the least. Let's face it—you're in bed with criminals. FIO documents and e-mail correspondence describe your pals in Mexico as having started those fires in the rainforests to burn out the Zapatistas in Chiapas and the surrounding areas. All the rebels were doing were peacefully protesting the government over their strict, oppressive laws and murderous racism." I had everybody's attention now and I could see some of the foreign press guys hammering their iPhones and Treos with worn styluses to call their editors and scoop my information.

Before Pritchard could open his mouth, I gave him my final answer. "And what about the companies you own in the U.S. and overseas that helped get you and keep you in office? Do they practice what you preach? I don't think the United States can afford such benevolence, do you, Senator?" Never, never mess with another man's wife.

Pritchard's mood changed from down-home diplomacy to downright pissed-off. Just then, from behind him, this vision of beauty walked up, placed her hand on his arm and squeezed. Jennifer Hoover was a voluptuous blonde; a staff member in her late twenties who looked like she had been taking more than dictation.

Pritchard winked back at her support then turned to me with anger in his eyes. "It's that kinda muck-rake'n yellow journalism that only sells tabloids, not newspapers, Son! I know the American public can see through those fabricated allegations." He looked at Dexter as though he had an ace up his sleeve. "I'm surprised you haven't learned to stop recklessly slander'n politicians after what you did to Senator Foster. Smear campaigns can't faze Dan Pritchard, remember that!"

All eyes were on me, now. That son of a bitch had turned the tables. What he said hit a nerve and everyone around me knew what Pritchard was talking about. Bam. Right between the eyes. I felt the blow like a baseball bat to the head. I was listing and wouldn't right myself today, not in front of these piranhas. At least I'd still gotten a jab in.

Pritchard took a step back as Dexter walked up to the podium. "Ladies and gentlemen, this press conference is over. The senator has a long trip ahead of him. See you when we return from Mexico. Thank you all for coming. Press kits are at the front," he said matter-of-factly. As Dexter and the other staffers whisked Pritchard away, he turned to give me one last glare. Yeah, up yours, too!

The crowd had already started to disperse. A couple of reporters bumped me on the way out. Rawlings from the *Times*, whose timing was always off, stepped up and snickered,   "Riley, you asshole, don't you know he's been waiting to trump you in public? Man, you just opened the door for him." Rawlings looked at his watch. "Aren't you gonna be late for happy hour? You oughta stick to drinking. You're better at it than journalism." He stopped for a female reporter to pass in front of him on the way down the steps. Big mistake. I couldn't resist. I gave him a little shove… Don't worry, he didn't fall too far.

I was nursing my pride on the walk back to my car when I heard a voice coming up from behind me. I turned to see an enthusiastic-looking man in a trench coat and big black horn-rims approaching. I thought, is this guy a fan or a stalker? Just in case, I stopped and planted my feet, readying myself to hear what he had to say.

"Wow! That was great," he said, huffing as he slowly caught up to me. "Too bad you didn't bring up the sex scandal—it was just getting good." I felt he wasn't too much of a threat so I started walking. He walked with me.

"It's against my religion," I said. He was like a Jack Russell Terrier jumping up and down as he stayed in pace with my step. "You're Riley, Terry Riley, with the *Post*, right?"

Here it comes. A single gunshot behind the ear, a knife in the square of my back. "Who wants to know?" I said in my best Humphrey Bogart.

"Come on, you're him aren't you?" He said begging.

"Terrence Francis Xavier Riley, of the Chicago Rileys, by way of Tralee, County Kerry, Ireland, if you must know." It was probably way too much information for him, but he was beginning to bore me and now I was close to my car. If he was going to kill me, I wished he'd done it by now. It was close to happy hour.

He reached into his vest pocket slowly. Here it comes. Let's get this over with. He pulled out something: a long, folded piece of paper. Ah, the poor slob just wanted an autograph, I thought. I guess I'd been on edge so long, I was beginning to get paranoid, suspicious of everyone.

Without looking down, I pulled out my gold pen. "Who's this for?" I said, about to give him my John Hancock.

He chuckled and said, "Marilyn, your ex-wife. She said you'd be here today hounding Pritchard. Here, you've been duly served."

Son of a bitch… a summons.

The process server laughed, then turned and walked away. I stood there dumbfounded and pissed off for a moment, the paper moistening from the sweat in my palm, then swore skyward at my ex-wife. The damnable upshot of it was that I spent so much time pitying myself, I never noticed the large black Mercedes that pulled up and parked across from my car. It was just not going to be my day.

IV

Boomba rode hard across the desert as he led the other twenty or so outlaws toward the tiny village of San Cristobal. He was considered an outlaw—not by his own people or others who knew what his people had endured for so many years, but by the Mexican government, the very ones who were sworn to protect their people.

They were *Zapatistas*, rebels named after Ernesto Zapata, a revolutionary war hero who, like themselves, had been betrayed. Boomba and his band came from all around the State of Chiapas: Tila and Salta de Agua in the north, Sapanilla, Los Positas—the last bastions of indigenous Mayan Indians and, with the exception of the Aztecs, the original people of Mexico.

They were called rebels, outlaws, scourge, because they fought not to monger war or win power, but to raise attention and garner consideration for eons of oppression. Until recently, there were even laws in the Mexican Constitution that forbade any Indian from walking on the sidewalk in the presence of a "Latin," a Mexican with pure or mixed Spanish blood. Indians were required to walk in the street, avert their eyes, and had better be dressed in their native clothing or face harsh retribution. Nazi Germany had laws like that for their pals, the Jews.

The mines in the mountainous jungle regions of Chiapas that contained valuable "Jurassic Park" amber—prehistoric hardened tree sap with insects trapped inside—were worked by enslaved children: the only people small enough to navigate the tiny passages and locate the gray-veined mother lodes.

His large chestnut steed frothed at the bit as Boomba, a man aptly nicknamed for his love affair with his sawed-off twelve-gauge shotgun, gave no signs of easing up on the horse. The other rebels followed close, flanking their *jefe* to protect him from any ambush or assault, like the Blue Angels at an air show. They covered their faces, always with black bandannas—though a red-and-white one would do in a pinch—to guard their anonymity and to spare their families from terrible reprisals by government death squads like *Paz y Justicia*. It was ironic that the Mexican government had named a paramilitary cadre whose sole goal was to kill and harass Zapatistas after two things—peace and justice— with which they were certainly not very familiar. The government wanted nothing more than to eviscerate any and all who opposed it, including Western journalists who would try to get word out of the country about human rights violations.

All this Boomba kept in the forefront of his thoughts; this and his long-lost friend, an exiled sub-commander of the Chiapas rebels who had gone into hiding in the United States in exchange for the Mexican government's vow to stop the rampant killing of his fellow Zapatistas. But we all know the value of political promises.

V

It was truly a sight to behold, the grand, old fountain in the center of the village of San Cristobal. It was old Mexican. Old Spanish. Old World. Beautifully sculpted, it rose fifteen feet above the plaza. The statue of Saint Christopher carrying the baby Jesus on his back that sat atop the fountain illustrated the biblical parable of a strong, young man slowly weighed down by the small child he carried on his shoulders across a river. When Saint Christopher asked Jesus, the young boy he was carrying, "How can such a small child be such a burdensome load?" Jesus responded, "You carry the weight of the world's sins upon your shoulders." It was the perfect metaphor for the spiritual destiny of San Cristobal, and the one thing tourists might actually go out of their way to see. But tourists never came to San Cristobal. It was forbidden.

An old, beat-up pickup truck with decades of rusty dents and four bald tires sat idle near the fountain. With little paint and of no certain color, it might have been mistaken for derelict but for the lack of dust on the hood and the fresh tire tracks leading up to it in the reddish clay. It was certainly from the 1950's—probably the early 50's. Chevrolet, Ford, Plymouth—it was impossible to tell upon first glance since no identifiable markings were still present and dents covered the front grill. It was old, but it was solid.

Doctor Ramos had to step back from the truck door as he swung it open. It screeched and thumped as the hinges strained. Flakes of rust sprinkled from the jamb. Once situated inside, he had to slam it shut.

In the distance, he saw the sweat-covered horses charge into the center of the village. It looked like a scene from an old western where Pancho Villa appears to save the villagers in Robin Hood fashion. But saving this village would take more than Hollywood theatrics.

Boomba walked his horse toward Doctor Ramos' truck as the others stood guard under the archway. He was exhausted, but remained effective due to his ornery demeanor, which could only be matched by his courage. Part Old West cowboy and part modern soldier, Boomba wore dusty canvas military clothes draped with dual artillery belts that made an *X* across his chest. The guns the Zapatistas carried were no longer single-shot rifles, but pump-action shotguns and automatic weapons: M-16's, arma-lites and M-60 machine guns. My, how times had changed.

"*Doctor!*" Boomba shouted. "Wait! We have come to help!"

From the driver-side window, Doctor Ramos stretched out his head and shouted, "Boomba, *mi amigo! Gracias*, but go home." The old man shook his head. "I must do this alone."

Boomba maneuvered his large horse in circles to protest, but Doctor Ramos was resolved. "If anything happens to me, send for my son, send for Carlos. *Adios!*" He waved to the other rebels at the far end of the village as Boomba huffed and turned to gallop straight at his men. In near military fashion, the rebels opened their gauntlet for him to ride through.

"*Andelay!*" Boomba bellowed at them as he led the charge out of the village.

Doctor Ramos could still hear Boomba shouting expletives in anger and frustration when he turned the old truck's ignition key. The engine coughed and spurted, making his foot bounce up and down as though he were tapping to a fast tempo. He hit the gas pedal repeatedly. The engine chugged and chugged. Nothing. Just then, the passenger-side door opened and Pepe glanced up with a playful look. Before Doctor

Ramos could admonish him, Father Gonzalez appeared behind the boy and scooped him up. Still undaunted, Pepe pulled himself up onto the car window just as the priest gave a final blessing to the old man: a last blessing asking God to protect his old friend. Just then, miraculously, the engine roared to life. God's one helluva mechanic.

Doctor Ramos looked straight ahead and avoided eye contact with everyone: Maria, Father Gonzalez, Isabella, his nuns. The few villagers that were left, the ones still strong enough, waved and wailed as they chased after the truck.

As he passed the old fountain, Doctor Ramos glanced up at the giant clay sculpture of Saint Christopher, patron saint of the village, carrying the baby Jesus on his back as he waded through a river with nothing but a walking staff.

The inscription read, "You Carry the Weight of the World Upon Your Shoulders." He knew the feeling. Doctor Ramos raced for the great archway that safeguarded the village and quickly passed under it. From his rearview mirror he saw the letters in reverse that he, himself, had carved into the stone: "San Cristobal - Vaya Con Dios!"

Thick, whitish smoke poured over the dirt road just on the outskirts of the village, mimicking fog. Doctor Ramos didn't even blink as he slowed to pass the workers that were systematically tossing human bodies and animal carcasses onto large bonfires. By now, the doctor was even used to seeing the faceless technicians in their biohazard suits, looking like they came from another planet except for their high-tech trucks and gear. But they were from a place far closer to home. Their Dante-esque forms against the hellish background of the fires could have been perceived as cloaked demons by anyone less pragmatic than the doctor. All the old man could do was shudder and say "*morbido*" as he gazed into the distance at the burning pyres that dotted the horizon.

VI

The brakes on the old pickup squeaked noisily. Doctor Ramos pumped them slowly to keep the sound to a minimum as he pulled up to a large, well-lit compound. An industrial facility of some kind. It was already night. Already dark.

He pulled the truck off the main road and onto the graveled shoulder to sit just outside the perimeter of the gated factory. Turning off the headlights, he checked the compound for movement under cover of darkness.

Now a few hundred yards from the entrance, he eyed the high, chain-link fence capped with razor-sharp concertina wire that surrounded the complex. Hitler's boys, he thought, couldn't have done a better job. This was a top-security facility, if nothing else. Everything about this place screamed, "Stay away!"

Doctor Ramos locked onto a sign that read: *Toluca Pharmaceuticals.* Above it, floodlights illuminated the grounds and the trucks and the soldiers as laborers dollied shiny barrels labeled: *Chlorino - TXC* onto stake-bed trucks.

From his vantage point, he could see a military officer, perhaps a colonel, barking orders to his underlings and workers, supervising the process. He took long, deliberate drags from his cigar then sent plumes of smoke into the hot night air. Without even seeing his face, Doctor Ramos knew this man was trouble.

Two workers pushing a large barrel snickered and complained quietly to each other as they toiled. From where Doctor Ramos was, he could only hear plaintive mumbling. Suddenly, the barrel slipped off the dolly, dropped to its side and rolled into a ditch, where it stopped with a thump. *Crack*. A break ran up the length of the barrel as the two workers exchanged horrified looks. White powder began to flow from the breach, covering the ground in front of them.

The military officer suddenly appeared behind both frantic men. He was Generalissimo Jorge Cortes, who claimed the dubious distinction of being the direct descendant of Hernan Cortes, Conqueror of Mexico and historically responsible for the deaths of over forty-five million Aztecs.

Cortes was also Secretary of Defense and none other than the right-hand man to the Governor of Mexico, Roberto Chavez. Cortes was cruel. No, he was more than cruel. He was maniacal. Sadistic. He gave no quarter and never, ever allowed anyone a second chance. Approaching the two workers, Cortes pulled his pistol from his waistband and raised it high above his head. All work on the site ceased as he pistol-whipped them bloody. Their pleas for clemency went unheard as the other workers, each terrified into the shameful role of passive onlooker, did nothing but quake in their boots. Cortes would not tolerate failure or mistakes of any kind: period.

Doctor Ramos was used to seeing his people take this kind of abuse: poor Mexicans, Chiapas Indians, Zapatista rebels, anyone unlucky to find themselves under the thumb of a man like Cortes. Human rights were merely thoughts in a man's head. They were words in outlawed publications or on-screen in a darkened theater. Only in America.

He had seen the horrible treatment of his own villagers in San Cristobal by the army and the murderers of the Chiapas rebels who often sought sanctuary or volunteered or assisted there. He was not complacent. He hadn't grown numb to the sight of such atrocities. In fact, what he was about to do would help end them once and for all.

Yet instead of charging full-steam ahead into the complex and stopping Cortes, he waited.

Doctor Ramos reached into the sack of tortillas that Pepe had given him. As he chewed one, he admired the effigies of Catholic saints and other trinkets that adorned his dashboard. After a moment in reverie, he rubbed his hands together to clean them and opened his black medical bag. He fidgeted through surgical instruments, gauze, bandages, alcohol swabs and scissors, clanging things together, then, carefully, pulled out a large camera complete with telescopic lens.

He quietly exited the pickup and made his way inside the compound through an old, unrepaired hole in the fence he had scouted on a previous reconnaissance. As he stealthily hurried downhill toward the complex, he kept his finger on the camera trigger, capturing multiple images of the clandestine operation taking place below him. He was now on a mission. He was now, finally going to make a difference.

Doctor Ramos was so focused, so blindly directed, he never looked back to see the mysterious silhouette moving toward his truck behind him. The interloper, the stranger, the gloved figure in a cheap, dark suit, stepped out from the shadows behind the hole in the fence where Doctor Ramos had charged into the compound, then slowly walked toward the old man's pickup truck. With more business-like efficiency than stealth, the shadowy form reached inside the driver-side window, then dropped something in.

Simultaneously, through an opened warehouse door, Doctor Ramos could see soldiers standing guard over a beaten and bloodied man. The man's long, dark hair, not yet matted by blood, flicked sweat from side to side as two soldiers beat him. His facial and cranial lacerations were still fresh, but bulging welts and bruises were already transforming his face into a grotesque mask.

The man, *Chucha*, as his friends called him, licked his split lips and tongued the roof of his parched mouth. He stretched and strained, smacking his mouth and coughing from the blows, trying in vain to bring his roped hands to his face and wipe the blood away. Maybe he was just in for a beating: no big deal, nothing he hadn't had a hundred times before, something he could recover from in a few weeks or even a month if it wasn't too severe. Maybe this was just a warning, Chucha thought.

It wasn't until these soldiers who were purportedly there to do nothing but stand guard stopped beating Chucha and swung him around in the swivel chair that he realized how bad his situation really was. His eyes pulsed with pain and he began to sweat profusely, wriggling, making the ropes that bound his hands burn deeper into his wrists. Now, in front of him, atop a simple old wooden desk—the kind you might see in a turn-of-the-century frontier schoolhouse—sat a large black box. Just a box.

The box was simple: nothing remarkable about it at all. It was as black as pitch, made of wood or some other kind of solid material and sealed up on all sides except for a silken black veil covering a small opening in the center. No sound came from inside and there seemed to be no logical reason to fear the inanimate object. It was just a black box. But Chucha feared that box like the Devil himself.

Now close to the warehouse, Doctor Ramos could hear footsteps marching hard across the cement floor as he placed the eyepiece of the camera's scope against his forehead and hunted for movement. Slowly, Cortes appeared in the sight—and this time Doctor Ramos could see him clearly.

General Cortes was tall and lean and official-looking in his greenish khaki uniform that sported silver-studded epaulets and colorful military medals and bars. His sharp brown features seemed to have been chiseled by a dulled blade. Pockmarks from acne or illness riddled his cheeks and neck, and a long scar ran the length of his face, just crossing his brow then shooting diagonally down to his jaw. Cortes had the look of Lucifer incarnate, and an attitude that would rival even his.

Doctor Ramos trained the crosshairs of the monocular on Cortes and racked back to a macro shot to see the others in the warehouse. *Click*. He began to snap photos. He could barely hear anything but footsteps until Cortes began to roar at Chucha, who was still sitting terrified in the swivel chair.

"You took what was mine, peasant! Now I will take what is yours." Cortes peeled off one of his black leather gloves and swatted Chucha with it.

The shock or the sound against his face finally broke the beaten man. He began to plead, "General Cortes, *por favor*, it was not me, the others stole the powder. I swear!" His cries went unheeded as Cortes prepared an ample punishment for the alleged crime.

The general suddenly snapped his fingers. An instant later, the soldiers grabbed one of Chucha's arms. One soldier withdrew a small knife from his belt and quickly sliced the bloody binding. Was he being released? The soldiers then took his hand in a firm grip, spreading his fingers wide and slowly pushing it toward the black box. Chucha begged for his life, pleading more fervently as his hand got closer. Slowly, but with great effort, the two soldiers were able to pass his hand through the silken veil and drive it deep inside the box. You had to give the guy credit—he fought and struggled valiantly, manipulating his shoulders, breaking the joint at his elbow, nearly tearing off his own arm like a coyote in a trap just to keep it from entering that innocuous-looking black box. But it was too late for Chucha. *Click.*

There was a moment of silence, a pause in the drama when Chucha stopped struggling, that made the soldiers relax their grip on his arm— but just for a moment. Then, from the depths of Chucha's soul came a blood-curdling scream. Doctor Ramos could see the man's eyes bulge as the primal fear we will all experience at least once in our lives expanded his face.

In less than a minute, Chucha's labored breathing eased as if he were growing calm. Suddenly, his body seized slowly for another moment, then went limp, then nothing. *Click.* Cortes narrowed his eyes like a crocodile feasting on the tastiest part of a water buffalo. Through his camera lens, Doctor Ramos could see that the general not only enjoyed killing, but found the murderous experience seductive, even erotic. *Click.*

Doctor Ramos snapped his final shots as he watched the soldiers carry Chucha's lifeless body to a giant vat of churning chemicals. Lifting him high above their shoulders, the soldiers pushed forward and threw him in. *Click*. Massive amounts of white powder flowed into barrels for containment. *Click*. Barrels being transferred by men and machine and loaded onto stake-bed trucks for delivery to parts unknown. *Click*.

After the last shot was taken, the old man hobbled back across the darkened part of the compound, back through the hole in the fence and across the dirt road to his pickup. He turned one last time to make sure he was not being followed, then quietly opened the pickup's door and climbed in.

Laden with too many barrels, an old stake-bed truck fired up its diesel engine and chugged into the night through the front gates. As Doctor Ramos watched in his rearview mirror, he could see the truck listing from side to side under the excessive weight of its payload as it drove onto the main road behind his pickup.

As the stake-bed truck turned to drive the opposite direction, its headlights passed over a darkened object across the dirt road a few hundred feet behind Doctor Ramos' pickup. As the image flashed in the rearview mirror, the doctor suddenly realized it was a parked car. An unmarked car. An official car. That wasn't there before, he thought. Then he began to panic.

"*Dios mio*," he shouted to himself as he frantically turned the ignition key. Nothing. He tried again and again. Nothing. He kept trying, but the engine only gasped. Was it flooded? Was the battery dead? Had they tampered with it?

He couldn't have heard it from inside the pickup, but gravel and rocks began to pop from the shoulder of the dirt road as the dark, unmarked car slowly began to creep forward. Still unaware of what was going on behind him, Doctor Ramos frantically tried to start the engine as he locked his eyes onto the Saint Christopher statuette on his dash. For a brief instant, it calmed him, and he almost gave himself up to his fate. He said a quick prayer, then suddenly, miraculously, the engine of his old pickup truck roared to life. The backfire from the release blew out of the exhaust pipe like mortar and lit up the pavement. Doctor Ramos wasted no time. He downshifted quickly and slammed the accelerator to the floor as the balding tires ripped onto the road. Just then, the unmarked car's headlights burst bright as its engine, too, roared to life. The chase was on.

Fighting to keep control of the steering wheel, Doctor Ramos sped up the narrow dirt road of *Montes De Mixtongo* Mountain and onto a curvy pass in the hopes of somehow shaking his pursuers. As the headlights of his own pickup rounded each turn, he caught a different view of ancient Aztec and Mayan structures. Millennia-old ruins loomed hauntingly on both sides of the dirt road and seemed to rise up like ancient skyscrapers as he began to slowly gain confidence that he could possibly, maybe, make it through this bad situation.

Then, suddenly, strange dark patches and colors passed over him, tricking his eyes with the play of light. He remembered what Father Gonzalez had foretold about strange shadows passing over the weary traveler. But there was no time for old wives' tales. The unmarked car was in hot pursuit, blinding Doctor Ramos with its highbeams and smashing his bumper in an attempt to drive him off the ever-present cliff. Then came bullets, whizzing past his ears, through the thick back window and sideview mirrors.

As Doctor Ramos frantically shifted gears in an effort to get to the mountain pass, he accidentally bumped the switch to the old AM radio. Mariachi music began to blare from the speaker in the center of the dashboard. The sharp sound cut through the tension like the bullets flying past him. He burst out a cry of emotion—part fear, part amusement—as the music set the pace of the chase. It was surreal, he decided, and managed to laugh.

The old pickup was taking a pounding. Everything inside it was being thrashed around, flying everywhere—everything except the bag of tortillas. The bag seemed to move oddly against the sway of the pickup and its violent turns, counter to everything else. Doctor Ramos didn't notice the queer movement as he had more pressing matters at hand.

He caught sight of a sign that read: *TEMPLE OF THE GREAT AZTECS - ELEVATION 6,000 FEET - PELIGROSO - DANGER - ROAD NARROWS AT CLIFFSIDE.*

Defiantly, Doctor Ramos began to sing along with the festive music as he realized he had pulled away from the car. Maybe ten or twenty car-lengths. As he climbed higher and higher into the mountains, he saw a chance that he might actually make it. He sang louder and louder.

As the great Aztec temple came into view, another shadow passed over him and he suddenly felt a strange sensation. He looked down towards his lap at the bag of tortillas. It was the only thing near his body. Everything else had blown out the window or fallen to the floorboards. There wasn't much light, but he could still see something, feel something against his leg. He just didn't know what.

As the old man became preoccupied with the sensations on his leg, the pursuing car caught up to the pickup just long enough for its highbeams to be effective. As the cab became illuminated, Doctor Ramos looked down once again to see two black masses creeping up his lap. They were *Bothriurus bonariensa*—giant scorpions. One methodically climbed up his shirt, delicately digging its bluish speckled claws and needle-tipped legs into the fabric, climbing slowly toward his chest as another crawled up his crotch. Still another crept out of the sack onto his thigh as the old man's eyes widened.

He tried not to panic, but instinctively began swatting at the enormous arachnids in an attempt to get them off him. *Sting.*

He tried to keep control of the steering wheel as he came to the narrow curve in the mountain pass. *Sting.*

He quickly felt the fire of the toxic venom as the agitated scorpions injected him over and over again with burning, acid-like poison. *Sting. Sting. Sting.*

Screams filled the night air as Doctor Ramos swerved, losing control of the pickup truck, which sailed off the side of the road and over the high cliff.

The dark evening sky was momentarily illuminated by a giant fireball that rose from the desert floor below. The unmarked vehicle that followed pulled off the road near the edge of the cliff where the tire tracks ended, and stopped.

A miniature mushroom cloud of smoke and flames blossomed skyward, its reflection mirrored in the driver's window. After a moment, the explosion subsided and the car drove away, leaving the Aztec ruins to fade once again into darkness.

VII

It's true my life was a mess. My only consolation was that I had a bitchin' apartment. Oh, and I owned it. Not that rental shit. On the East Coast you can own apartments. At least they call them apartments. They're really just small condos, but no one seems to call them that. Why the big mystery? Who the hell cares? After all, I had a place to crash complete with four dead trees, pots full of old potting soil, ten-year-old mall-bought lithographs and mold in my bathroom. I had been planning to get a maid, but since my wife had left me, what was the point?

I made it home from the press conference uneventfully. I unlocked the door and pushed half a hallway full of mail to the side with my feet. I suppose it was time to clean up a little, so I picked up a pile of overdue bills, magazines and junk mail and threw it onto the hall bureau. I stacked the post high and wide so it would be hard to knock over when I stumbled in late at night. I couldn't be bothered to spend an hour opening all of it, writing checks and paying bills. Besides, my girlfriend Jill should've done all that by now. "Jill?" I yelled as I walked in.

I made my way to the living room for a drink. I had this kind of makeshift bar that seemed to have taken on a life of its own. It was now larger than the sofa including extensions and add-ons, and stocked full with bottles of gin, tequila, mixer and, above all, whiskey. Hey, I was Irish—no need to fight the stereotype.

I seemed to be running low on Jameson, so I grabbed a tumbler, plopped a couple of cubes into it and finished up the bottle. "Jill? Jill, honey, I'm home," I called out, facing the wall but hoping my voice would carry into the back bedroom. Hmm, where could she be?

Out of the corner of my eye I saw the red LCD light of the answering machine blinking. I swirled my drink with my index finger, then sucked it dry before pressing the button to rewind the tape. I fell into kind of a quick trance to the rewinding tape's accelerating hum.

While I waited, I took a moment to look at my prize possession: my Wall of Fame. On one full wall of my apartment, I had framed photos and autographs of every interesting event in my life: Terry Riley with politicians, Terry Riley with celebrities, even one with Terry Riley smiling. That was a rare one. Worth a fortune someday.

In the center of the wall was a little wooden scallop and on it was my Pulitzer Prize. It gave me a bittersweet feeling every time I saw it.

Beep. Roll tape.

The first message started garbled, but I could tell it was one of Marilyn's attorneys. "Mr. Riley, you're three payments behind on your alimony. It's not worth it to garnish your wages; you don't make enough. Take out a loan or we'll have to take your car. Do yourself a favor, Pal, she's not gonna let up. She's a Lobbyist, remember." I hated attorneys.

The second message began. An angry voice screamed, "You fucking reporters can't leave well enough alone, can you? You dig and you dig until you dig up something that fucks somebody's life up. Well it's your turn to bite the pillow this time, Riley!" I hated stalkers too, but I still hated attorneys more than stalkers.

The third message began. It was Kate Walker from the office: "Give it up, Riley, you're a dinosaur. Be a good boy and just walk away. Take a cushy teaching job at Georgetown or NYU. I could talk to Charlie—I'm sure he could get creative on a letter of recommendation. Step aside and let a real journalist show you how it's done. See ya on the front pages." What a cute kid.

It was nearly a minute since I'd had my last taste of whiskey, so I powered the last bit down. *Beep*. This was a record: four calls in one day. "Terry… I'm sorry. I can't live with a man who doesn't even respect himself. I think you love drinking more than you love me. I don't know if you ever loved me. I'm sorry. Good-bye." It was Jill and it took me a second to realize I had just heard her version of a "Dear John" message.

Crash. The glass slipped from my hand as I tore through the apartment. Nothing. Gone. Not only had Jill moved out, but she'd taken most of my stuff with her. I hadn't even noticed that the stereo, the television and those new leather couches were gone. The bedroom was a wreck. She must've had one of her college buddies help her move out. And in a hurry. She knew I was coming home early today. She had even taken my clothes hangers. God damn it.

VIII

Smog covered the entire horizon of East Los Angeles. The ghetto. The *barrio*. Smog covered pretty much all of Los Angeles even on a good day, but it had a habit of being particularly bad over older sections of the city. There weren't many trees or manicured lawns here, but there was a river: The L.A. River—an oxymoron as well as a misnomer. It was not a river at all, but an enormous open flood basin that stretched from the northern part of the San Fernando Valley, south past Orange County and probably through San Diego down into Mexico. It was used primarily for flood control and run-off, but also got a lot of use from Hollywood for its car chases and explosion scenes. But you didn't have to look far to see damage of another kind around this part of town.

The barrio was made up of spiked iron bars, burned-out apartment complexes and corner *bodegas*. Nearly all the residents were Hispanic or Latino or whatever the politically correct term of the day was. Either way, they were mostly Mexicans that had crossed the border in Texas, Arizona and California, legally or illegally, to find a better life than what they had left behind. They were first-generation Americans, immigrants with nothing in their hearts but the pure joy of being here and the promise of success for their children and families. Sure, the streets were dirty, but the Latin culture was alive and thriving here.

Carlos Ramos was a handsome man: tall, lean. He had ruggedly high cheekbones and brown skin and looked as though he had been an athlete once. He could have rivaled Jimmy Smits or Benjamin Bratt or even Javier Bardem for a lead role in their movies, but over the years he had been in Los Angeles, he had never, thankfully, been bitten by the Hollywood bug.

He walked the streets of the tough barrio every morning on his way to the mission. On either side of him he'd see tricked-out Chevys and low-riding mini-trucks with gang-bangers lurking everywhere. Gang colors, tattoos and hand signals as well as graffiti decorated the neighborhood like parade flags. Like badges of honor. Yet here, Ramos could walk unmolested, unchallenged even amid a jungle of angry youths. He was respected here. This was his home.

He waved to a group of punks. Chollos. He didn't particularly care for those boys with their wife-beater tank tops, oversized workman slacks, chains dangling from their pockets and blue bandannas wrapped around their foreheads as though they'd been toiling in the fields all day. But he knew that if you were known here, you were safe here. There *was* a code of honor. Even here.

The East Los Angeles Mission could be seen from blocks away. It was at the end of a long street and was one of the oldest buildings around. Ramos walked up the steps and entered the mission through dingy double doors, stepping over a homeless man wrapped in a fleece blanket emblazoned with the mission's logo. He didn't stop and check on the man or wake him or try to move him. It was Sam, a Vietnam vet. He was a regular. He just liked to be by the door, close to the action.

The mission was sparsely furnished due to lack of city funds, but nonetheless filled with life. The men and women here were the homeless, the vagrant, the wandering souls of the world. For reasons of mental illness, poverty or choice, they came here, ate here, lived here. They may have been wretched refuse out in the world, but here in this shelter they had dignity.

Ramos passed one after another in the hallway on the way to his office. He always had a smile for even the lowliest dumpster diver or rat catcher, and doled out soft greetings and murmured salutations as he passed. "Good to see you, Shawanda," he said to a black woman holding a grease-smeared baby's doll. "How are your feet today?"

She looked up at Ramos and took her thumb out of her mouth, as she only did to talk. "Hi, Doctor Ramos. I got a new baby. See?" she said in slowed speech. She held up the little blond doll and stroked her hair. "She's lovely," Ramos answered as he kept heading down the hall.

He stopped at a door with aged, translucent glass, the kind from a late-1940's Art Deco building. The stencil on the door read, *Doctor Carlos Ramos, M.D. - Mission Medical Director*. He entered, tossed his keys on his desk and opened the window to air the office out. One of the drawbacks of having an office in an old building was the mildew and rot smell that kept the rents so low. Ramos cleared his sinuses with a huff.

Taking a long look across the concrete playground, Ramos emitted a deep sigh. He used to be a leader, he thought. He used to fight for a cause that meant something. He used to help his father in the hospice treating patients, learning medicine. Helping those who truly didn't have a chance. A moment of self-pity passed before he realized that the people outside his door were just as in need of his help as his fellow villagers back in Mexico. He dismissed the brief depression. He was just homesick. He missed his father. He missed his sister. He missed his people. His country. He missed his cause.

Ramos sat down at his desk. He was thumbing through his pencil tray when he suddenly saw a large manila envelope atop a stack of mail. It had brightly colored postmarks and he knew who had sent it—and that made him smile. He wondered what surprise was inside this time. But before he could open the package, a graying priest appeared at his door with a serious look on his face.

Ramos set the correspondence back down on the desk and asked, "What is it, Father Connor?" The priest rubbed his hands together. "Carlos, there's a woman on the phone for you. She says she's your sister." Ramos' expression changed as he quickly grabbed the phone and pressed the flashing button. From the other end he could hear a woman's voice, trembling and incomprehensible.

"Maria?" he asked loudly, in case the connection was bad.

"Carlos," Maria answered, sniffling and obviously holding back her tears. "Come home! Papi is dead!"

IX

It's quiet in the newsroom of the *Washington Post* after hours—a complete 180 degrees from the day's events, where the only sound you hear is the drone of far-off vacuum cleaners and backup servers. The only people you see in the building are security, maybe a janitor here and there and, of course, the over-zealous, over-ambitious overachiever. Kate Walker was the poster child for overachievers. Her father must have been a Marine drill sergeant.

"City desk! Hi, Duke. The presses keeping you busy down there in the dungeon? Riley? No, he's gone for the day. Went home after Pritchard's press conference. How's the story look?" There was a long pause as she listened intently to the typesetter's explanation. "Oh shit, not again!" she said in a half-disbelieving, half-angry, but certainly concerned way.

"Give me ten minutes, okay?" She hung up the phone quickly and began to pound the keyboard of her laptop. She furiously clicked the mouse as her story developed. It read: *PRITCHARD UNVEILS ECO-FRIENDLY POLICIES FOR MEXICO CITY.* Underneath this, she wrote a byline: *by Terry Riley & Kate Walker.* What an opportunist.

X

Any writer worth his salt in D.C. drank at the Writer's Block pub, a local haunt inhabited mostly by newsies and turncoat politicians-turned-novelists. You'd have you're occasional Tom Clancy wannabe and deepthroat informant, but all-in-all it was a respectable crowd.

Luckily the owners had hired a genuine paddy to give the place some color—an enormous Irish bartender from Donegal, Seamus Murphy. He looked like he'd eaten three lumberjacks and had a thick, red beard that made him look rugged and fierce. Surprisingly, though, he was one of the gentlest people I had ever known. Since I was a kinsman—an Irishman, a "Narrowback" as we Irish-Americans are called by the real McCoys—luckily, I got served as much and as often as I needed to be. And thanks to Seamus, eighty-six was never my number! I never got tossed from the Block no matter how bad I got—and I had just started to set a new personal best.

Traditional Celtic music blared from the jukebox. Not that *Riverdance* crap, but true pipes and fiddles, sometimes the Pogues, definitely the Chieftains and occasionally the odd Enya or Clannad. The bar tables were filled with reporters rehashing the day's events and waxing poetic about their greatest assignments, and they shouted and laughed and slapped each other on the back the way Americans do—as well as the odd Irishman or Brit, if he's well-oiled enough. I was of a different mindset.

I was fast on my way to the Betty Ford Clinic as I tried to arrange numerous empty shot glasses in front of me into a pyramid without sending them crashing over the edge of the bar. Please, we must have complete concentration. This was a challenge since the only thing holding my head up was one elbow and another soon-to-be-swallowed shot of twelve-year-old scotch. I must've looked like ten miles of bad road by the time Seamus approached.

"So much for the 'Luck o' the Irish,' eh, Shamey?" I garbled pathetically. "Line 'em up again!" Seamus always kept a toothpick between his teeth. I remember once he'd said it was the only thing that helped him to stop smoking. He was gnawing on what seemed to be a tree branch when he gave me a dirty look.

"Forget it, Terry-boy-O! You'll do right to stop drinking before I'm cleaning up your supper from off me bar. What's into you, Lad? I haven't seen you on a bender like this since you caught Marilyn with that Kennedy bollocks." He shook his head and scoffed. "That shagg'n bastard's giving the Irish a bad name."

"Marilyn, huh! She's screwing every last penny out of me, just because she can. Like she needs the money! She sent one of her goon/lawyers after me today and another's calling the house. I haven't written a decent word in months, I'm probably gonna lose my job soon and Jill left me today. Oh, yeah—and she took just about everything I owned with her."

Seamus sat back against the counter. "Ah, ya poor sod, listen to yourself! The son of one of Chicago's finest. Jesus, Mary and Holy Saint Joseph, I'm glad your old da isn't here to see you like this. God rest his soul." He made the sign of the cross then kissed the bar towel where the tip of his thumb would've been. "You know what you're suffering from? Irish Alzheimer's!"

I peaked up curiously and blathered, "I've never heard of that."

Seamus sucked in his cheeks, making them taut, and said, "You forget everything but the grudges." My laughter was in direct proportion to the amount of alcohol I had already consumed.

At that very moment, Kate pushed the brass-railed door in and entered the bar. I hadn't seen her yet, but Seamus had and nodded toward me as he wiped the heavily varnished counter down. I had gone back to happily feeling sorry for myself when I heard a familiar, yet uninvited, voice.

"Contributing to the delinquency of a slacker is a serious offense, Seamus," she said, then laughed at her own joke.

"Speak of the devil… and she will appear," I bellowed. I had unwittingly returned her volley in our ongoing match of insults. She loved this game.

"Stop trying to get on my good side, Riley."

Attempting to stave off the inevitable, or just to be hospitable, Seamus sounded in: "Aye, Sweet Katie, you're prettier than a bed of roses, but sharper than the thorns, you are, Love." He laughed as he poured an economy-size portion of Old Bushmills into a crystal highball glass. He went on to dry newly rinsed beer mugs, all the while gnashing the toothpick. Sure, it was easy for him: All he had to do was sit back and watch the show.

I was ornery, or rather plain mean-spirited at this point. "Who invited you?" I grumbled.

She cocked her head and forced her way into my field of vision, or what little was left of it. "You did. When you missed your deadline—again! Thought I'd buy you a drink to celebrate my pending promotion."

I tried to ignore her by focusing on my favorite bar wench, Colleen. She was a beautiful brunette from Dublin who had been a waitress while she put herself through Georgetown. She just kind of stayed on after she'd graduated. Why not? The world was full of over-educated, jobless students. If I was lucky, she could be the next ex-Mrs. Riley, or at least an unforgettable one-night stand.

In my condition, I was fumbling more than being cool as I fawned over her. I could hear Kate sigh with boredom as I made a spectacle of myself. "When are we gonna go out, Colleen?" I slurred as she went about her business dropping off empty glasses and waiting on Seamus to fill her orders.

"Follow you to your place so you can show me your etchings, is that it, Terry Riley?" she rebutted in a lovely lilt without even looking up. Seamus placed four twenty-ounce pints of Guinness on her tray, and Colleen twirled through the bar like a ballroom dancer while delivering them.

Kate just shook her head at Seamus. "Come on, Riley, I'm just kidding. Don't worry about Pritchard's press conference, I wrote the piece and got it in before deadline—adding my byline to yours, of course."

That was the last straw! I wasn't mad at Kate. Hell, she'd done me a favor. But her having to write my story and taking a byline credit made me realize how low I'd sunk. I guess, looking back, you could say I reacted badly. I backhanded my creation all across the bar. The pyramid of shot glasses I'd spent all night constructing flew in every kind of direction, spraying warm whiskey, bar backwash and glass to the four corners. It splashed half the patrons in the place, the lion's share going to Hank Klein and three other reporters sitting behind me.

"Riley, you drunk asshole!" said Hank as he stood up to brush off the liquor that was staining his Dockers. "Can't you stop embarrassing yourself for five minutes?"

That was just the excuse I needed. Just the outlet I was waiting for. Now I could kick some ass—or get mine kicked. Either way, it would get my mind off my problems. Game on.

I whirled around and jumped off my barstool, surprisingly agile for being so drunk. Liquid courage, I guess. I stumbled to my feet, struck a pose and poised for a fight. Hank was going to become a statistic. "What's the matter Klein, didn't you ever get messy on job?" I yelled over the music. Everyone had stopped by this time to watch, sizing me up and trying to figure out my next move. I had the crowd in the palm of my hands. I continued, "I guess the only action you stock-report pussies get is when you're going down on some inside trader." I was on a roll. "Does the *Herald* consider that kind of action worthy of hazard pay?" I was ruthless, relentless. I gave him both barrels and wouldn't give him room enough to respond.

Hank Klein was lean and balding, and probably hadn't been in a fight since he was in a sandbox. He had to stand up to me just to save face, but he did so reluctantly.

The crowd suddenly surged forward, encircling us. It was a classic tribal reaction when two angry males challenged each other. Heathens. Kate was pushed aside and had no choice but to climb onto the bar to see how I was doing. She knew it wouldn't be a good time for one of her sarcastic lectures. She knew I was pissed and meant business. She unfortunately blamed herself for the whole mess. She was a good egg.

Even though Hank was discouraged from fighting, I had nonetheless insulted him professionally and personally. He might have had to take a beating, but he was standing up for himself. I admired that. I'd never liked the little cocksucker, but I admired his chutzpah.

He decided to fire a return shot to advance the stand off. "I just write 'em, Riley. I don't bury 'em," he said, driving the sharp words into me.

Man, everyone was going for my throat today. You'd think they would've learned not to go below the belt with the first shot. I bolted for Hank and his pretty, unblemished face, but before I could throw my haymaker, I felt two huge arms lock me in a bear hug. It was Seamus. He pinned my arms against my sides and lifted me up like a small fence post. The crowd choked out a collective sigh, then made a lane as Seamus carried me out the back of the bar.

Hank stood there, awestruck. He could've enjoyed the moment as a victor—after all, he wasn't picking up his teeth from a pool of blood. Instead, he sat back down quietly with his friends and they all looked at each other, confused about what had just happened.

Seamus lifted his tree trunk of a leg and kicked the security bar on the back door. *Beep, beep, beep,* the security alarm sounded. It flew open. Maybe it was his tight hold on me that caused a loss of oxygen to my brain or maybe the whiskey had just kicked in. Either way, I was about out of it. Seamus set me gently down on a pile of bloated garbage bags filled with beer bottles and diapers. He towered over me, looking down as he pulled a toothpick from the back of his pocket, tossed it skyward, and caught it between his teeth.

"There's a lad!" he said motheringly in his thick accent. "Stay here and I'll call yaz a cab. Go ahead and puke now, Terry-boy, you'll feel better and you'll thank me later." As he turned to walk back inside the bar, he stopped and lamented, "Pity though—Hank Klein deserves a thump for the gobshite he was on about. I don't care what anybody says, Terry, you're alright by me." With that he headed inside and slammed the back door behind him. The beeping finally stopped.

I was really drunk now, my eyes getting heavy, starting to close. I was somewhere between sleep and consciousness when I began to slip into a trance-like state. It was a dream I'd had many times before. A dream that haunted me...

I am sitting at my desk in the newsroom. It's daytime, maybe afternoon. I am hard at work writing on my laptop when everything suddenly becomes distorted and begins to move in slow motion. The clock on the wall stops ticking. People next to me freeze mid-stride. Then this normal-looking guy comes sprinting around the corner from the elevators, heading right for me. When I say he's normal-looking, I mean he has on a sports coat and slacks—absolutely no remarkable qualities about him to speak of. He bounds toward my desk, obviously motivated by emotions. Looking past him, I see more movement: two security guards in hot pursuit behind him. I know this man, but can't remember from where or how. Since it is a dream, I just sit forward in my chair and watch the events unfold. Slowly, the man rushes up to my desk and throws something at me. It lands in my lap. It is small, not heavy at all. The security guards are almost on top of him when he slowly pulls something from inside his jacket. A large caliber pistol. As he cocks the hammer back with his thumb, I look down at my lap, then back at him and into his cold, dead eyes. Before the guards can stop him, he pulls the trigger... Bang! Bang!

I was jolted awake. I slowly opened one eye to see two shadowy figures slamming the doors of a long, dark car. A Mercedes, I think. One driver, one passenger. I had been untimely wrenched from my dream before it could finish and was not in a good mood; that is to say I felt like shit and by now being conscious should not have been an indication that I could function.

The white light of the car's highbeams blinded me and, for a moment, gave me the impression that maybe I was still dreaming. Or maybe I had died and this was the white light at Saint Peter's gate. I was wrong on both counts.

Two dark silhouettes approached me slowly. I could hear them chuckle, snickering as they got closer. "It seems alcohol doesn't agree with Mr. Riley. Wouldn't you agree, Mr. Smith?" observed the first man. "Quite right, Mr. Jones! Quite right!" the second retorted with impeccable timing.

Smith and Jones: how original. More like Beavis and Butthead. Mr. Smith looked down his nose at me and said, "We have a message from an old friend of yours. You may remember him. Foster. Senator John Quincy Foster?" It was funny—hearing that name cleared my head, and quick. I looked up sharply at the men. Both were dressed in snappy silk suits. I knew they were probably knock-offs, but they suited those two well. No pun intended.

I grumbled something incomprehensible then shifted about on top of the garbage bags. Not making any headway, I covered my eyes with my forearm from the blinding light of the car's highbeams and tried to make out their faces.

"Don't bother going to any trouble, Mr. Riley. The lights will be out in no time!" Jones said in smarmy singsong. With that, he raised his foot the way a martial arts experts might, whip-kicked me in the face, then stepped through and side-kicked me square in the chest as I tried to stand.

Strange, but I remember feeling no pain as my newly assaulted body flew across the darkened alley. He came closer, advancing toward me, but all I could think of was how bad a mark that kick would leave. Jones picked me up by my blood-soaked lapel with his hands then threw me back across the alley. What was I, a human piñata? I hit the graffiti-covered back wall hard. *Thud.* I tried to breathe, gasping to regain the air that had been pounded out of me. Next came the uncontrollable vomiting. Man, I was having a real bad day!

Mr. Smith decided to chime in. Looking at his watch, he said matter-of-factly, "Let's get this over with, shall we, Mr. Jones? We do have a schedule to keep."

Jones straightened his jacket, swiping his cuffs to the end of his wrists, and sighed, "Time is a harsh taskmaster and we are slaves to our work, aren't we, Mr. Smith?"

These two were beginning to sound like those two cartoon chipmunks, Chip and Dale. Cutesy and glib. Ironic and flippant. Witty and pithy, perhaps, but they were there to do a job, and that job was me. Jones pulled a forty-plus-caliber pistol from his vest. Nice. It was one of those new nickel-plated ones, the kind that shoot a 180-grain bullet that leaves a really big hole—if anything is left. He knelt down next to me, put the gun to my temple, pulled the slide back and bolted a round into the chamber. Was I still dreaming?

Suddenly, the back door of the bar flew open into the alley. *Beep. Beep. Beep.* It was Kate. Wow, what an entrance. What a gal! "Hey, what the hell is going on, here?" she yelled above the din of the security alarm, startling the lot of us.

Jones, with his back to the door, kept Kate from seeing the pistol he held at my head. I suddenly became very worried for her. Yet before I could try and stop him, somehow perform some heroic, albeit drunken, feat, he slipped the large caliber cannon back into a shoulder holster inside his coat.

Pretending to tend to me, Jones poured on the bullshit. "Poor man," he cooed for Kate's benefit. He abruptly stood and nodded to Smith, and they backed out of the alley slowly toward their car.

"It looks like your friend's had a few too many, Miss. We were just going to take care of him when you, his friend, arrived!" Smith said sympathetically, but with an evil grin. Kate rushed over to me and began to wipe the blood and vomit from my mouth. The next thing we heard was the engine of the German car firing up. It was the same black Mercedes I'd seen near me all day. I should've been more careful.

I never saw it coming. I used to have a healthy sense of paranoia about these things, but now the alcohol was really starting to affect me.

As Mr. Smith dropped the car into gear, Mr. Jones rolled down the passenger window and shouted, "We'll be seeing you, Mr. Riley!"

The Mercedes peeled out, barely missing Kate and me as it raced down the alleyway and disappeared through a cloud of steam spewing from a manhole cover. Kate gazed into my eyes with concern and fear. I'd never quite seen this side of her before. Man, she sure had pretty eyes.

XI

The newsroom was painfully bright the next morning. I'd been there since around seven A.M. I could never sleep—a total insomniac. On top of that, the combination of alcohol, deep tissue damage and throbbing bruises precluded my relaxing at all, and probably for a while to come. So I thought, why not get a jump on the day and get to work so that I can at least keep my job another day? A small trophy on my desk reflected my face when I leaned forward. I looked pale. Unshaven. I looked like I'd gone ten rounds with Mike Tyson with both hands tied behind my back. I struggled to keep an icepack on my swollen cheek.

The office was its usual cheery self, bustling with reporters. Just another day, at least for them. I repeatedly tried to open and close my mouth, loosening the strained muscles and inflamed soft tissue of my jaw. I could handle cracked ribs, even a broken leg, but not being able to drink because of a damaged mouth? That truly would have been a crime! As I pondered my situation, my editor flung open his office door and filled the office with his bark: "Riley, in my office. Now!"

Charlie sat at his desk as I slowly peeked around the corner like a disobedient child. He was lighting a cigar with one hand as he instinctively flicked on a humidifier next to a large wooden humidor with the other. The filter did little to stop the thick, pungent smoke from filling the room. I stepped into the doorway slowly and said, "You know those things'll kill ya!"

Charlie lowered his eyes and studied my battered face. "You should talk, Kid. What the hell happened to your face?"

He took a long pull off his cigar as he waited for my response. I didn't really want to get into great detail about my life's shortcomings, but it was nice that he was concerned. "It's kind of a long story and I don't really feel like discussing..."

He cut me off abruptly, "Good! Save it for your memoirs. What are you covering right now?" I stood there a little dumbfounded. It was an odd question and one that a reporter never wants to hear from his editor. It's always the prelude to a cutback or a layoff or worse. I knew I was sunk, so I just gave in.

"Three nationals, let's see, and a couple of locals," I said, feigning apathy.

"Not any more, you don't! I just gave them all to Walker," he coughed.

"Kate? Ah, why?" I said, surprising myself for even caring.

Charlie leaned back into his high-backed leather chair and interlaced his fingers behind his head. "Because she reminds of a great reporter I knew once," he said, his stogie tight between his front teeth. He tried to take another drag, but the fire had died. He retrieved a lighter from his desk and brought it to the dead tip. He pushed the flame nearly to the tip of the cigar and circled it over and over again. "These damn Cubans!" He puffed until he was sure it was going to stay lit. "Terry, I think you need to take a little time off," he said without looking at my face.

"Charlie, what the hell are you talking about?" I reacted as though I hadn't seen this coming for some time now. Charlie's demeanor changed quickly. We always shot straight with each other and now I was playing him for a sap. He took exception to that.

"You! I'm talking about you! You've got no heart in your stories anymore," he shouted. "The only reason I haven't canned your ass is because of your Pulitzer. It's good for the paper's image. But you're not!

Now you're not even in the same league anymore with prestige like that." I could take the lecture, but don't draw it out so long, I thought. "So I'm bucking you down to the minors until you get off your ass and show me you can deliver the goods."

I was becoming quite grizzled by now, getting tired of taking so much shit, even if I had caused it. "Or until I quit. Is that it, Charlie?" I slammed my fist down hard onto the desk then swept my hand in an angry gesture toward the newsroom. "I gave you better than you get from any of those hacks out there," I yelled. "I dug deeper and swam through more crap to get you stories; stories that, if you've forgotten, put this paper back on top." My voice began to crack. "I gave up everything for this job, Charlie."

Charlie listened intently, stood, and turned his back to me. He, too, had a Wall of Fame like I had at my apartment. Many of the photos he began to study were of he and I. "Nobody said it would be easy, Kid," he said pausing.

He began to narrate an old story. I didn't realize it was going to sound like a scene from a 1950's movie. He took a deep breath and recounted:

"About a hundred years ago, when I was riding the desk at the *Times*, one night, just before Christmas, a call came in from the city mission. They'd found some young deaf kid at their doorstep. The little guy was hungry, cold—a real frigg'n mess as I recall."

I decided this would be a good place to interrupt before he put me to sleep. "What's this got to do with me, Charlie?" I said callously. The interruption didn't help my position much.

"Just listen for a change, goddamn it!" He demanded. He took a moment to compose his thoughts then continued his story:

"I was ambitious. I smelled a human interest story. So I hauled ass down to this mission that was in a filthy part of Manhattan, had a look at the kid, scribbled some notes and snapped a few pictures of him." He looked as though he were about to have a revelation. "When I got back to the newsroom, it hit me what a shitty deal the kid had gotten. Right then and there I decided to do something for him. I sat down and wrote my best story ever. My editor liked it so much he ran a front page headline that read: *DEAF AND DUMB BOY ABANDONED ON STEPS OF MISSION*." He gestured broadly his hands. "I put his picture there in black and white for everyone to see. The next day, the whole city of New York opened up for this poor kid. Money, clothes, you name it—they sent it all to the mission to help."

He was really getting into the story by now, but I was starting to get impatient. I began to flip my gold pen over my knuckles as I often did when I was nervous or bored. Maybe I could speed up the story a little.

"But it turned out that this little boy was really a thirteen-year-old girl trying to hide out from her pimp!" Charlie's mood changed from nostalgic to maudlin. "She just needed to buy some time, you know, but I had plastered her face all over town with that headline. Three nights later, that bastard, that pimp, walked right into the mission and grabbed her up." His tone changed quickly to a dark, slow, guilt-ridden one. "They found her in midtown two days later, stuffed in a dumpster, her throat cut from ear to ear." He turned to face me.

By this time, I had become engrossed in the tale, and I was hanging on every word as he finished:

"The moral of the story... GET OVER IT! Not a day goes by I don't think about that kid, but I stopped blaming myself years ago. I advise you to do the same."

I stood there kind of humbled. "I get the picture, Charlie," I said sheepishly. He was the commander-in-chief of my world and when he wanted to make a point, there was no one better. "You had better get the point, Mister, 'cause this is your last chance. I suggest you ask yourself if you still wanna be a reporter. If you don't, we'll shake hands and part friends. If you do, I want total dedication. I want you recommitting to this job and yourself and kicking ass again," he said in no uncertain terms. He was a great one for never mincing words. He turned his back again to me and stared out the window. It was his way of punctuating his speech. He was an old-school guy who had never watched *Oprah* or listened to Dr. Phil, but had still somehow gotten in touch with his true feelings. He picked up a white plastic pail with a long thin spout and began to water a lush plant on the window sill. There was a long, pregnant pause. "I want your decision in seventy-two hours," he said in one quick breath.

I could feel the pressure. My natural reaction was to lash out. I didn't. I governed my tongue. Charlie was one of the few people I still respected and I knew he was right. I stood up quietly, maybe still in a state of shock from his insightful words, and walked out of the office. Just before I cleared the doorway, I heard Charlie let out a deep sigh. I felt like a kid who had just been scolded and the only one really upset was the punisher. He just stood there with his back to me as he continued to water the plant, all the time staring at a picture of him and me with two past presidents. Better days.

XII

An old, dusty army Jeep sped across the desert flats of the Mexican Badlands. It was a beater, like one of those Jeeps that was always driving in and out of camp on *M*A*S*H*. Clouds of dust seemed to pour over the windscreen out of nowhere as it raced over the sand and sagebrush.

The driver, Sonny Ortega, had pulled his red-and-white bandanna off hours before to reveal his dark skin and smooth, reddish-brown complexion. He was lean but had tight, bulging muscles that lay quietly under his shirt and thick, worn hands with dirty fingernails.

He was a driver, a bodyguard. A friend. He was an Indian. A Zapatista. A rebel with plenty of cause. He drove without question as another man wearing a black bandanna over his lower face, maybe his brother, rode shotgun, constantly surveying the landscape for any unusual movement, his goggles caked with dust.

In the backseat sat Carlos Ramos, his hands grasping the backs of the two front seats to stabilize himself against the jarring motion caused by the uneven terrain. He had no bandanna to hide his identity. He wasn't incognito. He was here to bury his father and he didn't care who saw him now.

As his face returned to its true color, turning darker from the intense rays of the Mexican sun, he began to look very like his father. After driving many hours across the desert in the heat, the dirt and dust and sand had blown his hair back and colored the normally dark strands to a light, sandy shade. Almost white. He was surely his father's son in many ways and soon would be in many more.

From a distance, San Cristobal looked like a dried-up oasis in a sea of desert. All you could see as you approached was the shocking white archway contrasted against the earth-toned Badlands. The Jeep barreled straight for the center of the archway and past the two giant wooden doors that had not been closed since Carlos had been a boy here. He maneuvered into the center of the village with dust clouds trailing in his wake, enveloping the Jeep, making it and its occupants invisible for a moment.

As the dust settled, Ramos stood up in the back seat and took a deep breath. He, too, had goggles on, and wiped them clean to pan the village with his eyes. Surprisingly, he saw it filled with people unlike the description his sister had given him on the phone. Could the sickness be over? Could San Cristobal be returning to its natural state?

Boomba and a group of men walked toward the Jeep and encircled it. Ramos was now an intruder. An interloper. The rebels approached cautiously, swaggering in their military fatigues and black berets. They, too, wore bandannas over their lower faces, leaving only their eyes for all to see. More men followed behind the others, some taking up position to kill their target if need be. Each man carried a rifle, a pistol, a machete—anything they could use to fight for their beliefs. They all drew their weapons then drew a bead on the Jeep's occupants as Boomba stepped up.

Ramos slowly raised his hands, removed the goggles from his dirty face and tossed them to the ground at the foot of a young soldier. The men leaned in and peered down the barrels of their guns. Boomba raised his hand then slowly lowered it so as not to cause confusion in his signal. He grinned widely and began to chuckle as he stretched out his arms toward Ramos. Slowly, man after man lowered his gun and straightened his neck. Looks of surprise, even revelation, came over their faces. Ramos jumped down from the Jeep and embraced Boomba, each smacking the other's back with thumps that could be heard throughout the village.

From the back of the crowd one woman shouted, "*Esta Carlito!*" Another shouted, "*Viva Ramos!*" Suddenly all the men dropped their weapons and joined in: "*Viva Ramos! Viva Ramos!*" They rushed the Jeep and lifted Ramos to their shoulders. The driver and shotgun turned to each other with pride; after all, they had accomplished something great. They had brought their leader home, Sub-Commander Carlos Ramos, living legend and local hero, like the Prodigal Son. As the rebels roared in adulation, they hoisted Ramos aloft like a rock star in a mosh pit and carried him to the hospice.

Maria couldn't see what was going on as she stepped out of the hospice entrance, wringing her blood-covered hands with a dirty, wet towel. She took a few steps outside and, for a moment, softened her tense face at the sight of her people celebrating something—anything. She curiously cocked her head as the cheering crowd came toward her. Closer. Closer. Then stopped. Like Moses parting the Red Sea, the rebels moved aside to reveal Ramos in the middle of their mob.

"Carlos!" Maria shouted as her eyes met his. She threw down the bloody rag and ran into his arms. "I'm home, *Mija*," he whispered just for her to hear.

He was taller now and seemed to swallow her up in his embrace. The normally serious, stone-faced rebels wept happy tears. This was territory that prided itself on machismo, but had a soft spot for all matters of family. Maria sobbed as she took refuge in her brother's arms. It was a bittersweet reunion. Ramos could now see what he hadn't before, and his brief happiness was shattered by the carnage strewn everywhere throughout the village.

XIII

It was late. After midnight, I think. Just out from under a three day bender, I was feeling dejected because of my meeting with Charlie, and I'd decided to chuck it all in. Fuck my career. Fuck reporting. Fuck journalism.

The media—newspapers, T.V., radio, you name it—all of it was now controlled by unrealistic, unwelcome and unseen bed-wetting liberal wannabes, anyway! Everyone had an agenda. Everyone. And it was always a hidden agenda. The media controlled how to dress, how to think, who to elect and how to live, and it was now the purest form of fascism since Hitler. Political correctness ruled our hearts and minds and had fucked up this country so much that Americans didn't know whether it was worth leaving the safety of their homes in the morning lest they be shot dead for speaking their minds. The "Land of the Free?" What a crock. That kind of subversive ideology was a thing of the past.

Sure, the country used to be tight-assed, puritanical, tough on crime—that's how we broke Watergate. But now it was run by the media. Whatever Turner or Murdoch or Redstone wanted, their media outlets force-fed to the country. If you pissed someone off in power, real power—media power or any copasetic entity—the least reprisal you'd suffer would be public humiliation and character assassination. It was the "New McCarthyism."

Mis-information. Dis-information. Partial truths wrapped within partial lies, quoted by night-school-educated "experts" consulting on the nation's behalf. I was sick of the hypocrisy. Sick of the lies. Nobody knew anything anymore and all everyone wanted to do was blame the president— or somebody else, anybody else—for their problems. And the media was there to feed on the disenfranchised public like a school of sharks. You couldn't get the truth, the real truth, in any story in America if you held a gun to a three-year-old's head. Hell, maybe I was just burned out.

I'd been wandering the empty streets of downtown D.C. for I don't know how long. I remembered being surprised that I hadn't been mugged or shot yet. That was odd. Then I walked past a storefront window and caught a glimpse of my reflection. Christ! The street people, the homeless, must have been shit-scared of me, the way I looked. They must have thought I was the king of these lowdown streets. At least that would have explained my physical condition. Unfortunately, nothing could either make sense of or cure my mental state.

I strolled past the Lincoln Memorial and tried to climb some of the stairs to the top. Forget it. I got up to the tenth or twentieth step and sat my ass down in exhaustion. I lay down and stared upwards. There he was, Honest Abe, in all his stoicism, sitting on his eternal throne. I used to think, hey, Abe's a smart guy, maybe he's got the answers. So I'd come here to try to get some. Answers that would help me find the truth in a story. Answers that might show me the way. Old Abe was like a priest I'd confess to when I needed guidance. I'd ask him questions like, "Abe, what would you do if you thought someone was guilty of crime? Would you hound him 'til he broke or do a hatchet job on him whether he was guilty or not?" After a while, I realized ol' Abe never really had the answers. He just afforded me the time to work it out for myself.

I stumbled past the Washington Monument then somehow made it to the Mall. I think I fell asleep on the lawn for a while because when I woke up, it was still dark. I never could sleep too long. No rest for the weary or wicked, I guess.

XIV

The lobby of the *Washington Post* was well lit even through the thick smoked glass. I must have looked like George Bailey from *It's A Wonderful Life* as he ogled at his past from outside in the cold. Anyone inside would've brushed me off as just another dreg looking for a warm place to lay my head. "No room at the inn," they'd say around here to vagrants.

I tapped on the glass lightly. "Hey!" I said, not too loud. "Hey!" A small head popped up from below the large marble guard station near the elevators. It was Leo. He'd been a security guard at the *Post* since Lindbergh, as far as I knew. I think I was the only guy who ever talked to him. Everyone was always in such a hurry.

Leo had a thick head of gray hair, but kept it cut short and tight. Probably an ex-Marine. I wondered if maybe he'd been in World War II or Korea. I'd never even bothered to ask him. Leo waved me off. I knocked and knocked again. From inside I could hear him shouting, "Take a hike! You can't use the bathroom in here. Go down the street to the park." I stopped tapping for a second and realized how I must've looked.

I stretched my hands out wide and shouted, "Leo! Leo, it's me!" Leo was just on his way back to his desk when he stopped dead in his tracks. He turned on a dime and, with a curious look, came closer to the window. "It's me, Leo, Terry Riley," I shouted with my mouth up to the glass. Leo quickly realized I was who I said I was and fumbled with the keys on his belt. He was nervous now and unlocked the double doors as fast as he could. I stood in place so as not to scare him further as he popped his head out and waved me in.

"It is you, Mr. Riley?" He said, bewildered.

"Yeah Leo," I said, a bit embarrassed. He gave me the once-over with his eyes, then his nostrils flared as he got a whiff of my three-day-old b.o. He'd never seen me unshaven or in such dirty clothes, and he couldn't quite figure out what was going on. "You all right, Mr. Riley? You been in an accident or something? You want I should call the cops?"

His concern was genuine and refreshing. I certainly didn't deserve it. I walked toward the elevators and he followed close, if for no other reason than to get the story. "No, nothing like that, Leo," I said, "just here to pick up a few things."

He pointed his finger up at me and a smile crossed his face. "You're undercover again, ain't you Mr. R? I can tell by the a..." He pointed at my appearance. "By the way you... your undercover clothes and the Hollywood-type make up. That's a great get-up, I didn't even recognize you." He said it as though he had uncovered a state secret and was going to take it to his grave. "Only you could pull off another coup like that crooked senator guy, eh, Mr. R?"

We got to the elevator and stopped. I didn't dare step on the old man's pride, so I leaned backwards as he stepped in to press the elevator button like an eager valet. "Something like that, Leo," I said softly as I looked up and stretched my neck. Booze can make your joints stiff.

Leo beamed as I suffered. "Haven't seen ya 'round in a coupla days, Mr. R., I shoulda put two and two together. After all, guys like you don't take vacations, do you?" he said proudly. "You're a real workhorse, a real pro, if you don't mind me saying so."

Ding. The elevator had finally come. The doors opened and I stepped in shallow, blocking any way for him to follow. I pressed the button and the doors slowly closed as Leo gave me a broad, collusive grin. I smiled and said, "Thanks Leo."

I stepped over a long orange extension cord as the janitor vacuumed the endless aisles. In between desks. Around desks. Under desks. These unseen, unappreciated workers had more discipline than most writers I knew.

I ambled down the hall into the darkened newsroom. The bluish green glow that illuminated each workstation lit my way. I could never figure out why they didn't just shut those damn things off. Everyone's so concerned about the power crisis, but no one wants to participate. I always got cranky about this time of night. Maudlin. This was it, the end of my career. I walked down the hall past the partitions and cubicles to clean out my desk. How long had it been? I recounted: I'd been a reporter, a writer, longer than I could remember. High school newspaper editor, college journalist, cutting my teeth in Foreign Service and the press corps. I was a real overachiever back then.

I pulled a wadded-up envelope addressed to Charlie Petersen from my pocket. I placed it in the crack of the door to his office just above the knob. I pushed it in deep, partly to convince myself to really do it and partly so it wouldn't fall out if a janitor bumped it. Ba-bye.

I had found an empty box in a broom closet and was nearly done packing my desk when I opened the thin drawer just under the front desktop lip. I'd almost forgotten about that little drawer. It only contained a couple of old pencils and some odds and ends, but they were mine. When I reached into the back of the drawer, I felt something. It wasn't a piece of paper or business card, but it was thin and had a smooth side. I retrieved it and sat back into my desk chair.

Oh, a photo. I didn't recognize it at first, but upon closer inspection after clearing my red eyes, I realized it was from my days in Mexico. There I was, drenched in sweat from the humidity in this obscure little village somewhere in the middle of nowhere. Steve Meyer from the *Boston Globe* and Kevin Price from the *San Diego Herald-Examiner* stood on either side of me. We all had smiles on our faces and cameras around our necks, looking more like a bunch of Japanese tourists than reporters covering a story, arms wrapped around each other's shoulders like college buddies. Around us, a sprinkling of little kids sprinkled ran and played.

You wouldn't have known we were there to cover the insanity, the killings. Our headlines would call it *The Chiapas Massacres*. I remembered that was the last time I saw those guys. The fighting was getting too close to the village and we all had contracts on our heads. "Death to Any Reporters!" was the edict. We didn't care. We were gung-ho print jockeys with an adrenaline-rush addiction and one foot in the grave.

She was there, too, in the picture. Yeah, it was her there standing next to me, her face blurred from me rubbing the picture nearly raw during my infamous drunken stupors. She was so beautiful. I could hardly remember what she looked like, but I remembered her beauty. This was the only photo of her I had, and now even that was only a memory. The haunting sound of her voice in the middle of the night somewhere between dreams was my only record of her now.

I still had a nagging ache in my head. Guilt, probably. She was etched deep in my brain. I closed my eyes, leaned back in my chair and tried to picture her face. It was a good chair that had served me well over the years, still comfortable. I'd spent many a night sleeping in it after working on a story for days on end. I held the photo tight between my fingers and held it up to my forehead like a card in liar's poker. I rubbed it against my head either to get a clearer picture of her or to get her out of my head altogether. Neither seemed to work.

I was about to wad up the picture and throw it into the trash when I opened my eyes and saw my laptop. In the corner of the screen, a tiny mailbox symbol was blinking. It had probably been blinking the whole time, but I had been too self-involved to notice it. I had an e-mail, and by the looks of it, it was important.

I leaned forward, grabbed the mouse and clicked on the icon. A message appeared. It was from Kate. I hadn't returned any of her calls or contacted her over the last few days. She must've been pretty pissed. I didn't blame her one bit. The message read: *Riley, I'll keep the presses warm for you! - Kate.* I'll admit it, she was sweet. She had a soft side, but she didn't know me as well as she thought she did. I was going to quit, tonight, never to be seen again. I'd probably spend the rest of my days at the bottom of a bottle. Why not? I wasn't going to ruin her life as well as mine, so I'd stay as far from her as possible. Even after all our rows and jabs and verbal sparring, I thought she was a great girl. Too bad it couldn't have worked out.

I walked to her desk to write her a "Dear Jane" letter, but couldn't find a pad of paper. I searched through her finely labeled top files, perused her detailed inbox, pushed some small stuffed animals out of the way and finally found a yellow scratch pad to leave a message on. As I started to write, I saw a file peaking out from under a top sheet that read: *AMERIMEX WATER PURIFICATION PROJECT.*

Maybe it was my years of professional investigating and maybe it was just curiosity that made me pick it up, but I did, and I was now standing there over Kate's desk reading page after page with the intensity of a researcher finally on the right track. My face began to fall and my muscles drooped. Was I so miserable, I hadn't even read files that had sat on my own desk **for six** months?

I sat back down in Kate's chair and read as my eyes opened wide. One page read: *SENATE SUBCOMMITTEE CHAIRMAN DANIEL PRITCHARD TO SUPPORT QUESTIONABLE NAFTA BILL DEREGULATING DRUG COMPANIES IN MEXICO.* Another read: *MISSOURI SENATOR PRITCHARD TO OFFER SUPPORT TO MEXICAN GOVERNOR CHAVEZ. VOWS TO CONTINUE AID TO MEXICO 'NO MATTER WHAT THE COST!'* I read on. A thick black cloud seemed to lift from my brain. Here it had been the whole time.

I'd known Pritchard was up to something, but I could never prove it. The link was Chavez. The link was Mexico. I suddenly felt a rush, a new sense of duty. All thoughts of leaving the paper quickly vanished. Quit? Hell, I'm no quitter! I read on.

If Charlie wanted me to take a vacation, here was the perfect opportunity. Whatever it was that Pritchard was up to, I'd find it in Mexico.

I quickly logged on to the Internet via Kate's desktop computer. We were on a network and I knew her password, although she didn't know I knew it. I searched the Web for additional articles on the AMERIMEX Project. I'd stupidly overlooked the fact that Pritchard was calling in all his favors and throwing around his considerable influence to push through his proposal. That water system was his baby. I'd been so busy chasing phantom leads that I never saw what was right under my nose. I bet it was money laundering. Maybe, but that seemed too easy. Oil for water? No, Pritchard didn't seem too popular with the oil companies and he'd need them to boost support. What was it? I was determined now to find out.

I perused a number of political archives that most people don't have access to and a few commercial sites that keep past articles and political proposals. Found one. I read well into the night.

Around six in the morning, I decided to go to one more Website, a travel hub. I booked the first flight out to Mexico City. It left in two hours. I walked to Charlie's door, grabbed the envelope and ripped it up.

XV

Even Hollywood didn't have as many limos as D.C. and all of them seemed to be in front of Dulles Airport that morning. They weren't full of rock stars or actors, but another sort of celebrity: politicians. Nothing said, "I'm spending all your money, America!" like a statesman in a new stretch. They had no shame whatsoever. They flaunted it. And they spent it so brazenly just to let you know they controlled it all.

Pritchard sat back into the soft leather of the Lincoln after finishing a phone call to a subcommittee member. His staff sat near him swapping pens and cell phones, Blackberries and laptops clicking away as Pritchard took a breather.

The limo sat at the curb of the terminal, but was never hassled by the Metro or D.C. Police, probably because of its very obvious, almost ostentatious senatorial seals and flags. It was an unspoken rule among politicians and cops that neither would tread on the other without just cause. This made for a strange, but profitable, relationship between two sets of public servants: law makers and law enforcers.

Dexter Grace sat next to Pritchard and studied his schedule intensely. He spoke in a robotic tone: "Senator, our flight's at ten o'clock. It's about a four-and-a-half-hour flight and we arrive in Mexico City this afternoon. We'll be met by Governor Chavez's people, then shuttled directly to our hotel where..."

Pritchard suddenly interrupted, "Fine! Fine, Dex! I trust your efficiency."

It was just about that time I walked past Pritchard's limo on my way to catch my flight to Mexico City. I stumbled a bit from exhaustion, lack of sleep and the fact that I hadn't had a drink in what seemed like days. I couldn't see through the blackened windows of the limo, but I knew Pritchard must have cocked his head sharply when I went by.

I had a bad habit that I wasn't about to stop now. I walked to the limo, glanced at my reflection in the darkened window and blew my nose into a handkerchief. Blood. My face still hadn't healed from the beating a few nights before and alcohol only acted like Heparin. I still had the occasional bloody nose, but it wasn't as bad now. The swelling had gone down and there was just a little bruising and a small gash on my lip. I'd had worse.

Pritchard began fuming: "Make sure that son of a bitch ain't crawl'n up my ass this trip. Je-sus-Christ, Dex! I can't even get any quality time with my own staff with him around. Ain't that right, Miss Hoover?" He turned to the leggy staffer just across from him. The striking blonde, Jennifer Hoover, wore a seductive smile and a low-cut dress that accentuated her plentiful God-given endowments and seemingly endless legs. The shocking red of her dress just bordered on being inappropriate, yet she wore it like a modern day Jackie O.

"That's right, Senator. I think we'll need to go over those new congressional briefs... thoroughly," she said in a husky whisper. Everyone in the limo, both men and women, stopped as she spoke. All the men wanted her and all the women sneered in a catty way, secretly wanting to be her.

An evil grin slowly pursed Pritchard's lips and he said, "Dex, make a note of that. I'll be tied up later this afternoon."

Dexter glanced up from his paperwork and gave Jennifer a leer. "Yes, Sir," he said with a stone face. "Oh, and Senator, don't forget to call your wife upon your arrival. How's she feeling these days?" Dexter couldn't help slipping in a jab.

Suddenly, the doors flew open and the staff members jumped out. With the help of some private security at the curb, they secured a safety perimeter and everyone exited the vehicle. First the staffers, then Pritchard. Jennifer came next and Dexter followed last, his eyes cold to the back of her head.

Pritchard waved at a small crowd that was beginning to gather. A number of reporters charged up as someone shouted, "Its Pritchard!" They scurried up and surrounded him, the staffers and guards holding their ranks. Pritchard put his hands up to ease their formation.

"How y'all do'n today? On to Mexico City. Let's hope we get some great results! See y'all soon," Pritchard said with a plastic politician's smile. Jesus, he sounded like Jed Clampett on steroids. The wave of people poured into the terminal as Pritchard disappeared behind the sliding doors.

First class air travel is everything it's cracked up to be. I, of course, was in coach, or steerage, as they called it on the Titanic. I wasn't just sitting uncomfortably, with my legs against my chest and some kid shooting weird looks from the seat in front of me, but at the far back against a squeaky panel, next to a lavatory that had malfunctioned or hadn't been cleaned the last few flights.

I tried to imagine the pilot pulling some long, yellow lever, like a bombardier's release stick, and jettisoning the entire contents of the plane's toilets. I could imagine the dirty fluid as it crystallized into a huge chunk of blue ice speeding towards earth at hundreds of miles an hour and crashing into some poor slob's living room, somewhere in Kentucky. He'd be headline news, his shocked face plastered all over the papers. Nothing worked. No amount of imagination would protect me from the nauseous smell. What next, hijackers?

I tried to get the stewardess's attention as she walked by. She kept walking. I instinctively focused on her ass and quickly measured her up, but was abruptly ripped from my fantasy by the sight of Dexter Grace. He was sitting forward in the first class cabin. Of course. I hadn't realized I'd be on Pritchard's flight. It added a sense of irony to my day. This was going to be interesting.

Dexter diligently pored over files and paperwork as Pritchard sipped champagne and flirted with Jennifer. Although her legs were crossed, the slit of her dress went up to her thigh. I couldn't understand how any of Pritchard's staffers could get any decent work done with her around.

Pritchard tapped her glass in a toast of some kind then whispered something in her ear. She giggled. Dexter took umbrage and looked up, but Pritchard was too quick to let him get in a word. "You must know Mexico pretty well by now, Huh, Dex?" Dexter nodded, wondering what Pritchard was groping for. "I'll bet that ol' scoundrel Chavez has already offered you some kind of cabinet position, hasn't he?" His voice took on a slight timbre of impropriety.

Dexter put down his pen and paper and looked at Pritchard emotionlessly. "You know where my loyalties lay, Sir," he said in an enigmatic way.

Pritchard took a moment to study Dexter's reaction. Dexter was hard to read, a definite nerd, half sociopath, but he was also shrewd in a way. He perplexed Pritchard, but the senator knew his aide was loyal and looked out for his best interests. Pritchard sat back and broke a smile as wide as a country mile. "I'm just mess'n with ya, Dex! Come on, have some bubbly before we land. I won't tell your mama."

Just then, the captain came over the loudspeaker. "And if you look to your left, we're just passing over the green Caribbean waters of the Yucatan Peninsula," he said in a mundane voice, sounding more like a lackadaisical tour guide than a pilot.

A drunken college student a few rows ahead of me spilled his drink as he stood up and shouted, "Just fly the plane, Captain Kirk!" His fraternity brothers roared with laughter, high-fiving each other. It was kind of funny, I thought, but you would have had to be there.

Pritchard began a conversation with two of his staff members as Dexter looked down the aisle into coach. He zeroed in on me. I was taking notes. His jaw tightened.

Backwards. Forwards. Backwards. I had to keep pressing the button on my microcassette recorder as I fed my oral notes into it and backed up to check if the sound level was right. It sounded pretty good. Like Charlie, I was old-school. I didn't trust technology, or it didn't trust me. Either way, I still used real tapes in my recorder. The stewardess finally arrived with my third Bloody Mary and I tried to steady my hand as I brought it to my mouth. "God, I needed that!" I said under my breath as I downed half of it in one gulp.

Maybe I should seriously think about cutting down on my drinking... Nah! I reached for the airphone buried in the headrest in front of me. The kid ahead of me hadn't bugged me in a few minutes, so I pulled the phone out softly and fed the long cord around my hand to make sure I'd have enough to bring to my ear. I was beginning to feel pretty confident by now. I dialed the *Post* and charged the seven-dollar-a-minute call to my well-used expense-account credit card. "Charlie, it's Riley!" There was a momentary pause due either to a poor signal or Charlie's surprise.

"It's about goddamn time!" he shouted in his usual boorish way. "So, did you make your decision?"

I smiled as I looked out the plane window and said, "I'm following a hot lead right now. I think I might be onto something big."

Again a pause. "Are you fucking with me, Riley? I'm in no mood to be fucked with today."

I huffed out a laugh. He was so predictable. "No, Charlie, I'm serious, I'm on the job."

I could hear his voice changing from disappointed skepticism to beaming pride as he said, "Okay, now you're talking. So fill me in! After all, I am your editor and the idiot that pays your prima-donna salary."

I swirled the red-stained ice cubes in my little plastic glass and inhaled the vodka. "Can't give you any details yet, but you'll have to trust me on this one," I said, knowing full well that it would drive him crazy.

"Riley," he said, beginning to raise his voice.

I knew he wasn't going to like what I was about to say. "I'm on my way to Mexico City," I said straightforwardly.

Another pause, but this time it was longer. I could feel the mood change over the airwaves. Charlie began to shout, "Mexico! Jesus-Fucking-Christ, Riley, you know you can't go back there!" We were too far away from each other for him to have any real effect on me and he knew it.

"Too late, Charlie! I'm calling from the plane and we're about to land. You wanted commitment, I'm giving you commitment."

Again the mood change, but this time it was serious. "Listen, Terry, forget what I said. Come back now and I'll give you some nice stringer work, I'll put you back in the field, you name it. Just don't do this," he said paternally.

I looked down as we passed over some clouds. It was a bright sunny day outside and I couldn't remember the last time I'd stop to notice one. "Charlie, you were right about what you said the other day, right about everything... I'll call you in a couple of days."

I heard Charlie scream, "Riley!" as I hung up the phone and sat back into my seat. I smiled then pressed the record button on my tape recorder.

I was leaning forward to bring the cassette recorder to my lips when I looked up. It was Dexter. He was looming over me with this Cheshire-Cat grin on his face. "A friend of mine got a call from your Girl Friday, Kate Walker. Seems she's buck'n for your job, Riley," he said in a smarmy, prep-school way.

I swirled the ice cubes, trying to accelerate the melting process. "You got any friends, Dexter?" I said without looking up.

After a moment, I could see his shoes were in the same place, so I continued. "Do you mind? I'm working here." I said it loud enough for a stewardess in the aft kitchen to hear me. I felt like a woman at a bar trying to get rid of an unwelcome suitor.

Dexter's face turned serious as he said, "Keep trashing Senator Pritchard and you'll look a lot worse than you do now."

I looked down at my tray table to see the tape running. I wasn't even in Mexico yet and I was already getting juicy stuff. "Is that a threat, Dexter?"

He pointed at my face and barked, "You bet your ass, Riley!" then turned to walk back up the aisle to the forward cabin.

I hit the stop button on my recorder. "Wow, what a dick!" I said to myself quietly. Now I'd caught a senatorial aide threatening a reporter. This was great stuff.

I looked down through the clouds as we descended. All I could see was a huge expanse of ghetto. Gray and black, rust-covered corrugated-tin shacks. Half-built apartment complexes and millions of people stacked upon millions of people. From one end of my field of vision to the other was nothing but an enormous city laid from top to bottom with poverty. Even from thousands of feet above, I could see little dots moving about. Cars, people, everything and everybody crammed into one space. A dense, yellow-gray sky loomed over Mexico City and obscured the sun, casting a dingy shadow over the endless ghettos. It was a sickening sight.

XVI

Mexico City had an airport that most Americans would laugh at. It was simple in its layout. Green tile flooring polished to a high gloss, with yellow signs everywhere in ten different languages. The airport didn't have terminals or security gates or immigration lines like others. They had their own way of doing things here.

People left unattended bags everywhere around this place. After all, Mexico City wasn't exactly on Al Qaeda's top ten list. They take siestas in the middle of the day, for Christ's sake! The occasional policeman or *Federale* cruised the foyers and surrounding area, but never got too involved in airport matters. They seemed more concerned with passing the day chatting up sorority girls and Brazilian models. No harm done. Relax. It's Mexico!

The most stunning oddity at the Mexico City Airport was the traffic signals. No, not the lights outside on the street, but the traffic lights inside the terminal. They directed human traffic, not cars. Mexican officials either feel no need or don't have the manpower to greet each and every arriving tourist and immigrant. Instead, they have a rather ingenious way of weeding out ne'er-do-wells. A simple traffic light. Red means stop. Green means go. That's it. Whether you are entering Mexico legally or illegally, you step up with your bags to a small traffic light and push the tiny silver button, and it will either turn green, allowing you free access to the country, or turn red, which means, basically, you're screwed.

If the light turns red, you're moved to a large table where customs agents begin their long, tedious and irritating process of inspecting your bags. If you're lucky and get a considerate agent, he or she may rifle through your belongings quickly and carelessly, and send you on your way. If you're unlucky, you'll get the royal treatment, which may include a thorough inspection of each item you've carried—"tossing a bag," as they like to say—and then being told to repack your luggage in front of them. And it better fit. All this, of course, is due to the outcome of a simple game of red light, green light. Suspicious or not, you're gonna push that button.

I just knew I was going to get screwed on this deal. The last five people in front of me had pressed the button and gotten a green light. It was a percentage game, and with my luck, I'd be there all day, maybe even get a little hassle because of the state of my face. I walked up to the little silver bastard and pushed it in contempt.

"*Oyé, Señor!*" I heard from the customs officer in front of me. "*Señor, venga.* Come through, please." I knew it, I just knew it. I looked up at the traffic light. It was green. Now I was holding up the line. Maybe my luck had changed....

As I stepped out of the terminal onto the walkway, the bright Mexican sun momentarily blinded me. I'd been pretty much a vampire the last few years and hadn't spent a lot of time in direct sunlight. I reached into the sleeve of my carry-on bag and pulled out a pair of sunglasses. I might've been beat up, but I was going to try to look cool. I searched over the crowd of people waiting for their rides and tried to hail a cab. "Taxi!" I shouted over the din. I could tell it was going to be impossible to get a ride into town.

There was an overwhelming stench of diesel fuel, and puffs of soot belched from the hindquarters of the old, slapped-together vehicles. Cars with names I'd never seen, like *RAPIDO* and *EL POCITO,* went whizzing by. Superglue and worn rope held bumpers together and broken lane dividers meant nothing to these drivers. They wanted to get where they were going, and nothing or no one was about to get in their way.

Across the street, a group of old cabbies were leaning against their cars, smoking cigarettes and bullshitting. Next to them stood a young Mexican boy, probably only around thirteen. He looked like a street urchin, a runaway, homeless, yet seemed playful and sensible. His thick black hair was coifed to a perfect pompadour and he mimicked one of the other cabbies, making broad gestures with his hands as he told a story. He looked like one of those pain-in-the-ass mimes you see in the park, but he cracked me up. As a group of young Catholic schoolgirls in plaid skirts walked by, the boy jumped up, making sure his hair was smoothed back.

I had already raised my hands towards the men and shouted, "Taxi!" Nothing. No response. I decided to cross the busy road. Big mistake. I never saw the pickup truck change lanes and barrel right towards me. Like a slow-motion scene from a movie, I glimpsed the cabbies frantically waving their arms at me, shouting, "*Pare!*"

I remembered that meant stop.

They say your life flashes before your eyes right before you die. It doesn't. What does happen is the other guy's life flashes before your eyes. I had just enough time to lock eyes with the driver of the pickup truck and I could see the fear in his face. He looked like a family man, maybe two daughters and a young wife, probably a dog. He was a gas station attendant or construction worker and he really, really didn't want to kill me. I gleaned all this from the fleeting second of connection we shared just before he ran me down.

I felt my body sail through the air, and it wasn't what I'd imagined. Death. Talk about cremation! My head hit the pavement. *Bam*. Well, this was one way to cure my problems. I was thrown back into the crowd. I slowly opened my eyes, expecting to see Saint Peter or Christ or Gandhi, but what I got was what I didn't expect.

It was the young boy. He had raced across the busy the street while I froze in a state of shock, then dove at me, knocking me right on my ass.

"*Buen día, Señor!* You need a taxi?" He crawled off my chest and smiled as though nothing had happened. What few teeth he had were brown from malnutrition and vitamin deficiency. I was in no position to criticize. "I am Sancho, Sancho Lopez," he said with the innocence of a child. He extended his hand and tried to pull me up. I got a quick look at his T-shirt. It was dingy white with a picture of Elvis Presley across the entire front. The caption read: *EL REY! The King!* This kid was a real character.

Sancho may have been thin and wispy, but you could tell he had a good heart and a sense of determination. "Come on, *Señor*. I get your bags and we go to my taxi, okay?" He grabbed my two carry-ons and jumped off the curb. Fearlessly, he stopped the onslaught of cars with his hand like a traffic cop and led me to an awaiting cab.

Sancho stooped low and walked between the cabs, signaling to me to get in one of them. Instead of putting my luggage in the trunk, he pushed it into the back seat behind me, tossing my bags to the floor. It was odd how he crept in the driver's side so as not to be noticed by the other hacks. I thought his cab was out of turn and the taxi captain would probably have his ass for taking a fare before the next guy in line. Hey, nobody else saved my life that day, so I'd back his play if the others gave him a hard time. Still, I thought, he did seem awfully young to be driving a cab—or driving at all, for that matter.

Sancho slowly slid into the front seat and closed the door softly as he pushed down the lock button. He began to frantically search for something under the floor mats and under the seat.

"Thanks again for what you did back there," I said, "and listen, your secret's safe with me. My name's Riley, Terry Riley." He continued his search as if he hadn't heard a word I'd said. I began muttering some more: "I mean, I understand there are rules, you know, the first-come-first-serve rule and all that, but I think there are enough cabs for everyone at the airport..."

Sancho reached up to the visor above his head and pulled it down. The car keys dropped right into his hands. "A-ye!" he yelled. He quickly jammed the ignition key into the steering column and forced it forward. The engine coughed and sputtered for a moment as Sancho rapped on the gas pedal with his foot, then it roared to life. He began to pull forward. *Bam.* He hit the bumper of the cab in front of him. He put the cab in reverse. *Bam.* Another ding.

To his credit, the spots were tight, but he seemed to be in a bigger hurry than was called for. "Hey, no sweat, Kid. I've still got some time. You don't have to ruin your cab on my account." Of course, I was only half-kidding.

I looked through the window and saw that Sancho's maneuvers had agitated some other cabbies who were gathering around. One of the older cabbies looked up sharply. The large, gray-bearded hack pointed his finger at us and shouted, "*Oyé!*" I knew that meant he was pissed. "Hey, Kid, I think you pissed that guy off when you hit his cab," I chuckled as I thought of trying to catch a cab in New York City. I turned back around to watch what was going to happen next. The large cabbie shook his finger and ran toward us, still screaming, "*Oyé!*"

Sancho finally got the taxi loose from its moorings and headed into traffic. This was also a trial since no one in Mexico really wants to let you into traffic. But this kid seemed to have less patience than I did. He swerved in and out, cutting off three or four cars as he cut across the lanes into the fairway.

Bang. Bang. Suddenly there was pounding on the driver-side window. It was the large cabbie and yes, he was pissed. His face was red from running and screaming and sweat was beginning to bead on his brow. His eyes seemed crazed as he shouted and banged on the window, trying to open the driver-side door. "*Cholito! Puto!*" and other Latin expletives spewed out of the old hack's mouth as Sancho's attention remained fixed on driving through the heavy congestion. Suddenly, Sancho turned and began to taunt him, thumbing his nose at the cabbie, who was now struggling to keep up.

Seeing a break a break in the traffic, Sancho pressed the accelerator down hard. He waved at the old man as we zoomed away. I turned around and watched the old man slow, then stop, panting as he reached down to sit on the curb and catch his breath.

Sancho giggled like a schoolboy. "What the hell was his problem?" I said, laughingly.

"*No problema, Señor.* You sit back and relax. You are with Sancho now." He pulled a pair of rhinestone sunglasses from his back pocket and put them on, saying, "When you ride with Sancho... you ride with the king!"

I leaned forward and happened to catch the driver's ID placard draped over the stereo knob. It was a hack license with a picture of the large old cabbie and his name in bold letters: *RAUL DOMINGO.* Sancho had stolen this cab with me as an accessory. Man, I'd just stepped off the plane and already I was in trouble.

I couldn't stop laughing. This kid had just pulled off something I would never have the balls to do. I slowly leaned back and took the kid's advice. "Hotel Intercontinental... and take your time," I said.

"*Sí,* Señor Riley!" Sancho smiled.

XVII

Mexico City's a pit. I'm not bashing Mexico or Mexicans *per se*, but Mexico City's a shithole. And when it's hot, like it is almost year-round, it's worse. What makes it so unpleasant isn't the architecture or the language or the people themselves, but the nauseating pollution and old cars and millions of bodies meandering through the streets and back alleys nearly on top of each other. It's the most overpopulated city on earth, even rivaling Calcutta, and when you're there, you never question that little piece of trivia.

Sancho drove past a monument of some guy who'd done something heroic. It was covered in soot. A cloud of smog had layered the atmosphere and gotten darker and darker as it descended upon the city. We passed long, dark alleys and ghettos where clotheslines hung from the rooftops and people threw their trash in the street until it piled up knee-deep. Half-naked children played anywhere they could, giving no access to a passing car or bicycle. They learned to own the streets here from the time they were in diapers and didn't give them up until their lives ended from starvation, drugs or a bullet. A chill ran down my spine when I thought of how good we in the States had it. No wonder they were willing to risk everything to get to *El Norte*. What else did they have to live for?

Sancho careened down Revolution Boulevard toward the *Plaza De Mexico* while I admired the hundreds of colorful campaign posters that lined the streets. Some promoted a grassroots campaigner named Jose Vasquez, who was running on the Socialist ticket, while some endorsed PRI candidate Elena Katrin Alonso, but most of the advertisements favored the charismatic incumbent Governor of Mexico, Roberto Chavez.

Chavez seemed to control the lion's share of ad space and revenue, and no matter where you were in Mexico City, it seemed he was looking down on you. Yet despite their veneers of pomp and circumstance, nearly all the political posters had been vandalized. Spray-painted graffiti that read *VIVA ZAPATA!* were evident everywhere.

I'd known the Zapatista movement was powerful and had grown since I nearly got killed covering it years ago. It was gaining acceptance because it was comprised of the common Mexican: the farmer, the laborer, the native. The regular Joe. The government had oppressed the Zapatistas, or Chiapas rebels as they were called for years, but now they seemed to be gaining a large underground following.

Just then I got a tingle in my belly. That meant my journalistic instinct was kicking in and I should follow my nose to a story, wherever it led me. What was I saying? Those days were over for me. I had to focus on what I'd come down here for.

"Do you see her? Ah, she is the Great Angel," Sancho said, breaking my concentration.

I looked up to see a towering monument of an angelic woman with wings. "Yeah! She's something else," I retorted. As we passed underneath the statue, I couldn't help but stare at the beauty of the relic. It was kind of a weird feeling.

It was just before siesta time and the crowds were getting heavier on the streets as we pulled up to the Intercontinental Hotel. There were no valets or bellhops—the sidewalks couldn't support idle bodies waiting for guests to arrive. It was each man for himself. Sancho nearly drove over two tourists crossing the busy boulevard as he pulled up to the curb in front of the lobby doors. He reached behind his seat and began to grab my bags.

I pulled out a twenty-dollar bill and snapped it in front of his face. Sancho's eyes lit up like a Vegas slot machine. I let him get a good look at it, inspect the bona fide greenback, then moved my fingers to the center of the bill and ripped it in half. "Listen, I need a siesta," I said, "but I'm gonna need a good driver who knows his way around the city." I handed him half the twenty. I kept the half with the seal—you can always cash that end. "Be here when I wake up, *comprende?*"

The little guy took the half note, and a devilish smile crossed his face. "Señor Riley, I live on these streets. No one knows them better than Sancho Lopez! You can count on me!" He buried the cash in the fob pocket of his tattered blue jeans. "We are amigos now, you and me, Señor! I will stay with you everywhere you go!" He got out with my bags and slammed the door. As I fought the crowd to the lobby entrance, I could hear Sancho drop the taxi into gear and shoot across traffic. Tires screeched as he narrowly missed a street vendor whose mule reared up and spilled a load of vegetables, knocking over a painter's easel and destroying her nearly finished watercolor. Adding insult to injury, Sancho raced toward an open parking spot on the opposite side of the street, brushing past a group of nuns that had to jump into a decorative fountain to escape his maniacal driving. It was either sink or swim with Sancho behind the wheel. I had to smile. It was the first time I had smiled in a long, long time.

When I got to my hotel, sweat was already dripping from my forehead. Christ, this country was hot! I threw my bags at the end of the bed and licked my parched lips. "Man I could sure use a drink," I said to the empty room as I headed for the bathroom and the small utilitarian sink. I turned on the cold water to splash my face seven or eight times, trying to somehow saturate myself and regain the gallons of moisture I'd already lost. I quickly pulled the plastic off one of the drinking glasses so generously provided by the house and filled it with the tepid water from the faucet. I was imagining how good it was going to taste when I saw a small placard on the mirror in front of me. It read: *FOR YOUR SAFETY - PLEASE DRINK THE BOTTLED WATER PROVIDED FOR YOU - MUCHAS GRACIAS!* I dumped the glass of water down the sink in disappointment and reached down to the dorm-sized icebox below. I usually never opened those little hotel refrigerators just out of principle. Ten-dollar beers, four-dollar juices or even a three-buck soda would set you back the price of a decent meal, but in this case I made an exception. I was dying of thirst.

I jimmied the lock and practically tore the door off it. Empty. I was left with a choice: drink the tap water and take my life into my hands or die of dehydration. I grabbed a hand towel from the rack and soaked it under the tap. I dabbed my neck as I walked back to the room and fell backwards onto the bed. *Whoosh.* At least it was a soft landing. I put the wet towel over my sweltering face and gave a sigh… and I was out.

XVIII

Across town at a swanky luxury hotel, Pritchard and his staff of young, slave-driven overachievers had bivouacked, setting up a makeshift camp in the ante-room of a large presidential suite—quite befitting a man who seemed to have nothing else on his mind but the White House. Cell phones rang, chirping constantly like a swarm of annoying parakeets as faxes came in almost non-stop. Congressional update this. Senate approvals that. Politics as usual. Pritchard's cabinet was online and running on full steam despite his venue change.

High above Revolucion Boulevard, overlooking the best of Mexico City, Dexter stood near the window and looked out over the masses. Someone looking up from below might have mistaken him for a black Mussolini or some stoic statesmen about to address his subjects. He looked cocky. Arrogant. A pain in the ass, but loyal. He was ambitious and there were no two ways about it.

Dexter periodically glanced behind him to eye Jennifer Hoover mixing Pritchard a drink. Pritchard had loosened his tie by now and was smiling at her from across the room. Staffers and aides seemed to be trickling out slowly as the business of the day began to subside.

Jennifer crossed the suite carefully while a blue-suited freshman staffer crossed her path with his nose in a clipboard. *Swoosh*. He just missed knocking the drink out of her hand. "Oh, I'm sorry, Ms. Hoover! I... I," he groped for a reasonable excuse.

She just smiled and placed her hand on his shoulder. "Tommy, you just make sure you leave a little time to enjoy yourself this trip," she said in a mothering way. Nearly lulled into a trance by her soft, sexy voice, the young man stumbled on his way out of the room.

From his vantage point, Dexter watched Pritchard give Jennifer an evil grin while stretching out on a stuffed chaise. She strolled over to where he was sitting, bent over to purposely expose her perfect cleavage and handed him a tumbler that was more bourbon than rocks. Dexter was coldly eyeing her from the balcony when his cell phone suddenly rang, tearing his attention away.

"Yeah." He listened a moment, then exploded in a calculated flurry of instructions. "I don't want to hear that! The Zapatistas could strike anywhere, anytime. The Senator's safety is paramount! It is all I care about, do you understand? Good!" He could be charming when he wanted to be. "We arrive at the Governor's mansion at eighteen hundred hours. I want the press contained, and I mean contained! When Senator Pritchard and Governor Chavez unveil the new AMERIMEX plant this week, then we'll begin the media blitz, not before. Remember, no mistakes. Any screw-ups now could cost us the election." Dexter smacked the flip-phone closed, barely taking a breath.

As Jennifer sat next to Pritchard on a couch, touching his leg, pretending to go over the latest news briefs, Dexter clenched his jaw in anger.

XIX

The hot sun sank toward the horizon, filling the city with a strange, pollution-thick, orange haze. Traffic had died down a bit as the afternoon wore on. Many Mexicans would be midway through their daily siestas by now.

Across the street from the Intercontinental, Sancho was slumped behind the wheel, snoring loudly as cars and pedestrians passed by unconcerned. His thick black pompadour was pressed up against the headrest and a long stream of drool leaked from the corner of his gaping mouth. Asleep, he had a childlike quality that belied the very adult stresses his poverty and homelessness caused him to suffer.

As Sancho snored, a single hand slowly reached from behind the door, through the open driver-side window and straight at him. It moved toward his throat, then slowly crept up and stopped at his face. Two fingers suddenly pinched his nostrils closed. "Schnaack!" Sancho gasped himself awake. I couldn't help myself. I chuckled like an idiot, jumped into the backseat and slammed the door.

Sancho shot up in the driver's seat with wide, crazy eyes. "Ah, Ah!" he shouted as he tried to focus and step out of his dream.

"Rise and shine, Amigo, we're off to the U.S. Embassy," I yelled just behind his ear. I was going to have fun torturing this kid. "Vamanos!" I yelled again to make sure he was conscious.

"*Sí, Sí*, Señor Riley," he said, pretending he hadn't fallen asleep at his post.

XX

Philip Gutierrez was a well-dressed man in his early forties with dark, slicked-back short hair and light brown skin. He enjoyed being the Secretary to U.S. Ambassador Sparks. Although he was an American citizen, Gutierrez had been raised in a part of Southern Arizona that was predominantly Mexican, which afforded him the best of his culture in the comfort of the North. He had been with the U.S. State Department for over fifteen years: first with foreign service, diplomatic training, and so on, and now this post. He was hoping someday to be appointed ambassador himself. Since his wife had just had their third child, though, he was in no hurry for a promotion. He was happy to spend his day running interference for the ambassador and reaping the benefits of being an American diplomat on foreign soil. Diplomatic immunity was a trump card if you knew how to use it.

Gutierrez stepped out of his office and walked to the long, spiral staircase above the embassy lobby. He seemed to glide down the off-white stone steps to the shiny marble foyer as he headed for the enclosed reception desk. He hardly noticed the embassy guard chatting with a visitor as he began looking through the daily mail and checking the security lights on the panel behind the desk. He popped his head up over the top of the counter when he heard the pitch of the guard's conversation change.

"I'm sorry, Sir, if you don't have an appointment, you cannot see the ambassador," the guard said in a subtle, but authoritative, tone. He was a large Marine, probably six feet-five, with an enormous chest and biceps. He could talk as quietly as he'd like and people would pay attention. Any deviation in his voice could instantly cause someone to reevaluate their presence there.

Gutierrez looked at his watch and decided to intervene. He walked up behind the guard and assessed the situation. There in front of the guard was Carlos Ramos, dirty and disheveled from the hours spent being blown around by the hot wind in the open-air Jeep, caked with the dirt and sand of the Badlands. Ramos was in no mood to dicker. He had come for help and that's exactly what he planned on leaving with. He had grown impatient.

"Listen, this is a matter of life and death," Ramos barked at the guard as he leaned into his face. The guard's ears raised and his brow narrowed just as Gutierrez stepped up. The guard didn't snap to attention, but stood back in a respectful manner. Seeing that the secretary was willing to help, the guard briefed him quickly. "Mr. Secretary, this man claims to be a doctor. He says his name is Carlos Ramos. He says he has an urgent matter for the ambassador's ears only, but he doesn't have an appointment." Gutierrez smiled and shook his head slightly, then placed his hand on the Marine's shoulder.

"It's okay, Mike, I'll take it from here." Ramos knew that he was slowly climbing the ladder to the right people. Gutierrez took the place of the guard, who went back to his desk and sat down, but kept a tight eye on Ramos to ensure no threats would ensue.

"*Buenos dias, Señor*, I'm Philip Gutierrez, Ambassador Spark's personal secretary. How can I help you?" Gutierrez said as he extended his hand in friendship. Ramos reached out and shook it slowly. The act seemed to calm him, as though someone were finally going to listen. Suddenly, a strange look flashed across the secretary's face. A realization.

A look of remembering... But as a diplomat, Gutierrez could never afford to show his hand. He continued with the pleasantries.

Ramos knew he had been recognized and now felt he was in great danger. Would this man call the Mexican authorities as he was bound to do by international law or would he instead be more apt to listen in sympathy with the plight of his Mexican brethren? Ramos rolled the dice. "I can tell by the look on your face that you know who I am," he whispered.

Gutierrez tilted his head slowly to see if the guard was within earshot. He turned back to Ramos, never blinking, and pursed his lips, leading him to the end of the large rotund desk. "Yes. I know who you are, and the fact that you're standing in the lobby of the United States Embassy tells me you've taken a great risk in coming here," Gutierrez said with the tone of a priest. "I suppose I should give you a few moments of my time."

Ramos looked over Gutierrez's shoulder and up the staircase. "With all due respect, I really need to speak with the ambassador."

Gutierrez raised his chin, bringing Ramos' eyes back down to his. "When you're speaking to me, you are speaking to the ambassador. Everything, and I mean everything, goes through me first."

Ramos realized his impertinence and nodded slightly. "Since you know who I am, I'll get right to the point. I've been exiled in the U.S. for five years and have just come back to bury my father. He was murdered by conspirators in this government!" Gutierrez gave him a quizzical look. "My father was a doctor in the village of San Cristobal when the entire village began showing signs of an epidemic like we've never seen before. A combination of diphtheria, plague and hemorrhagic fever-like symptoms. People began dying within a week. My father was the only one who could help them."

Gutierrez rubbed his chin with mild interest. "Go on."

"He soon learned other villages in the Valle de Luna were infected and that people throughout the desert, the Badlands, the mountains, the foothills—throughout those rural parts of Mexico—were dying at an alarming rate." Ramos took a breath. He knew he had only a short window of opportunity to present his case before he would have to flee. "My father discovered something in the desert, I don't know what, but it was at a high-security facility. Something the military was hiding. A vaccine, a drug maybe, that would prevent this epidemic… something. He had been gathering evidence to send outside Mexico that would expose a conspiracy the night he was run off the road."

Gutierrez pondered this information like a yogi. He decided to play the devil's advocate. "Valle de Luna? That's in Chiapas, isn't it, Zapatista territory?" Gutierrez inquired.

Ramos looked sternly at him. "Yes, that is what I'm talking about. This epidemic seems to be spreading to every pro-Zapatista village and community."

Gutierrez showed the first signs of doubt. "Are you telling me that only the villages that sympathize with the rebels are affected? No one else?"

Ramos became slightly flustered. "No, I don't know! All I'm saying is that I know whatever the military was doing out there is directly related to the rebel movement and we both know the Mexican government and the military would do anything they could to quash that." Gutierrez was straight down the line when he said, "These are strong accusations you're leveling, and as you probably already know, U.S. policy frowns on foreign intervention of any kind. I don't know, this sounds more like a matter for the Mexican authorities, don't you think?"

That agitated Ramos. "The police? All they care about is their fucking *mordida*—nickel and dime payoffs, their drug money. Corrupt cops aren't about to stick their necks out for anybody. Why would they?" His toned suddenly changed to one of desperation: "Here. Look. My father documented everything." Ramos pulled a number of manila folders from an old leather satchel and threw them onto the marble countertop. Enlarged black and white photos and documents spilled out everywhere.

Gutierrez brushed his hand over the pile of photos and began to inspect them, picking up two and three at a time. He was taken aback by the graphic nature of the pictures: mass graves, rows of dead infants. Death was everywhere in the photos, each one more gruesome than the next. The secretary could almost smell the rotting corpses as he pored through as many as he could. He was truly affected, but knew he had to come across as indifferent. In his position, he could never show the slightest sign of prejudice or allegiance—especially to an outlaw like Ramos.

"This epidemic is sweeping the valley," Ramos continued as Gutierrez surveyed the photos. "Men, women, even babies in the womb, are dying horrible deaths by the hundreds, thousands. Infant mortality has risen tenfold in the past thirteen months and we cannot isolate this bug."

Gutierrez looked up and responded, trying to misdirect his feelings and play the consummate diplomat: "Doctor Ramos, you should know better than most that infant mortality in rural Mexican villages is not uncommon if for no other reason than lack of proper medical facilities. Why haven't you contacted the CDC in Atlanta? I'm sorry to sound so dispassionate, but the U.S. could only assist in a 'Humanitarian Effort,' and that would be after months of investigation and committee approvals."

Ramos knew that meant stalemate. Gutierrez was not going to help, and his frustration began to mount. "Sir, you know I am a Zapatista subcommander. A rebel leader. I've put my life on the line just to come here. If they caught me it would mean certain torture and death. I do not ask this for me, but for my people. Please, I'm begging you to help us!" Ramos said in a deep tone as his face flushed and eyes welled.

"Believe me when I say I realize the risk you have taken, and I want to thank you for entrusting me with this information, but I cannot give you the answer you seek. The position I am in precludes it. I am truly sorry." Gutierrez nearly bowed his head in shame as he said the words.

Ramos picked up a number of photos and shook them in Gutierrez's face. "Look! Look at what's happening to my people. Your people. You must do something. You have to!"

Suddenly the Marine guard looked over and slowly rose from his chair in a protective manner. He placed his hand on the leather holster of his Glock .22 and was about to flip up the locking strap when Gutierrez gestured with his hand. It was okay, he motioned. The guard nodded then slowly sat back down, keeping a close eye on Ramos' every move.

As photos flew in Gutierrez's face, he suddenly saw something that caught his eye. He waited for Ramos to drop the pictures then nonchalantly picked up one from the counter. It was a photo of Cortes: He stood at the center of a secured facility supervising the transfer of hundreds of barrels. Gutierrez pulled out three similar pics and put them aside, but without raising any hopes.

"I'd like to help you, Doctor, and I will note our conversation in detail and with the utmost discretion, but there's really nothing we can do at this time. I would, however, like to keep these photos. Maybe they could become useful if we decide to offer any aid."

Dejected, Ramos became even more frustrated. "By the time you bureaucrats get off your fat asses, my village will be wiped out and they'll be no one left to help! *Muchas Gracias, Amigo!*" he said sarcastically. That didn't help.

It was about that time when I strolled up to the reception desk. The guard still had his eyes tight on Ramos when I interrupted him. "Yeah, I'm Terry Riley with the *Washington Post*. I've got an interview with Ambassador Sparks," I announced in a droll way. I had to wipe the sweat off my brow just to make small talk. "You got anything to drink around this place? Christ, this country is hot! How can you stand it?" The guard turned his attention to me and loosened up his demeanor.

He pulled out a clipboard from under the desk and scrolled down an attached list. He took his pen and made a check mark next to my name then pointed to a small glass panel built into the top of the reception desk. "Yes, Mr. Riley. If you'd be kind enough to place your hand on the plate, I'll scan your fingerprints and you can sign in," the guard instructed as he placed the clipboard near my hand.

I complied with little resistance. I had no choice: This guy was a monster. I placed my hand on the glass plate and a green neon light scanned my fingertips, my palm then my wrist. I could see the guard scrutinizing a color computer monitor as my hand digitized, materializing on screen. A color picture of my face suddenly appeared next to my palm. Nearly my entire life history popped up in summary:

Riley, Terrence Francis Xavier. Born May 1963, Chicago, Illinois. Father: Patrick Michael Riley- Chicago Police- Deceased. Mother: Mary Patricia- Deceased. Criminal Convictions- None. Prior Arrests- 1: Drunk & Disorderly. Employed: Washington Post. Occupation: Journalist. Threat assessment: CLEARED FOR EMBASSY.

Man, I was used to the routine, but somehow this security check made even me uneasy. It was just way too scary how much private information was out there now and how just about anybody with a laptop and a *Dummies Guide to Identity Theft* could fuck your life. Thanks again, Osama.

The guard looked at me and smiled. "Your old man was a cop, huh?" He gave me a stare as though he was giving me the club handshake, letting me know I was okay.

"Yep! A Chi-town flatfoot!" I answered to speed up the process. I was in no mood to start talking about my father. Luckily he wasn't either.

"Hang on a sec, I'll get ya somebody," he said as he walked down to Gutierrez.

The foyer was vast. And clean. It had a shiny floor—the kind your mother would have a heart attack over if you ever walked on it. It was tastefully minimalist, with merely a few pieces of artwork and sculptures from both Mexico and America. I admired the lobby. I inspected every nook and cranny with my eyes. Squinting, I could see tiny video cameras in each upper corner. Metal detectors next to every place a person would sit or stand, pressure-sensitive monitors and outlets that were probably souped-up infrared scanners. I followed a thick, grid-like opening in the floor that mirrored the same kind of opening in the ceiling. These would produce bullet-proof, blast-proof acrylic panels that would shoot up within an instant in the case of an entry assault. A series of gunmetal-bordered holes in the walls and ceilings were probably actual gun turrets that would ensure the return of enemy fire from any angle. I couldn't stop pondering how expensive the art of war and paranoia had become. This place had all the comforts of insecurity. I'm glad it was going to be a short stay.

While I was busy waiting on the ambassador, the guard stepped up and whispered into Gutierrez's ear. The secretary immediately ended his conversation with Ramos. "Forgive me Doctor, but I have to take an interview with an American journalist. I hope you find your answers soon. *Mucho suerte.*" But before he walked away, Gutierrez scooped up the photos. As the secretary approached me, I looked over to see Ramos scowling at me from the other end of the desk. Who the hell was this guy and why was he giving me the evil eye?

Gutierrez extended his hand. "Mr. Riley, *Buenas Tardes!* The Ambassador apologizes, but he's been detained in meetings all day and asked me to supply you with any information you require for next week's summit. I'm Philip Gutierrez, the Ambassador's Secretary." Shit! I was being blown off already, and I'd just got there.

Gutierrez continued with classic diplomacy: "If you could give me a moment, we'll go to my office. We'll be more comfortable there." He turned and stepped away to the opposite side of the reception desk, where he pulled a panel aside. A small red phone appeared. He extracted it and put his ear to the handset. His call was obviously routed by an operator in some safe basement somewhere since the phone itself sported no buttons, keypad or carousel.

The guard was sitting in his chair diligently watching the multi-screen security monitor when Gutierrez began speaking quietly into the handset, all the while inspecting the black and white photos in his hands.

Ramos, though still agitated, decided to make his move. He cautiously sidled up towards me, and I was too preoccupied with thirst to see him coming. Big mistake. I should've sensed something was about to happen. Nothing in Mexico was ever easy.

"So you're a reporter?" I turned and realized Ramos was right in my face. No place to run.

"It's debatable these days, but yeah," I said acerbically. "Do I know you?" I could see a weird glimmer of what seemed to be unexpected hope cross his face. He had found his patsy. Me.

"Listen, there's no reason for you to believe me, but trust me, I have a story for you. An important story that you'd be a fool not to cover," Ramos said with desperate enthusiasm.

Oh my God, here it was: whack-job central. This kind of shit happened to me all the time. I couldn't have become more bored. I looked him up and down, thinking he might be a vagrant. I smacked my parched lips in a disinterested way and said, "Jesus! If I had a dime for every time someone used that line on me, I'd be a fucking millionaire."

Ramos quickly pulled out the manila folders and withdrew the black and white photos. He leafed through them, spreading the goriest, most horrid ones in front of me to get my attention. I was more sickened than impressed.

"Nice. Really nice. What are you, some sort of amateur pathologist, or do you just get a kick out of documenting horrible illness?" I thought I was gonna puke, but I wouldn't show this guy the satisfaction. It was probably just what he wanted. The sick fuck!

Ramos beat his index finger down hard on a photo and said, "This! This is the story! There's a disease, a terrible plague, wiping out the villages in Valle de Luna, The Valley of The Moon. It's just outside Mexico City. I could take you there so you could see for yourself what's happening. My people are being wiped out." He grabbed my arm at the tricep. He was a strong guy, had a grip like a vice. "A reporter like you could blow the whole thing wide open. Please, you have to help me," he said forcefully.

I could tell this guy wasn't going to take no for an answer, but I had bigger fish to fry. I was in Mexico for one reason and one reason only. "Sorry, Pal. I don't do that kind of reporting anymore. You want an investigative journalist. I do the nice easy stuff, now." I didn't know how this lunatic would react, but I suddenly felt this guy looked familiar too. I couldn't place him off-hand, but I swear I thought I'd seen him before.

My answer didn't sit well with him so I turned away and crept closer to the guard's station. Moral support. Ramos grabbed my arm again, this time whipping me around like he was going to knock my block off.

Out of the corner of my eye I could see the guard leap over the counter. Wow, this guy must have taken a course in high jumping from Michael Jordan. Gutierrez threw down the phone at the same time. It all happened so fast. In an instant, the Marine popped up behind Ramos, then pulled his arm off mine and yanked it behind his back in one motion. I think they call it "joint manipulation" in mixed martial arts.

Gutierrez appeared. He was more civil about the matter; nonetheless, he moved quickly to intercede. He maintained his composure as he instructed the guard, "Please escort the doctor to the exit. He is distraught over the death of his father."

Ramos struggled a bit, but was no match for the Marine guard. I take back every bad thing I ever said about gym rats and juicers.

Gutierrez walked with Ramos as the guard led him through the revolving door, whispering in his ear, "Go home, Doctor. If you are right about the government being involved, they will never let you live long enough to prove it. Remember, you're still a wanted man in Mexico!"

With that, Ramos gave one last tug to pull his arm away from the guard in protest. As he exited the embassy, he gave it one last look. I could see him as he leapt down the long stairs and onto the street. He disappeared into a crowd.

XXI

Kate Walker was settling into her chair with a cappuccino and croissant from the guy on the corner when she realized her desk was not in the tight and pristine and anal-retentive order she'd always left it in. It was like some Goldilocks had been rummaging around her things, eating all her porridge and sleeping in her bed. She began to thumb through papers on the top of her desk. She slowly pursed her lips and lowered her eyes like one of the Three Bears and grumbled aloud, "Who's been using my desk?"

Jean Smiley looked up over her computer screen and said, "Who else would leave a mess like that?" Smiley never talked without a cigarette dangling from her lips like it was an appendage, a permanent part of her facial structure.

Kate reared her head back in curiosity and said, "Riley?" Smiley sneered as a puff of smoke shot from her nostrils like a dragon, and went back to work. A combination of affection and downright pissed-off-ness came over Kate's face. She walked over to my desk. She scratched her head. It had been nearly a week since I'd been out of the office and it didn't look like anyone had been at my desk since. She marched down the aisle.

"Who is it?" Charlie barked as Kate banged on his closed door. "The fact that the door is closed should be abundantly clear to whoever it is that I don't want to be disturbed," he yelled as his voice got closer to the door.

Bang. Bang. Bang. Kate was in no mood to be intimidated by the likes of Charlie Petersen even if he was her boss.

"It's me, Charlie, open up!" she barked back. Charlie flung open the door to scare whoever was there, but Kate pushed right past him, nearly knocking him off his feet. She snapped, "Where's Riley? I know he's been here, because my desk looks like his apartment."

Either in fear or as a quick exit strategy, Charlie kept his office door halfway open. "He's on assignment. Now get out, I'm on a phone call," he said as he returned to his desk. He picked up the receiver and was about to finish his conversation when Kate slammed both her hands down onto the top of his desk and said quietly, "What assignment?"

Charlie covered the receiver, knowing full well he'd have to give this woman a good answer or she'd hound him forever. "He's away on assignment, that's all you need to know. Now get...," he began to say, but Kate raised an eyebrow.

"Where, Charlie? Where is Riley? And don't mess with me today or I'll turn this office over and tell security that I'm having my period to justify my psychotic episode and worker's comp case!" Charlie was from another era. He could swear like a truck driver with the boys, but at the mere mention of a woman's... you know, time-of-the-month, he'd walk a mile out of his way to avoid it.

He spoke into the receiver, "I've got a situation here. I'll call you back," and hung up the phone. He composed himself and gestured for Kate to sit. Nope. She was gonna stand. "He's covering the International Ecological Conference," he said sheepishly, waiting for the other shoe to drop.

Kate stood up and processed the information for a second with a tilt of her head then said, "The International Ecological... That's in Mexico!" Charlie nodded. Kate continued in a sarcastically questioning fashion, "Charlie, I thought you told me once that Riley could never go back to Mexico. Isn't that what you said, CHARLIE?! " Charlie reached for a cigar from his humidor to evade the question, but Kate was getting impatient. She slammed her hands on the desk again. Charlie took the cigar from his mouth and pointed at her with it.

"Now slow down there, Missy. All right. I don't like it anymore than you do... Riley went down to Mexico on some half-baked idea that he's got some big story."

Kate relaxed a little, but still had suspicion in her voice as she said, "What big story? The Eco-conference is a no-brainer. It's just a bunch of politicians patting each other on the back." Suddenly she threw her head back in a sort of exasperated realization. "Pritchard! He went after Pritchard, didn't he?" Now she was truly annoyed.

Charlie threw his hands up in disgust and said, "Kid, I don't know what the hell he's doing down there, but if he's not careful, he's gonna got himself killed. Now get back to work and don't mention this to anyone. As far as everybody's concerned, Riley's taking a long overdue vacation and is incommunicado."

Kate decided then that Charlie's deal wasn't good enough. "I want to know where he is and what he's doing. If he calls you I want to know what he said. Charlie, you better keep me posted or I swear to God..."

He knew she was serious. "All right, all right!" he said with a paternal tone, studying her worried face as she backed up toward the door. "You got a little thing for him, don't you, Kid?"

Kate hesitated just long enough for Charlie to get his answer then huffed defensively, "No! God, no, Charlie! I just... I just need to know where he put that, that thing... you know, my thing for the deal... Oh, forget it!" Charlie popped the cigar back into his mouth and smiled as Kate slammed his door on the way out.

XXII

Gutierrez leaned back into a comfortable high-backed leather chair. It suited the room, which was designed in a dark wood with thick paneling and deep, plush carpet. A diplomatic seal was woven into the center of a large area rug, giving the place an official look and feel. He had the usual framed pictures around the room: wife and kids, fishing in the Gulf on a chartered boat, sky diving in Puerto Vallarta; photos where he looked more like a USC frat boy who liked to party than a Harvard grad, which he truly portrayed when you met him in person. Bright. Sophisticated. Tactful. He had good taste in clothes, too. I pulled out my microcassette recorder, checked the tape, turned it on, and grabbed my notepad and my favorite gold pen.

"You don't mind if I record this interview, do you?" I asked.

Gutierrez waved his hands in an unconcerned fashion as he swiveled in his chair. "Here, have a cigar," he said as he opened the humidor in front of me on his desk. "Some of Castro's finest! We in the foreign service can occasionally turn a blind eye to exports of questionable origins. One of the perks, you know."

I thought, what the hell, I'm no politician; I'm just a regular guy. These things were like gold to a working class stiff like me. I reached in and scooped up three cigars, then dropped two back before he saw what

I was trying to do. This guy was beginning to impress me. "Hmm, this could be confused with leftist sympathizing, Mr. Secretary."

He chuckled and said, "Call me Phil." He fired up his stogie with one of those fancy flameless jet engines then reached over to light mine. We plopped down into our chairs after drawing off the first deep puffs and took a brief moment to relax.

Gutierrez nonchalantly picked up a dossier with a diplomatic seal on it. He removed the red ribbon from its hook and began to peruse the material inside. I let him take all the time he needed; I hadn't had a decent cigar in years.

The folder was still in front of his face when he began, "I hope you don't mind, but I took the liberty of having the girls downstairs do a background check on you, Mr. Riley."

I leaned back and took a long drag off my cigar, then sent a thick smoke ring into the air and said, "Call me, Terry... I didn't realize I was a security risk!"

Without moving the folder, he retorted, "Actually, it's S.O.P. for just about everybody who enters a U.S. Embassy nowadays. Look at Nigeria!" I could hear him muttering behind the folder, "Hmm, interesting. Very colorful. I see this isn't your first trip to Mexico."

I had hoped he wouldn't go there. I began to feel a little uncomfortable. I squirmed in my seat. "Yeah, I covered the Chiapas Massacres a few years ago."

Gutierrez placed the file on his desk and gritted his teeth. "An ugly, ugly business, that. Unfortunately, the growing pains of a country struggling to become more of a democracy," he said, careful to stay neutral.

"More like fascism, if you ask me!" I answered. "Government troops charging in, soldiers shooting rebels and everyone else in sight. It was like Vietnam without the rice."

Just then I saw a twinkle in Gutierrez's eye. "Remember, their president did pull the army out of those territories. It's pretty stable now."

This guy had pushed the wrong button. "Of course! It's an election year."

He knew I knew my politics, so he switched gears and changed the subject: "Good point. That's why this International Ecological Conference is so important to Mexico. And it may just end up the most important summit of our lifetime."

I could tell he meant what he said, but I was not so optimistic. I volleyed back, "Come on, Phil, that's just U.S. protocol talking. It's a fucking tree-hugger's convention. A chance for the old boys to throw back a few tequilas, a couple of señoritas, and pat themselves on the back for talking about making positive changes to the environment, but never enforcing any of them. It was bullshit in Paris and it's bullshit here."

Gutierrez leaned back into his comfy chair and folded his hands behind his head. "You seem to be quite a cynic, Mr. Riley. I like that. Cynics make the best journalists. You realize that you reporters are the best check and balance system we have?" He studied my face. Stop jerking me off, I thought. He thought for a moment, then spoke candidly: "I'll speak frankly with one caveat: Don't quote me. You know the drill—not from my lips!"

I sneered a bit, but knew it was the only way I was going to get any decent information out of this guy. But I wouldn't let him off without letting him know I knew his game, so I said, "'Plausible Deniability,' right?"

Gutierrez took a moment, looked around his office as though he was checking to see if the coast was clear, then said, "Are you familiar with U.S. Senator Daniel Pritchard?"

My eyes rolled almost to the back of head. "Oh, yeah, I'm his biggest fan. Because of him, I'm required reading for all the crooked politicians on Capitol Hill. To be honest with you, Phil, he's the reason I'm here in Mexico," I said, letting the proverbial cat out of the bag. Gutierrez returned to my file. "It says here that you won a Pulitzer Prize for investigative journalism. What was that for?"

I squirmed again as I replied, "Farmgate."

Gutierrez sat back and pointed his finger at me, saying, "That was your story? That really shook the tree on the Hill, didn't it?"

I really didn't want to talk about that, so it was my turn to change the subject. "Yeah, it did... now, you were saying about the conference?"

Gutierrez got the picture. "This conference was designed to put serious pressure on those countries that continue to create Global Warming by destroying our environment and natural resources with impunity."

He had me a bit curious. "What kind of pressure?" I asked.

At that point, Gutierrez reached over, grabbed my microcassette recorder and promptly shut it off. Things were about to get interesting. "This is off the record!" he said seriously. "If these violating countries don't start playing ball, we, meaning the U.S., NATO, etc., have certain contingencies we'll be forced to implement."

I said pensively, "Go on."

Gutierrez stood up and began to pace the room as he got to the nitty gritty of his explanation: "Beside the obvious fact the world is using up resources and destroying the environment at an exponential rate, there seems to be a way to make a profit in ecology. Getting the rest of the world to comply, well... Let's say it only makes the United States look better."

I don't know, it sounded a little vague, so I thought I'd get him to go deeper when I said, "Tough talk, but what about the compliance? Most of the violating countries are Third World, anyway: China, India. How do you think we'll be able to force them into doing anything?"

He paced the room and snickered, then said, "That's the easy part. Trade sanctions. Embargoes. Heavy import duties. Serious economic manipulation—you name it. It's all about dollars. Big Euro-dollars. Big Yen. Get the picture?"

I acquiesced, "I'm starting to."

He changed tack: "Take Pritchard, for instance. He was relentless down here. He really tightened the screws after NAFTA passed. He was so powerful in lobbying that he got his AMERIMEX Project funded in merely two months." I hated the thought that this guy, a cool guy, admired Pritchard. "Thanks to his dogged effort between Washington and Mexico, AMERIMEX is already in Michoacan, Jalisco, Toluca—and by 2014, this country will be a world leader in agriculture and industry, not to mention tourism. He's one of the power brokers who put his money where his mouth was and came up with a good, safe alternative that would supply fresh water to every Mexican while remaining safe to the environment."

My ears were beginning to bleed. I nearly shouted, but contained myself when I said, "Stop! Stop! You're making him sound like Mother Teresa."

Gutierrez laughed. "Perhaps, but there's no changing the facts. Besides, it's good public relations for the U.S. and Mexico."

I checked my handwritten notes and said, "Phil, you know a guy like Pritchard's got his fingers in a pot down here somewhere. I know he does. I can smell it."

He sat down on the corner of his desk near me and said, "Don't believe everything you write. Not all politicians are crooked."

With that I stood and shook his hand. This interview was over. "Only a politician would say that. Thanks for your time," I said politely, "and give the ambassador my best regards." Gutierrez stood and placed his hand on my shoulder, saying, "Take care, Terry. If you need anything at all, please feel free to call me." He handed me a handsome business card complete with a red, white and blue diplomatic seal in the upper corner.

"I'll keep that in mind," I said as I packed up my recorder and notepad.

You could hear a pin drop as I walked down the long staircase and onto the marble lobby floor. My interview had run long and now it was dark. I crossed the foyer and the reception area where the Marine guard was sitting. I nodded to him as he sprang up and intersected my trajectory. He hurried to beat me to the revolving doors, pulled out a large set of keys, then reached up and unlocked the side door so I could exit.

"Have a good evening, Mr. Riley," he said, still giving that old fraternity-brother look.

"Thanks, I'll try!"

The door shut and locked behind me. There I was, standing at the top of the high steps, looking over the normally bustling street, now quiet and dark: no sign of anyone. Even Sancho was nowhere to be found.

"Shit!" I scoured the dark area with my eyes. There were some cars on the street: a couple of Toyotas, some beaters and a dark, polished Mercedes with blackened windows, one cracked open with a thin stream of smoke seeping out. Probably some rich drug kingpin getting high with his posse, I figured. I didn't think twice about it. All I was concerned about was that the little street urchin had left me in the lurch. Oh well, I thought, get to a populated street and catch another cab back to the hotel.

In the distance, I heard music. I made my way down the embassy steps double-time. Behind me, the only noise from the otherwise silent street was the Mercedes' engine roaring to life.

XXIII

Heading down Revolution Boulevard is like walking into Times Square for the first time. It's fairly subdued on the outer blocks—the odd restaurant, minor hustling, your average downtown fare—then you come to the *Zona Rosa*: The "Pink District," an old American hippie enclave that grew at the rate Greenwich Village did in the 60's and 70's. Now the Zona Rosa was a combination of open marketplace and carnival.

Zona Rosa. It seemed like a dumb name to me, but what did I know? I was just a stupid American trying to do my job in a country that was just waiting for me to fuck up and expose myself. I'd see playbills and theater slicks posted in windows and on store fronts and began to feel the next one would have my picture with the caption: *WANTED - TERRY RILEY-DEAD OR ALIVE (PREFERABLY DEAD)!* I looked behind me from time to time, as a good paranoid will, but all I saw was the Mercedes a few hundred yards away, surrounded by some scumbags who seemed to be speaking to the occupants. I knew it: drugs.

I was still pissed about Sancho ditching me and a bit apprehensive about not being able to find a damn cab in the middle of the largest city on earth. Then I slowly began to let my guard down as I strolled through the *mercado* that was so alive with Mexican culture.

Street vendors pushed their wares: fried apples, tacos *al carbon*, pewter, lead, silver jewelry (the cheap kind)—you name it. If you could buy it, they'd have it here.

From the center of the Zona Rosa, you could see the golden angel atop the Independence monument illuminating the city skyline. It was really an idyllic place if you didn't mind crowds. An old man was serving ice cream from a tiny kiosk that he pushed around on a small flatbed cart. I approached him and asked in my best Spanish, "*Tiene cerveza?* Do you have any beer?" The old man looked at me cockeyed and just pointed to the ice cream. I abandoned my Spanish since it would take too long to remember how to formulate a proper sentence and said, "*Cerveza!* Beer! Where can I find a beer?" I spoke slowly and gestured like a mime. He understood me perfectly, but wanted to make me look as silly as possible for some reason, maybe just to get me to buy a cone. After enjoying his moment of humiliating me, he smiled and pointed down a long, dark alley.

"*Cerveza, Señor!*" he said. He laughed as he put his thumb in his mouth and tilted his head back, mimicking a drunk who needed a fix. He'd gotten more out of it than I had, I guess.

"*Gracias!*" I shouted over the music and din of the crowd.

It was eerily friendly, yet strange, that he kept waving to me as I walked down the alley. "*Adios, Amigo!*" he'd shout and laugh, then shout again. It gave me the creeps.

XXIV

Washington, D.C. was a party town, but you had to look hard to find one. Most came in for a convention or corporate retreat, but all were wild, out of control and never, ever covered by the press. This night was no exception.

Kate Walker arrived at the circle drive of the Biltmore in her late-model battery-operated hybrid eco-car. I used to give her a hard time about it, calling her a hippie and leaving packets of granola and peace stickers on her desk, but deep down, I admired her for being that person to go out of her way, spend the extra money and actually drive one. At least she was putting her money where her mouth was when it came to actually doing her part to reduce her carbon footprint. It gave her great street cred.

"Checking in, Ma'am?" A dark-skinned valet said as he approached her car. He took a moment to give it the once-over, fighting to hold back a laugh.

Kate was unfazed. "No, thank you, I'll self-park if you don't mind," she said proudly.

He ripped off the stub and handed her a parking ticket. "Down the ramp to the third floor," he said. He immediately ran to the next car queued behind her.

As the elevator doors opened, a blast of crowd noise burst through, jolting Kate. She was so busy rereading some handwritten notes she didn't realize she'd have to push her way through the lobby to get to her destination. Looking at her watch, Kate saw she had fifty seconds until her scheduled appointment. Man, she was anal about being prompt.

Buffeted from the side, she exited the elevator and dropped her notepad. She immediately fell to the ground amid a jungle of shoes and bare feet and tried to retrieve her papers. It was impossible to blame just one person; there was no use looking up to chastise whoever had bumped her.

The lobby was out of control with drunk men and women in cheap suits sporting soiled nametags. *John Holmes. Susie Schwartz. Ken Jones.* Where do they find these people?

"Hey!" she shouted as a woman walked right over her purse. She wanted to add, "Bitch!" but was too proper. Yet she wasn't going to take this lying down. Kate stood up, grasped her belongings and held them tight to her chest. She was ready to shove anyone back twice as hard if need be.

Just then, a young woman in her twenties stepped through the crowd and shouted something. "What? I can't hear you," Kate yelled as she tried to read the woman's face.

The young woman stepped in closer and shouted, "Are you Kate Walker?" Kate nodded and gave her a look as though she had been rescued from a desert island. "I'm Holly Goldfield, the Speaker's Aide. We're up this way."

Holly took Kate's arm and led her through the minefield of people. Kate had to shout in Holly's ear as they made it toward the lobby bar, "Who's in town this time?"

Holly answered back, never looking away from their goal, "Appliances! It's the National Appliances Convention. These guys make the CPA Convention look like an Amish picnic."

Luckily for Kate, the bar was through a single, thick glass door that swung shut after you entered. The noise slowly dissipated until it was virtually silent except for the elevator music playing in the lounge. The two approached a table where an attractive woman in her fifties sat sipping what looked like a small glass of sherry.

Holly walked over to the woman and introduced her. "Kate, this is Nebraska Congresswoman Kathleen Shannon, better known as The Speaker of the House," Holly said proudly. Turning back toward Kate she said, "Mrs. Shannon, this is Kate Walker, she's a reporter with the *Washington Post*."

Congresswoman Shannon rose slowly and deliberately, and extended her hand. Kate had always thought *she* had a firm handshake, and she was suddenly a little intimidated by this politician's strength. She was older and lean, but beautiful, elegant and confident.

"Thank you, Holly," Shannon said, "Ms. Walker, won't you please join us? Here have a seat."

Kate nodded and put her purse on the floor as she pulled out a thick, vinyl-covered chair on casters and plopped herself down. "Please, call me Kate," she said cordially. "I really appreciate you taking time out of your busy schedule for an interview, Mrs. Speaker. I know it's tough to fit these things in."

Shannon looked over at Holly, who was now sitting next to her and sharing an insider's smile. "Not in an election year, it isn't." Shannon waved to a waiter who was just finishing at another table. "What would you like? I'm having a Manhattan," Shannon said to Kate as the waiter approached. "On second thought, make mine a double."

The waiter nodded generously. "Very good Mrs. Speaker," he said as he turned to the other women. "Ladies?"

Holly abruptly raised her hand, nearly shouting, "I'll have a double!" then hesitated as she looked at the congresswoman. "I mean... I'll take a lite beer." She folded quickly back into her seat to avoid any visual retribution from her boss.

"Just a Diet Coke. I'm still on duty," Kate said, more interested in getting back to the interview. "Mrs. Speaker..." she continued as she retrieved her notepad, a pen and a microcassette recorder from her bag.

Shannon held up her hand slightly and interrupted: "No need to be so formal. We're not on the Senate floor. Please, call me Kathleen."

That reassurance took the edge off, relaxing Kate. She roamed through her notes for her first question.

"Okay, Kathleen. You're the most influential woman in politics today. Governor of Nebraska, congresswoman, and now you're in the enviable position of Speaker of the House. The Republican Party is going to announce you as their nominee in the next election and the GOP thinks you're the strongest contender to run against Senator Pritchard. Does this mean you'll be the first female President of The United States? Any predictions?"

Shannon, taken aback by the flurry of questions, was nonetheless impressed. "Boy, you sound like a one-woman fan club!" she said, chuckling.

Kate backed down, realizing her zeal. "I'm sorry, Ma'am, I just admire you so much. You're in the third highest office in the land. You're living proof of what strides women have made."

Shannon settled into her chair as her face became somewhat serious. "Let me go on record and say a lot of people seem to think I'm here to champion their cause. I'm not. I have no Feminist agenda and I try to treat all the issues that come before me with equality and fairness. I'm here to serve the American public as a whole, unlike many in politics today. When you're in this position, you have to be blind to color, race, religion and sex. It's the only way you can remain open to see how the sum of this country's people makes it the greatest on earth. Don't get me wrong. I'm not saying I don't cherish the diverse cultures, religions and issues, but the U.S. can ill afford to keep heaping money and swaying politics toward the minority-*du-jour*. All you can do is do your best to make the right decisions and back the right bills. You owe that to the people who got you there."

Kate took a moment to absorb this information. "I never really thought of it that way," she said, then switched gears. "But what about the trappings? You know, the perks, the interns, all the seductive stuff? How do you deal with all that?"

Shannon smiled and responded, "I think it was Lord Acton who once said, 'Absolute power corrupts absolutely.' It's true, but it only corrupts the weak in character." Shannon saw an opportunity and took it. "Take my would-be opponent, Dan Pritchard… How do you think he got where he is today? With his past track record, you'd think he was bulletproof, some sort of Liberal Messiah... but I wonder if the American people would still want to elect him President if they knew the truth... the whole truth."

A cloud of intrigue descended on Kate. Her eyes widened as she attempted to understand the cryptic message. "What do you mean by, 'the truth?'" she asked slowly.

The congresswoman nodded to her aide. Holly reached down to a dark leather briefcase at her feet. She fiddled with the lock then slowly pulled out some sort of thick package. She looked around the room to make sure they weren't being watched, placed the package on the table then slid it over to Kate. It was a tightly packed manila folder with a colorful seal on the front. Across the face in bold red letters read: *DEPARTMENT OF JUSTICE - OPERATION CASABLANCA - CONFIDENTIAL.* Holly grinned at her powerful boss as Kate began to rifle through the pages.

XXV

Armed guards paced the precipice of a large hacienda just outside the Mexico City limits in a wealthy, protected suburb. They walked the edge near the eaves like robotic characters on a Swiss village clock. Tight. In unison. Marching in opposite directions in order to cover a maximum area.

This was the Governor's mansion, meant to house the man who represented the people, yet it was anything but indigenous in style. It was not built in the typical Spanish mode so often seen in these parts, with amenities like vaulted ceilings inside and turret-like spirals on the exterior. It was more reminiscent of a European chateau, complete with parapets and a catwalk that encircled the entire roof as well as the adjoining buildings, looking more like a king's castle than a humble politician's abode. But Roberto Chavez was no humble politician. He was as grand as they came, whether he was corrupt, as most contended, or merely eccentric.

He put the finishing touches on his bow tie, straightened his tuxedo then checked his looks for any minor flaws as he liked to do in a full-length dressing mirror.

Roberto Chavez had campaigned hard for the Mexican people. He was the most popular candidate in the upcoming presidential election not because he had all the answers or because he was the most trustworthy, but because he was the closest thing to a celebrity Mexico City had. He dressed in three-thousand-dollar suits and nine-hundred-dollar shoes. He brought style and a sense of taste to Mexico and tried hard to leave the stereotypical Mexican wardrobe of cowboy boots and western shirts in the past. It was time for a *"New Mexico,"* he'd say at his political rallies, and he'd be damned if it didn't start with his appearance.

Valets dressed in discount versions of Chavez's tuxedo assisted guests as limousines arrived in the circular drive of the Governor's Mansion. Each guest was draped in formal attire, the women in gowns they were careful not to dirty or catch in hinges as they exited their towncars.

As guests arrived, they queued up to a receiving line that moved slowly from the bottom of the mansion steps into the grand foyer. There was a feeling of excitement in the air as diplomats and dignitaries from all parts of the world kibitzed and laughed and chatted politely while they patiently waited to advance into the party.

Chavez took a moment, then a deep breath, and stood at the top of the spiral staircase to see his foyer filling with people. He was polished. Refined. A youthful man in his fifties, never married, but always looking. He knew it was his big night. He was hosting the first event of its kind—a bash that would have all eyes on him, the man to watch during the environmental conference over the next few days.

Below him, waiters and waitresses sashayed between the guests as the butler led pairs and groups of people into the main room for cocktails. A harpist played soft, classical music with nimble fingers that strummed the instrument's chords like wind does a chime. A banner hung high over the foyer that read: *WELCOME DELEGATES TO THE FIRST INTERNATIONAL CONFERENCE ON ENVIRONMENTAL AFFAIRS.* Just below it, a slightly smaller one read: *ROBERTO CHAVEZ - MEXICO'S PRESIDENTE FOR THE 21ST CENTURY!* A picture of Chavez on the banner showed him holding a baby and kissing its cheek. It was humorous and certainly self-serving, but Chavez knew that politics was all about perception and marketing, and he wasn't about to stop—not even in his own house.

He made his way down the staircase, sauntering like a debutante at her coming-out bash, as the international diplomats entered through large double doors onto the terra cotta-tiled floor. Chavez's butler, Jaime, a sixty-plus stern-faced man, announced guests in English as they entered.

"Señor Kriskoffski, General Secretary of Russia, and his wife, Natalia!" Jaime shouted over the party noise.

Chavez hurried down the last step and approached Kriskoffski and his wife. He reached out and shook the Russian's hand with a strong grip. His stoic political face suddenly melted into one of suave admiration as he grasped Natalia's hand in his and slowly bent to kiss it, never allowing his eyes to stray from hers. He was a smooth operator. The quintessential "Latin Romeo."

"*Mucho gusto, Señora,*" he said slyly, but not so slyly as to avoid the Russian's wrathful gaze.

The butler continued, "Señor Lo Han Yeow, Prime Minister of the People's Republic of China."

A limo with United States diplomatic seals on the doors and flags on the hood pulled into the semi-circular drive. Valets rushed to open Pritchard's door and help out the senator and his staff. As usual, Dexter brought up the rear.

He exited slowly, surveyed the grounds then searched the area for any signs of trouble. He spied the soldiers atop the mansion then scanned the front and side yards, including the soldiers beyond the front gate. He nearly jumped out of his skin when he suddenly felt a hand come down hard on his shoulder. It was Pritchard.

"Don't worry about those boys over there," Pritchard said, pointing to the outer perimeter. "It's just that Asshole Cortes flexing his muscles. He may be in control of the military, but the governor keeps him on a short leash. Wouldn't want him to up and start his own coup d'état now, would we?"

Pritchard began to chuckle at his own words when Jennifer appeared next to him. She looked ravishing, wearing a low-cut, red evening gown. Stunning. "It's too damn hot out here," she said in a demure, Marilyn Monroe-type voice as she dabbed her neck with a small hanky.

Pritchard turned to her and gave her a wink. "Quite right, Ms. Hoover. Shall we?" He began to lead her inside the party.

Bang. A shot rang out. The loud report and ricochet sent soldiers and guards scattering. Instinctively, Dexter grabbed Pritchard, threw him to the ground then dove on top to protect his body from any bullets. Jennifer was left to her own devices. She crouched down behind a car. "*Claro!*" a guard shouted from outside the fence-line near the gate. He stood and waved. All clear. The soldier gestured with his arms and began to laugh. He walked over to a clearing with his flashlight and shined it on a wild boar still convulsing from the hit. A large rogue pig had caused the commotion and the guard who had shot him was lucky he hadn't been taken for a sniper. It was all clear now. The other soldiers advanced to the spot where the guard was relishing his kill. No danger. All clear.

Dexter got up from Pritchard slowly. They'd hit the ground hard, and now he rose dirtied and shaken. Dexter's employer was about to read him the riot act for making him look like a fool. Pritchard stood up and straightened himself, wiping the dust from his suit pants. He was covered in it. Jennifer, still jittering, ran to his side and began to wipe off the back of his jacket.

"Oh, baby, I thought that bullet had your name on it!" she whispered in his ear. "God I'm glad you're okay."

Dexter could only look down at his feet in embarrassment. The other staff members, who had gone into immediate shock and scattered everywhere, slowly came back to assist. Damage control. Immediately, they prepared Pritchard for the receiving line, flanking him as they walked up the steps toward the mansion.

"All right, all right! Quit fuss'n now, I'm okay!" Pritchard grumbled.

As the staff queued up, Pritchard said, "Jesus H. Christ, Dex! You sure take your job seriously, don't you?" As he looked over the rest of his staff, his tone changed from jokingly disparaging to dire: "And that's a damn sight more than I can say for you all."

The staffers now looked down in embarrassment. Pritchard slightly smiled as Jaime the butler announced them inside: "Señor Daniel Pritchard, United States Senator!"

Through the crowd of gatherers, Chavez suddenly appeared with a wide grin on his face. He marched up to the senator with open arms, hugged him then kissed him on the cheek. "Senator, I'm so glad you came. I've been waiting to settle an old score with you," Chavez said in a jovial tone.

Pritchard shot his finger out like it was a revolver and shouted, "Bobby, you old wetback! How the hell are ya? Stud poker in the parlor later?" Chavez smiled and nodded in agreement. "And don't try using those devalued pesos this time. That dog don't hunt, Boy!" Pritchard finished.

Chavez snapped his head up and his eyes caught Jennifer. He was instantly smitten. "And who is this vision of beauty?" Chavez drooled. Wrong question. Pritchard fumbled for a word and finally said, "Ah... well, this is my 'Staff Liaison Officer,' Miss Jennifer Hoover."

Pritchard turned to Chavez. "Allow me to introduce you to the next '*El Presidente*' of Mexico, Governor Roberto Chavez."

Chavez grinned devilishly as he took Jennifer's hand. "*Mucho gusto, Señorita!* Please, come, I will take you on a private tour of my humble home." Chavez wrapped his arm around hers and led her through the foyer to an adjacent anteroom where drinks were being served.

Pritchard chuckled. "At least the man's consistent!" he said under his breath.

Following Pritchard, Dexter decided to grab his ear at that moment. "Sir, with all due respect, she's going to complicate things for this administration," he said discreetly.

Pritchard never broke stride as he corrected him: "Point taken, Dex! But I want you to be crystal clear on this. Ms. Hoover over there is the reason this administration isn't complicated! Since Mrs. Pritchard's car accident three years ago, certain amenities, if you know what I mean, no longer exist in my household. Now I love my Betty, and I'm no 'Slick Willie,' but goddamn it, Son, I'm still a man!"

Dexter stood corrected, but felt another word was in order and said, "I understand, Sir, but with the election..."

Pritchard was following Chavez and Jennifer to the bar trying to ignore Dexter's last remark, but interrupted, "Let me worry about the election! Got it? Good! Now go and mingle, you need the practice. It's about time you make the transition from science to politics." Pritchard then slapped Dexter's shoulder again in a fatherly way and said, "Relax, 'cause that's what I plan to start doin' right now!"

XXVI

Kate's apartment was sprinkled with the usual fare: IKEA lamps and rugs, a matching chenille sofa and love seat, black-and-white prints of lovers walking in a park, and a couple of those French retro posters of some genie bouncing on top of a hot cup of coffee with some untranslatable marketing tagline scrawled elegantly across it: all the ditzy trash designed to make the occupant look tasteful and feel classy.

Her bedroom wasn't much different. She had a large four-post bed with dainty, sheer material draped everywhere to give the impression you were in the lap of luxury or somewhere in the Great Saharan Desert awaiting the emir to return to his harem. She was a lost cause. A hopeless romantic who wouldn't know the right guy if he stepped on her foot at the coffee stand.

Jackie, Kate's roommate, stood in the doorway of the bedroom as Kate furiously packed a large suitcase. Jackie watched as Kate ran from her bedroom to her bathroom and back again more times than she could count. Kate would race in and grab whatever nylons and dripping garments were hanging over her shower curtain and toss them into the case one at a time, never realizing she could make one trip, grab everything she needed, then return with one load. Jackie enjoyed watching her run around like a four-year-old after eating a candy bar.

She stood and scraped the top off her ice cream, whirling the rest in the bowl. "First big assignment, huh?" Jackie mumbled with her mouth full. "Where you heading?"

Kate tried to ignore her but she knew she'd have to answer in order to get Jackie to let her finish packing. "Mexico!" Kate responded without looking up.

The pitch of Jackie's voice raised a notch when she said, "Since when did you start covering international?" Silence. Jackie knew something was up. "Wait a minute! This doesn't have anything to do with..."

Kate stopped packing and instantly stood up. She held out her hand like a traffic cop and halted Jackie by saying, "Don't start with me, Jackie. He needs my help!" She'd said her peace and stood up to Jackie's inquisition. "He just doesn't know it yet," she said in a lower voice to herself—an attempt to justify her actions.

Kate pounded clothes into her case in frustration. Seeing her friend conflicted, Jackie began to lend a hand. But just one. She picked up a single item here and a sock there then dropped it in the case, all the while careful not to spill her bowl of ice cream.

"I know you don't want to hear this, but you've been obsessed with this guy since even before you met him," Jackie said, trying to make a point without upsetting her roommate further.

"I'm not obsessed!" said Kate, still trying to escape the obvious. "I admire him as a journalist, that's all." She plopped down on her bed nearly in defeat, but Jackie wasn't going to give up that easily.

"Bullshit! He's a burnout. He's never gonna be what you want him to be," Jackie exhorted emphatically.

Kate took a deep breath then sighed, "You don't know him like I do. There's a good man on the other side of that wall he puts up, I just know it."

Jackie shook her head and winced, then said, "Who are you trying to convince, me or you? For God's sake, Kate! You wanna screw this guy, so stop pretending he's Prince-fucking-Charming and just jump him. Get it over with already."

Jackie marched to Kate's bureau and grabbed a small jewelry box. She rummaged through it and pulled out a small packet. Diaphragms. Jackie cocked her head and gave Kate a strange look, then tossed the packet onto the bed next to her. Jackie smirked and said, "And by the looks of that expiration date, you'd better hurry!"

Kate quickly scooped up the diaphragms and shoved them deep into her suitcase. She stretched out her neck like a peacock and said proudly, "There's more to life than just sex!" Jackie scooped a large spoonful of ice cream from the bowl and seductively began to make love to it. She moaned and squirmed as she licked and sucked. Kate nervously fidgeted, the uncomfortable spectator. As Jackie continued her suggestive performance, she cooed, "Yeah, chocolate ice cream!" She laughed then exited the room, leaving Kate alone to finish packing.

XXVII

I was going nowhere fast. The dark alleyway was getting even darker as I wandered deeper into the blackness. There was nothing on either side of me but shanties and corrugated tin-roofed shacks. Absolute poverty. It was everywhere. I couldn't get away from it. I began to rethink the decision to feed my fix rather than use my head just as I came upon a sign over a wooden door that read: *AMIGO'S CANTINA - CERVEZAS - CHICAS*. It sounded like a fun place—after all, they were marketing what they had: beer and women.

Like Pavlov's dog, I licked my lips and imagined what a cold Mexican beer would taste like after a day like mine. The neon sign flashed: *CERRADO*. Closed. I couldn't believe my luck. It was like God was punishing me, forcing me to become sober by putting me through rapid detox. I wasn't ready to stop drinking yet, but in the whole of fucking Mexico I couldn't even find a shot of tequila. What was that bar owner thinking?

I turned back toward the Zona Rosa, where, maybe in the carnival-like atmosphere, I could find a drink. Before I took a single step, I heard a bottle roll down the alley. It was like something from a scary movie—that kind of sensation women must feel when walking alone in a parking garage upon suddenly hearing an unfamiliar noise. The kind of noise that men don't usually fear unless they're dumb enough to be walking down a dark alley, late at night, in a foreign country, alone. Don't say it, Smart-Ass!

I had just enough time to about-face before three swaggering characters were upon me. They came out of nowhere, but I'd recognized them from standing outside the black Mercedes. Drug dealers. I hated drug dealers.

They were rough-looking hombres and the last thing I wanted to see that evening. Before the first one spoke, I could see something in the distance behind them, down the darkened alley. It was a shadowy figure hiding in a dark doorway. Great, now it's *four* against one. I was in it again, and this time I was in deep.

I prepared myself for the second beating in so many days. I felt like a scrawny fifth-grader. Maybe they just wanted my lunch money… I was pissed off now. I decided this time I wasn't going down without a fight.

I tried to ignore the three men by walking in a straight line, but they closed their ranks, stopping before I ran straight into them.

The leader of this motley crew was even uglier than the other two. A real *puta*. "*Buenas noches, Señor!*" he drawled. I wasn't biting.

I decided to cut to the chase. "Come on, guys, give me a break, huh?" The three men looked at each other and laughed. They found it a lot funnier than I did.

Another sounded in, "Okay, first we break your arms, then we break legs." Wow, this guy was clever. I probably would've laughed if that had been a line from some action movie, but I wasn't laughing. These guys meant business. They would sooner stick me forty times in the chest with a pen knife than walk away. I pulled out my wallet and began to count my change.

"Look, I've only got like a couple hundred dollars and a company credit card. Here, I'll give you the PIN code so you can get some more cash with it at an ATM." Maybe they just wanted to bargain. Nope. They laughed even harder.

The third man pulled out something long and shiny. *Thwap*. It was a switchblade with a ten-inch, razor-sharp blade. There was no way out this time, but I wasn't gonna be a victim. A statistic. A Mexican cliché. I mustered up as much courage as I could and moved toward the leader.

I never saw the fourth man emerge from the shadows. If I had, I'd have seen it was Carlos Ramos—probably still trying to convince me to do a story on his sick little village. Man, I would've promised him a front-page article if he had stepped in to help me at that moment. He didn't. He didn't have to.

A sudden screech of tires tore the tension and stopped me from making my move. White smoke and bright lights raced down the alley towards me and my three amigos and I were momentarily blinded. It was Sancho. That little bastard. How the hell did he find me? Who the hell cares? He did!

Sancho pulled a *Rockford Files* move, driving right at the bad guys and scattering them. He pulled the hand brake up hard and flung the taxi around so that it came to a stop with the passenger-side door right in front of me. It was a perfectly executed move. This kid knew his stuff. He was good. I'd really underestimated him. This was the second time he'd saved my ass. "Get in, Señor Riley! Hurry!" Sancho screamed at the top of his lungs.

It was about that time the three ne'er-do-wells were regrouping for a frontal assault. They ran up to the driver-side window, reached in and grabbed Sancho. In an instant, they were pulling him out of the cab window, nearly breaking his neck. I had to think fast. I looked around the cab, but all I could find for a weapon was a fire extinguisher braced to the floor. I pulled the chrome tab up and yanked on the little red blowtorch. Sancho screamed and fought, locking his feet in the steering wheel for leverage but getting torn apart in the process. I pulled the pin, shoved the nozzle around Sancho and blasted the three from point-blank range square in their faces. The high-pressure foam retardant covered their heads, blinding each one in turn for a few seconds. Man, that felt good.

The shock to the hombres caused them to immediately release their grip on Sancho. I pulled him back into the taxi before he could fall out the window to the ground. Just then, in the distance, I heard a long, whiny noise. Sirens. I had never been so glad to hear them. Then I realized I was in Mexico. Shit! "Come on Sancho, let's go! *Vamanos!*" I screamed.

Sancho sat back into the driver's seat and quickly turned the ignition key. Nothing. The goddamn engine had died as a result of all his stunt driving. With the sirens getting closer, the three hombres were now more interested in revenge than in avoiding incarceration.

They wiped the drying chemicals from their eyes and faces as they writhed in pain to regain their focus. "No more fun and games, *muchachos!*" their leader shouted as he pulled a forty-five-caliber revolver from his waistband and cocked the hammer. I threw my arm across Sancho and pulled him down to the floorboards. He was just a kid. He didn't deserve to get involved with this shit. This was my problem. I tried to shield him as best as I could, but it was too late. The bullet came through the window and toward my face...

Bang. An officer shot a round into the air. *Federales* suddenly appeared from every angle. Police cars screeched down the alley with headlights blazing like the Mexican version of the cavalry saving the day. Everybody froze: me, Sancho, the three *bastardos*. My only hope was to give them some bullshit tourist story and hope they would let us go before they found out my real identity.

XXVIII

The sun came up with me scratching what felt like lice crawling around my three-day-old beard. I was a chronic insomniac as it was, but stayed awake all night worrying about my health as well as my virginity in that rotting jail cell. It was a place that looked like something out of a John Huston movie: mold-covered gray stones ten feet thick, water from God knows where dripping in the corners and Mexicans on top of Mexicans; and me, a gringo, the only gringo for miles, with my little space to curl up in.

The cell doubled as a drunk tank, and the night before must've been a fucking holiday because it was filled to capacity. Drunks, pimps, addicts, you name it. My only consolation was that my three amigos were in another cell buried in the basement. At least it was one less problem to deal with. I could think now. It was quiet. I have to hand it to the Mexicans, they know how to sleep. Between their siestas and what I could see in the jail cells, they had my little sleeping problems licked.

The only sound in that dank jail cell was an ear-pounding, frustratingly peaceful sound of snoring coming from none other than Sancho. In the corner, away from me, he lay curled up like a dog sleeping on a mat, snoring so loud and strong that he looked like one of those cartoons where the blanket goes down to the feet then up to the neck with each breath. It galled me that Sancho could sleep so well, just like any other child. I guess, after all, he didn't have a guilty conscience. I should have kissed the kid's feet. He'd already done two good deeds in one day just for me. Why shouldn't he get a good night's sleep? Shame on me for envying a kid and his nocturnal slumber, no matter how much it pissed me off.

In the half-light, I could feel someone's eyes on mine. I slowly looked down and saw an old man, maybe in his seventies, sitting on the floor and studying my face. His face was weathered and wrinkled, but his eyes had a lot of life in them. He had a good face. He had those woeful, understanding eyes. I don't know why, but I started to talk to him.

"My old man used to bring me down to the drunk tank at his precinct. He'd point to the lushes and say in a heavy Irish brogue, 'That's the curse of our people, Lad. Don't waste your life in a bottle, do some good for the world, it'll do good for you someday'." I picked up a stone from the bench and tossed it across the room. I knew the old man couldn't understand me, but the sound of my voice seemed to pep him up a bit, so I continued. "This from a man who was shot dead by the mob or one of his own who was dirty. They never found out which. The only cop in Chicago who wasn't on the take. Huh, a lot of good the world did him!" I said with resentment. I didn't know if I was talking to hear myself talk or to help this old guy out of his loneliness.

From down the hall I heard a clanging of keys and a banging on the bars. It was the jailer. He was an enormous tub of shit who looked more like a Turkish bathhouse regular than a prison guard. He ran his wooden baton over the iron cell bars, annoying everyone, or at least everyone who wasn't asleep. The oversized cell keys swung from his hip and clanged and jangled, making it impossible not to hear him when he was about. He waddled by, eyeing the human contents of the communal jail cell, pulled the keys from the hook and swung them teasingly, like the giant prick he was.

He scratched his ass as he unlocked the cell door and swung it open. "*Venga, Gringo!* You made bail," his majesty grunted. I jumped to my feet. He didn't need to repeat himself. I climbed over the floor of snoozing bodies until I got to Sancho.

An atomic blast couldn't have roused him. His nostrils flared with each deep, relaxing breath until his breath poured out of his lungs in the form of a volcanic snore. I shook him as firmly and quickly as I could, saying, "Wake up, Little Man. Let's go, Sancho. *Vamanos!*" Slowly he opened his eyes, rubbing them as though he had just had the most restful night's sleep of his life. He was really starting to piss me off. I picked him up by the armpits and pulled him to his feet.

Out of the corner of my eye, I could see the jailer leer at my little friend with a pedophilic grin. Sancho followed me as I walked straight out of the cell. Suddenly, the jailer stopped him dead in his tracks. "*Oye!*" Sancho cried. The jailer wrapped his thick forearm around Sancho's neck in a chokehold and smiled devilishly as he said, "Not you, my little car thief."

I began to protest in earnest. "He comes with me! He's... he's my assistant." There was no way I was gonna let anything happen to this kid after what he'd done for me. Sancho tried to bolt, but the whale had him in his clutches. His little arms flailed as the jailer put pressure on his throat to subdue him. "Your amigo only pay for you, Gringo, not my little burro, here," the pig proclaimed.

I was confused, "Amigo? What amigo?"

From around the corner Ramos appeared. He stepped up, looked me up and down then went right to Blubber Boy. Pulling out a twenty-peso note, Ramos waved it under the jailer's dirty nose. By now, Sancho had nearly passed out, his arms no longer flailing wildly in the air. The fat bastard waved to Ramos with his free hand. "*Mas dinero.* More!" he barked. Ramos reluctantly pulled out another twenty-peso note and held it up to his face in disgust. The jailer slowly released his grip and Sancho dropped to the floor, gasping for breath.

I hurried over to help him up. "Come on, Kid, let's get outta here!"

Ramos gave me a look, turned and walked back down the hall. I grabbed Sancho by the sleeve and pulled him along. Behind us, I could see the bloated fuck blow a kiss as he rubbed his crotch.

XXIX

Looking up at an old clocktower, I realized I was late for the first event where I'd have access to Pritchard. I half-jogged, half-staggered from exhaustion as Ramos and Sancho followed.

"What's your hurry? You haven't even thanked me yet for bailing you out back there," Ramos huffed.

I never broke stride on my way to the intersection. I jumped onto a crowded bus with a banner that read: *CHAPULTEPEC PARK* above the windshield. Ramos and Sancho had to race to catch up. By the time they jumped onboard, we were all out of breath.

"Where are we going?" Ramos gasped.

"We?" I retorted. "I don't know about you, but I'm late for work. I told you before; I'm not down here on vacation. I've got to get to Chapultepec Park for a political rally. Just give me your name and address and I'll have my paper send you a check for all your out-of-pocket expenses." I dug through my pockets. "It seems I've been relieved of all my traveling funds sometime last night."

Ramos stood in front of me with a somewhat snide expression on his face. He shoved something into my chest. It was a pink carbon copy of what looked like an official document. I took it and perused it. All

I could make out were the words: *RILEY,* and in Spanish, *CUSTODY* and *GUARDIAN.*

"What the hell is this?" I said, tired of explaining myself, "a bail receipt? I told you, I can have my editor wire me the money to pay you back by this afternoon. Is that what this is all about?"

Ramos grinned, saying flatly, "It's a custody form. I'm responsible for your ass the entire time you're here in Mexico. It was the only way to keep you from being immediately deported. You belong to me now. It's like we just got married!" I was quickly studying the paper in an attempt to make out any other decipherable words when Sancho glanced over my shoulder curiously.

Suddenly Ramos snatched the pink carbon from my hands and stuffed it back into his jacket before Sancho could see anything. He sneered at Sancho, "Who are you?"

Sancho looked up at him and smiled wide, then said, "I am Sancho Fernando Cantado Enrique Lopez Trujillo! But you can call me Sancho." The Mexicans kept their descendants' namesakes. It was a pain in the ass trying to remember all of it; even they had trouble with it, but it was kind of cool, the tradition thing. Sancho continued, "I'm Senor Riley's personal valet!"

I was in total denial by this time. "No way, Jose," I said. "This is bullshit! I've got a big story to research, then I'm hauling ass back to the States on the first flight out of here."

Ramos gave me the once-over again and said, "By the looks of it, you'd only be wasting your time in the local cantinas. With me, you can write a real story."

I wanted to pull my hair out. "Ahh!"

The bus slowed then stopped at a busy street corner, where I decided to make my exit. I pushed my way through the crowd as the back doors hissed open. I turned to shout back at Ramos when I got bogged down in the mix, never seeing the spit-polished *Federale* waiting to board.

"Hasta la bye-bye, Amigo!" I shouted over the crowd. I turned and walked smack into the *Federale*, nearly knocking him over. Man, I just couldn't catch a break. He looked me up and down, taking offense at my rude American behavior.

Ramos didn't take any chances. He stepped forward and began speaking to the officer in Spanish. The *Federale* listened intently, then after a moment, he blew out a laugh—and kept laughing. He climbed aboard the bus as I slowly backed up through the crowd until meeting Sancho in the middle. We could see Ramos slapping the officer's shoulder: I was now the butt of the joke. Ramos walked back to meet us. He'd made his point. I was stuck with him for God knew how long.

XXX

I disembarked as the bus slowed for a traffic jam in front of Chapultepec Park. Ramos and Sancho would simply have to keep up. We had to cross the busy and dangerous boulevard as we made our way to a long stretch of beautiful park land.

Chapultepec Park: the gem of Mexico City. It spanned as far as the eye could see in all directions. It was a lot like Central Park, but then again, it wasn't. It was ancient. Mysterious. I marched toward a crowd of thousands, making my way as close to the front as I could get. I never looked behind me, but with my current luck, there was no way my two traveling companions would desert me.

Ahead was a large stage with scaffolds on either side supporting spotters, snipers and other police. I had come to this political rally not to support the Governor of Mexico's bid for the presidency but to hear what his gringo buddy was up to, maybe find a few clues about why he was chumming up to Mexico in such a big way.

I stopped by the side of the stage and watched Chavez stroll center stage to meet the microphone. The crowd went mad, shouting, cheering, throwing their hats—and their babies—into the air in jubilation.

Chavez wore a perfectly tailored suit, looking more like an NBA coach pacing the sidelines than a politician. He took a few self-serving bows, then went right into his speech. He used broad, forceful strokes with his hands to make a point. His rich baritone turned sympathetic and friendly as he spoke about the plight of his *hermanos y hermanas*. His brothers and sisters. Behind him, the breeze buffeted colorful banners that read: *CHAVEZ PARA PRESIDENTE!* It was an election year and Roberto Chavez was going to make sure every Mexican, certainly every voter in Mexico City—the most overpopulated city on earth—knew he was the man to watch. He was going to make sure that no one would forget his name for an instant. A pure politician.

Pritchard, Dexter and the staff members applauded each major point Chavez made in his speech, just as all good little suck-ups do. I was busy witnessing Chavez dispense with the pleasantries and charge right to the heart of the campaign when Sancho and Ramos appeared. Damn, they had found me.

"I thank you for this warm welcome, *amigos y amigas*. We've traveled far to get here today. My predecessor told me, just before he was assassinated by the leftist cowards, to carry the torch of personal and economic freedom for all of Mexico. That, *amigos*, is why I campaign to become your next *presidente!*" Chavez slapped his hand onto the podium and the crowd erupted in applause.

Ramos leered at me while Sancho busied himself playing with two little children near their mother. I wasn't taking notes at this point—I pretty much knew the drill. Besides, I could always get a transcript from Reuters or off the wire service if I needed it for my story. It was Pritchard I was concerned with. What was he up to? Why did he have his head so far up Chavez's ass that they'd have to use the "jaws of life" to pull it out? I wanted to get closer to the stage, but soldiers stood guard everywhere.

Suddenly, from behind the stage curtain, Cortes appeared. General Jorge Cortes, the most maniacal, sadistic bastard alive, and runner-up only to the likes of Hitler, Stalin or Milosevic. I knew him from my days covering the Chiapas Revolution and cringed at the sight of him. He was the reason I was a wanted man in Mexico.

Cortes slowly made his way onto the stage and approached Chavez. It was his right, he felt, since he was the leader of all the armed forces and the *de facto* governor if anything, God forbid, should happen to Chavez. He was very popular with Mexicans, albeit through his strength and ruthlessness. He was more respected only because he was feared.

Although the crowd listened intently to Chavez's speech, all eyes were on Cortes as he walked up to take his place behind the governor. His menacing eyes pierced the crowd as he searched like a hawk for any signs of dissent. I was a bit nervous as he looked my way, so I stepped behind a fat woman to avoid his glare. As I looked to my left with my head bowed, I saw Ramos doing the same thing, hiding behind some red and green balloons a child on his father's shoulder was holding.

"What are you doing?" I mouthed to him.

He sneered back, "What are *you* doing?"

It was a pissing contest and I wasn't about to lose. Ramos stood up and exposed himself to trump me. I followed suit.

"You're a real asshole, Riley!"

That was profound, I thought. "You ain't seen nothing yet, *Vato!*" I salveoed back.

Suddenly, Sancho interjected, "Your Spanish is getting better, Señor Riley!"

Chavez poised himself for his grand finale. He took a deep, slow breath and changed his tone. The podium he was now clutching with all his might resonated as he spoke: "And our people are healthier today thanks to the AMERIMEX Water Purification Project developed by this man..." He turned toward Pritchard and said in a slow crescendo, "Senator Daniel Pritchard! He's supported our administration for years and helped us realize our dream of a free and prosperous Mexico."

The governor waved Pritchard from his chair to take a bow. The thousands of fans and supporters cheered as the senator graciously acknowledged their praise. In an instant, Chavez locked eyes with Cortes and something unpleasant passed between them.

Out of the corner of my eye, I suddenly saw Ramos bolt toward the stage. Oh shit! He was gonna make a hit on this guy! I stupidly chased after him as Sancho, my trusted lapdog, followed right behind me.

As the cheers from the crowd subsided, Ramos shouted, "Governor, people are dying in the villages of Valle de Luna. An epidemic is sweeping the country. How will they live to see your miraculous accomplishments without your help?"

Soldiers suddenly poised and postured, readying themselves, pumping shotguns and tightening ranks.

Chavez paused to think for a moment, but Cortes locked onto Ramos like a shark to its prey. I reached out and grabbed his arm, trying to reason with him before he got himself shot. "Are you fucking loco?" I said. "You're gonna get yourself killed."

Sancho stood with mouth agape as the crowd became hushed by the outburst. Looking around, Ramos realized he had everyone's attention: This was the time to get his point across—now or never.

Unfortunately, Cortes had zeroed in on Ramos. The corner of his lip crinkled as he nodded to his underling soldiers.

"Governor," Ramos continued, "your people—our people—need you! If this plague isn't stopped, it could reach this city and jeopardize all of Mexico."

Intrigued, but confused, Chavez listened. A dozen soldiers and undercover police suddenly appeared around Ramos and tackled him to the ground. *Damn it.* My old Superman Complex kicked in out of nowhere. I knew he needed help, but why me? I jumped in and started peeling cops off of him. Big mistake. They grabbed me, wrestled me to the ground then handcuffed us both before we knew it.

Luckily, Sancho had slunk back and hid behind an old woman, pretending to be her son. The soldiers never gave him a second look. Well, at least he saved himself.

Onstage, Pritchard caught a glimpse of me and snapped his head toward Dexter. "Jesus H. Christ, Dex!" he chided. "I thought you had a little talk with Riley. He's gonna blow all our work straight to hell."

Chavez managed to brush off the interruption as a mere heckling. Cortes supervised our capture with his own eyes, about-faced, then marched off the stage. His remaining soldiers snapped to attention as he marched by.

"I'll tell you what is killing our people: Drugs!" Chavez shouted. "That poor soul has seen the evil in the villages of the Valley of the Moon. As *presidente* I will unite all Mexicans and beg them to help stop the flow of drugs into our cities and rural areas. With your help, we can together create a new Mexico!" Chavez threw his hands high in the air. The crowd roared to life with cheers and adulation as Ramos and I were dragged back behind the stage, manhandled without the slightest care. I had one chance to turn around to look for Sancho. I saw him following covertly, serpentining around trees and people, staying at a safe distance. What was that kid gonna do? I really admired the little fellow, but somehow, I felt I was going to be responsible for something bad happening to him.

XXXI

Ramos got in a few slaps and punches, as did I, but nothing that hurt too bad. We were whisked across the grounds to an older section of Chapultepec Park, past a centuries-old cathedral and galleries—ruins dating back hundreds of years to the Age of the Aztec. I'm sure it was a great tourist destination, which would have suited me just fine at that moment. I could just make out the words *MUSEUM OF ANTHROPOLOGY* as they shoved us through a basement door into the large brownstone building. Great, a field trip!

Once we were securely inside, the soldiers began to disperse, peeling off and returning to their fascist duties or well-deserved siestas after violating my civil rights.

With only three soldiers to escort us now, they pulled us down a few flights of stairs, then down a long hallway illuminated by nothing but those shitty green fluorescent lights. I was more pissed off than scared as I sneered at Ramos, who, to his credit, was getting a little more negative attention than I was.

"Thanks a lot, Amigo!" I said with as much disdain in my voice as I could muster. He said nothing—just gave me this doe-eyed look that meant, *Oh, I didn't think that would happen!* I scanned around for Sancho, but he was nowhere in sight.

Giant glass showcases displayed diachronic scenes from throughout Mexican history. Models of Aztec and Mayan communities in all their splendor and suffering depicted the diverse cultures of the Spiritual Age. I was becoming painfully aware of the suffering part now that I was nothing more than a lamb being led to slaughter. I did my best to enjoy the tour. The Museum of Anthropology in Mexico City is definitely a "must see" under better circumstances.

The soldiers led us to a large, metal door then stopped. It was large and looked like it had been taken from an old prison—the kind that was rusted in all the corners and nooks and secured every which-way by large metal strips. It was almost like an Old-West bank-vault door. A soldier pulled the slide and unbolted it.

A strong stench of mold smacked me as we entered the dark, dank room. It was a rotting, nauseating stench that permeated everything. A single lightbulb dangling from a wire over an old wooden table burst to life when a soldier flipped the switch near the door. I could see the room was empty except for the table and two small wooden chairs barely big enough for an eight-year-old girl.

The three soldiers slammed us down into the tiny stools, unlocked our handcuffs, then recuffed one hand each to the bottom chair legs then stood in silence. This new and painful inconvenience gave me more time to observe the room with clarity. It had four stone walls with a large, bay-like window facing the hallway. I didn't remember seeing a window looking into the room as they were dragging me in, but a large, reflective pane. I wondered about its purpose as I peered through the window to a glass case containing a Mayan village replica across the hall. "What is this place?" I said to Ramos as he made a fist, opening and closing his hand to get the blood to flow back into his digits.

"It's a torture chamber, I think," he said, unaffected, as though he had been in a place like this before. Oh what drama.

"You mean an interrogation room, don't you?"

Ramos threw his head to the side and his dark, sweat-covered hair flew back over his temple to point at the back wall. There wasn't much light, but I could just make out what looked like thick, dark crimson clay covering the wall with pieces of… I don't know what.

"That's not…?" I said abruptly.

"Yep! Dried blood," he answered.

I suddenly wanted my private museum tour to end. "There's no way! I mean, look. People are just there, walking on the other side of that wall. Look. You can see them. Surely they'd hear screams or something."

Ramos pointed with his head again, this time toward the window. "That's a four-inch-thick tempered plexi one-way mirror. If you fired a shotgun at it point-blank, it would hardly scratch it. It's designed so the victim inside can see salvation just outside as people casually stroll through the museum a few feet away," Ramos explained.

"What the fuck!" I yelled profoundly. A soldier hit me on the back of my head as I screamed. I couldn't see him, but I yelled at him next: "You're on my shitlist, Jose!" They were hardly intimidated.

A young, brunette guide led a group of tourists through the museum and past the window. As the group stopped at each display, she narrated the scene with a microphone connected to a headset. Each tourist wore a matching headset that would translate her Spanish into English, Japanese, German or any other appropriate language.

Tourists snapped photos and *ohh*'d and *ahh*'d as the guide began the set up for *MASSACRE ON THE CAUSEWAY - LA NOCHE TRISTE*, depicting the night the Aztecs had their revenge on Hernan Cortes and his cadre of Spanish mercenaries.

I could relate. There was nothing more I wanted at that very moment than to have some revenge of my own on Cortes. Buried deep in the crowd of tourists was Sancho. He had lost us by being overly cautious, but was now just outside the chamber. Problem was, Ramos and I had no way of getting his attention. Did he even know we were there?

A bad smell preceded the general. Even from down the hall, with all those tourists in front of the window through which not a sound could be heard, I sensed he was coming. The door flung open in dramatic fashion. It was Cortes. He looked like a caricature of some post-junta despot entering his digs at the palace he'd just overthrown. His khaki military jacket, adorned with black insignia buttons, was newly pressed and the epaulets he'd acquired from years of mass murdering and genocide were spit-shined. His uniform was made of a thick material, thicker than the regular grunt soldier's and far too thick for the heat of Mexico. A black leather strap crossed his chest, securing his gun belt, complete with a forty-five-caliber automatic revolver in a holster. His black leather gloves seemed to be tailor-made for him; in fact, they were so perfect, they actually looked like a set of black, molded hands. He carried a medium-sized black box under his left arm, with his right hand always on his revolver. As Cortes stood in the archway of the door, Sancho had just enough time to catch a glimpse of us. I only had an instant to relay the peril we were in with my eyes. He got the message. At least I hope he did. I'm gonna buy this kid his first beer, I thought, if he can get us out of this.

Cortes slammed the door behind him and made his grand entrance, sneering as he eyed us up and down. He walked to the table and carefully perched the black box on the edge. His finger tapped the top of the box as he retrieved a long Cuban cigar from his vest pocket with his other hand. He struck a wooden match on the rough surface of the wooden tabletop and brought the flame to the cigar. His gloves creaked as he rolled the stogie, taking long, deliberate draws until the tip glowed red.

"That was a very foolish thing you did," he said as he blew out the flame, then rested his hand on the holster of his gun.

I decided I wasn't going to be a part of this. "Look! There's been a big mistake. I don't even know this guy. I just..."

Cortes snapped his head in my direction. "*Silencio!*" he interrupted. "Why did you come here? Are you with the rebel forces? Are you a Zapatista?"

Ramos cleared his throat, knowing Cortes had not yet recognized him, and said, "I came to speak with Governor Chavez, not one of his flunkies." Great, that was really gonna help.

Cortes snickered. "Ah," he sighed, "our little dog has not lost his bark. You may be assured I speak for the governor."

I knew it was a pissing contest now and I didn't have time to waste. "You have no right to detain us," I said confidently.

"I have every right!" snapped the general. "I am Generalissimo Jorge Cortes, direct descendant of Hernan Cortes, conqueror of all of Mexico. You have disrupted a political rally for Mexico's next *presidente* by resisting arrest and assaulting my men!" Man, I thought, what an ego!

He began to pace the floor. "Who sent you? Did you come to assassinate the governor, or just his character?"

Ramos looked right at Cortes and stated, "I'm a doctor visiting from the United States. He is a reporter with the *Washington Post* doing a story on the spread of the epidemic and whether this government will do anything about it or let their people languish and die." I looked sharply at Ramos, but held my tongue. I was primed to give this guy a good thumping when we got out of there.

Cortes narrowed his eyes as he paced between and around us. I could hear a touch of smugness in his voice when he said, "I know of no such epidemic. There have been no reports of unusual illness in the outlying communities except for those caused by the outlaw rebels. Reporters only write sympathetic propaganda. They are not wanted in Mexico. I have no use for them."

That one got my goat. I should have blown it off, but I had to say something—it was burning up inside. "You were looking for reporters when you torched the villages and massacred the people of Chiapas four years ago, weren't you?" I yelled. Suddenly, I realized my inner monologue was screaming forth.

Cortes didn't respond well to my jibe. His tone changed quickly to a shallow, perfunctory one, as though I'd just given the answer he'd been looking for: "Gringo, I have killed many men, and if you were in Chiapas during the uprising, then you are an enemy of mine—and an enemy of the state."

Well, it was all downhill from there on in. My mind went into kamikaze mode and I didn't even think when I started to speak—it just all came flowing out of my mouth like verbal diarrhea: "I could give two shits about your little power trip. I'm just here to do a story for my very influential American publication. If you try to impede me in any way, I'll have Washington crawling so far up your taco-eating ass..." Before I could finish, a soldier grabbed my arms and pulled them behind my back. "*Ah!*" I screamed, lurching forward in pain.

Cortes came closer and said calmly, "Señor, you are a long way from Washington."

I was past the point of no return, so I decided to fight it out, maybe somehow intimidate him. "I'll be contacting the U.S. Embassy and my personal friend, Secretary to the Ambassador Philip Gutierrez, and let them know you have illegally detained a Western journalist for the reasons of censorship, violating my civil rights." I couldn't believe the bullshit I was spewing, but I hoped, somehow, it would work.

Cortes stood his ground, but hesitated. Maybe I had finally made my point when I mentioned Gutierrez's name. "You are not being held against your will, Señor," the general assured me. "You are free to go anytime you wish."

Cortes nodded to the soldiers, who immediately released their grip on me. I hesitatingly stood up and wondered what he was playing at. Cautiously, I maneuvered toward the door as Ramos followed me with his eyes. I opened the door slowly only to see Sancho peek out from behind an Aztec warrior in full headdress. He whispered, "Señor Riley, what do I do?" I couldn't speak without Cortes hearing and grabbing up Sancho too, so I mouthed, "Help!" It was all I could get out before we both heard the sound of a pistol's slide as a bullet was bolted into its chamber.

I stopped dead in my tracks—no pun intended—but before I could shut the door, I flipped the small button on the knob to the "unlock" position. I pointed at it with my eyes to Sancho, knowing he would have to come up with something on his own now. I only hoped it would be in time.

"... Of course you'll be shot as a suspect in an assassination attempt trying to escape custody," Cortes went on. I never made it past the inside of the doorway. I walked back to my chair and dutifully sat back down. I was getting pretty tired of the games, but I knew our only chance was to buy some time.

"What's your problem, Adolph?" I heckled him. "Not enough migrant workers and homeless people to knock around?"

That did it. Cortes wheeled his arm back and cracked me in the mouth with his open hand. It took a second for my eyes to refocus. My tongue began to search the inner corners of my mouth for the source of the new taste. A taste of iron. It was blood. "You slap like a little girl!" I taunted him. "What are you, a faggot?" I laughed then spat a mouthful of blood and mucus into Cortes' face. What was wrong with me? I couldn't tell, but I think at that very moment, I secured Ramos's respect. In my peripheral vision, I could see his eyes widen and his jaw drop in disbelief.

Cortes took a handkerchief and slowly wiped my blood from his face, mouth and jacket, then replaced the soiled hanky in his vest pocket. He had a look on his face like that of a man who had finally found a worthy opponent, but was now going in for the kill. He looked at me, but spoke to Ramos, saying, "You say you're a doctor, well, we will soon see how good a doctor you are." Cortes took a step back and smacked the top of the black box that had been sitting idle at the edge of the table all this time.

XXXII

Panicked and sensing impending doom, Sancho searched his thoughts for a plan, a distraction. He squinted, closing his eyes tight, like a child making a wish. He grumbled in a self-deprecating way then pounded his thighs in consternation. Suddenly he had an idea. He quickly reached into his pocket and withdrew a small shiny object. It was a lighter. A cheap silver lighter complete with the face of Elvis on it. Slowly a wicked grin emerged on Sancho's face. He looked up and saw an old, rusted metal sprinkler head hanging upside down just above his own.

Sancho plucked two large peacock feathers from the Aztec warrior's headdress and popped open the lid to the lighter. "Forgive me," he said to the wax warrior in the diorama, then he touched the flame to the feathers. Instantly, a flame jumped forth, then thick, white smoke lofted toward the ceiling, getting thicker and thicker.

XXXIII

Cortes tapped the box with his fingers and unhinged a small, black veil that covered a hidden opening. "I call this 'Pandora's Box!' It is quite effective in extracting the information I require and convincing unruly Americans of their true worth," Cortes said calmly. He snapped his fingers like an annoyed father. Two soldiers simultaneously grabbed me while the other grabbed Ramos and pulled his arms behind his back. Each soldier gripped one of my arms, pulling one behind my back and extending the other toward the box. "You will now witness true power!" Cortes intoned. "I won't tell you what is in the box, but your ears will deafen from the sound of your own screams!" Cortes nodded to the soldiers holding me and began to pull my hand closer to the box. First was my index finger, then the other three, then the thumb.

I should have been proud of myself. I really didn't want to find out what was in that box. I presumed it was not good, so I fought and struggled and truly put up a good fight. Unfortunately, it wasn't enough. "What the fuck are you doing? I'm an American citizen!" I shouted in vain.

Cortes leaned into my face as my hand inched deeper into the box. "You will never print lies about my country again," he shouted.

I could see Ramos struggling, too, as he screamed, "Stop, Cortes, he is guilty of nothing!"

Finally, my hand went all the way into and almost to the other side of the box while the soldiers leaned with their weight on my back, pressing me forward. For a moment there was a foreboding silence. Waiting. All shouting stopped. All struggling stopped. Maybe this was just a bullshit scare tactic. Maybe there was nothing in that box after all...

Not a word was said for what seemed like and eternity. Then I felt it: a tiny pressure on the back of my hand; a feeling something was investigating me, my fingers, my muscles, my veins. Then came an instant rush of fiery pain. Before I knew what was happening, I began to shriek in excruciating agony. It felt like my hand was being blow-torched from my fingers up to my wrist. "Aaahhh!" I bellowed. I knew I didn't have long before I passed out... or worse.

I never saw her, but the tour guide had just finished her speech when the sirens began to blare. The lights in the corridor blacked out, then red emergency lights clicked on and began to flash. The combination of the sirens and the strobe lights were merely a prelude of what was to come.

Sprinkler heads burst open and water—lots of water with tremendous force behind it—gushed out everywhere. Not one corner of the museum basement would remain dry. You had to hand it to the engineers who had designed that fire extinguishing system: They did a helluva job. The lights in the torture chamber had gone off and it was pitch black. Ramos must have shot forward and pulled my hand from the box in a split second because I could feel the pressure of whatever was in that box subside. But not the pain. That just got worse. I could feel my body going into shock when the sudden sensation of cold water began showering my burning body. Although the fire in my veins was intensifying, the cold water was keeping me conscious. I felt my eyes roll into the back of my head until I hit the concrete floor hard. My body was already starting to shut down and I knew it.

It was then this weird, violent ballet began:

Everything became surreal: the way I saw Sancho rush through the door amidst the pulsating red strobe lights looking like some kind of superhero sidekick as I awaited unconsciousness… I only had an ounce of strength or tenacity or fear left in me, so in the confusion, I kicked the soldier standing above me in the nuts. It must've worked because I felt a body fall over mine. How do you like that, fucko?!

Ramos took Sancho's cue and wheel-kicked one of the soldiers, sending him to the ground. Making a fist, he punched the second in the throat, crushing his hyoid bone and making him fall to his knees, gasping for air. Seeing my quarry writhing in pain over me, Ramos hammer-kicked him just at the base of the skull. I'm no expert, but there seemed to be three less soldiers now. Before Ramos could make sure they were all neutralized, Cortes, half-blinded by water, drew his sidearm and tried to get a bead on anyone he could see. He fired indiscriminately until his body suddenly flew across the room. It was Sancho again. He had raced forward and, with his tiny, malnourished frame, dove headfirst into Cortes with the body-slamming power of a WWE wrestler.

I felt Ramos quickly scoop me up, and he grabbed Sancho by the shirt as we headed for the already closing door. He couldn't resist kicking one of the soldiers in the ribs, breaking at least three as a parting "Fuck you!"

Before the door could close behind us as we fled, Cortes locked his eyes onto Sancho, burning the boy's image into his rotten brain.

XXXIV

Each taking an arm, Ramos and Sancho carried me out of the chaos through the basement exit and into the park. It didn't matter that the alarm had sounded as we shot through the security door; no one would notice in all the commotion under the blare of the fire alarms and horns. I remember the shocking sensation of going from utter darkness into bright, midday light as they rushed me toward a crowd dispersing from the rally. My saviors ran quickly to bury us deep among the thousands of supporters as they made our way to a secluded area at the top of the park near the congested boulevard.

At the same time, Cortes hurried toward the opened exit door, but it was too late: We were already lost in the human exodus. There was no way he could find us now. He scanned the landscape like a falcon looking for a field mouse from high above. Nothing. Dripping wet and humiliated, Cortes furiously pounded his fist against the steel door.

In the thickets near Revolution Boulevard, Ramos and Sancho laid me down to access my injuries and treat the wounds. Glassy-eyed and in and out of consciousness, I retched in pain, my hand badly swollen. I was in agony. "It burns! It burns!" I cried as Ramos tried to muzzle me with his hand.

"Hold on, Riley!" he whispered sharply, trying to settle me down.

"What do we do, Doctor?" Sancho whimpered as he looked down at me with pitiful eyes.

Ramos grabbed him by the sleeve him and said, "Sancho, I need something sharp. Do you have anything sharp?" Sancho nodded then slowly pulled out a long switchblade from his back pocket. He pressed the button. *Thwap.* A long piece of steel flew from the hilt and locked into place.

"Your lighter! Give me your lighter," Ramos instructed. Sancho pulled the Elvis lighter from his front pocket and kissed the face. "'The King' will help," he muttered. Ramos grabbed it quickly and said, "Listen, we can't stay here. Riley needs medical attention now and they'll be looking for us in the city. We need a car, *comprende?*"

Sancho's eye lit up at this. "*Sí!* A nice car for a long trip, no?"

Sancho smiled then bolted from the thickets to the boulevard as Ramos flipped the top of the silver metal lighter. He brought his thumb down hard on the ridged wheel, sparking a thick, butane flame to life. He ran the sharp blade under the hot flame over and over again until the steel glowed red.

I could feel myself going into shock at that point, my body freezing, sweat pouring out of every pore. I couldn't control the fluttering of my eyes—couldn't control anything—as I felt Ramos slowly cutting deep into my hand.

"Sorry, Pal, this is gonna hurt!" he said as he drove the knife under my skin and ripped open my flesh.

XXXV

This is a good day to die.

A Great Plains Indian brave would shout that as a war cry just before mounting his fastest paint or pinto and charging bareback into battle. And he meant it. He didn't fuck around. He was the kind of unique warrior who lived each day to its fullest, enjoying the simple things that were so abundant in his world. Sunsets. The cool waters of a stream. Peyote. Nature. Everything in his realm he could taste, touch and see he relished, his very existence seeking enlightenment through adventure and spirituality. He was truly a tough guy. Brave. A complete man. A man to be admired.

Unfortunately, I wasn't born of his breed.

I refused to relish, or even acknowledge, each day of my thirty-something years on this ball-busting earth; that is, until I found myself in this godforsaken place. Here, I thought to myself, I get it. I understand what the Indians meant. Put aside all the petty bullshit; forget everyday trivia and mundane circumstances. They had choice, I thought, but I didn't.

Today was truly a good day to die.

I screamed out in a moment of lucidity and a beautiful young nurse came to tend me. "Your wounds were very extensive. Please lie still," she said softly. She reached for a towel in the wash basin, wrung out the excess and began to compassionately dab my perspiring forehead. She wiped my face gently, cooling the ravaging fever. It worked. I slowly calmed, relaxing under the moist towel and gentleness of her touch. I was half-naked. Surely it embarrassed her, but she stared at my chest, transfixed by the silver Saint Christopher's medal that was still safe around my neck.

As she washed me, she touched the medallion softly and looked me in the eyes as though we'd met before. I could feel her touch and something odd stirred in me, but I couldn't focus on her face.

"Who are you?" I muttered in a euphoric state.

"Maria," she answered quietly.

A strange thought popped into my head and I began to sing that stupid song from a movie I don't even think I ever saw: "*Maria, Maria, I've just met a girl named Maria...*"

Maria blushed, saying, "You still have a beautiful voice. Sleep now." With that, she passed her hands over my eyes like an angel or a hypnotist and I fell into a deep sleep.

A little while later, Ramos appeared at the bedside. He touched Maria on the shoulder and said with concern, "How is he?"

Maria checked my pulse and inspected the bandages. "The fever hasn't broken yet. He's still delirious, but he is a very strong man," she said proudly.

"*Mija*," Ramos whispered, "I shouldn't have involved him. I didn't realize he was..."

Maria gently touched her brother's face and smiled. It was a half-smile: part happy, part sad. She returned to tend to me. "You did what you had to do. Thank God Cortes didn't recognize you."

Ramos' face turned ugly. "That pig!" he yelled.

Maria quelled his anger by changing the subject: "Are they sending anyone from the lab to collect more blood samples?" She checked my I.V. tube for the hundredth time as she asked.

"I don't know. I don't know if anyone got the message," Ramos replied dejectedly.

I began tossing in my bed, mumbling and shouting as fever gripped me, swelling my brain. I began to flash back to a nightmare I'd been having for a long time; it would not stop haunting me:

I'm in the newsroom at the Washington Post. *I'm at a desk writing on a laptop, probably finishing a piece on some congressional bill that has just been passed, when I look down the aisle to see a man running towards me. Except this guy is running in slow motion and I realize the entire dream is in slow motion. Curiously, I stop writing and watch as this man, who I think I recognize, heads right for my desk. Just beyond him, I see two security guards chasing after him, running too, but slower. The man stops at my desk, throws something onto my lap then pulls out a gun. I'm not scared because I think I'm dreaming, but I can hear my own heart beat faster and faster in my ears. The man points the gun, squints his eye...* BANG! *I see blood splatter everywhere.*

Suddenly I gasped awake. The fever had broken.

I had just enough strength to comprehend the fact that I was still alive, just enough concentration to observe the little corner of my remaining world. That's all I had: an eerie beauty in the middle of all the chaos around me. I couldn't speak, couldn't say a word; all I could do was stare at my blurred surroundings like a child transfixed on a colorful mobile. Was I in a coma? Maybe paralyzed? Could anyone hear me, or even see me, for that matter?

Outside, the sun burned bright and life went on as a stark contrast to the dying that defined what happened inside the hospice. Life was outside. The world was outside. The future was outside. But I was inside, and I wasn't alone. Inside was surreal, like a depressing scene from one of those foreign movies that guys like me only saw with a date or when we wanted a decent nap; the kind you'd only see on a rainy Sunday at a dilapidated theater or yuppie arthouse. I remembered I used to like movies.

If you looked sideways, like I was forced to, and watched carefully as the sun moved, you'd see rays of light pierce dark patches of the room like shadows crossing a sun dial. Outside, in the world, back in my old life, I would never have stopped to see a thing so beautiful as the unfolding of a day. But here, my mind was imprisoned by a withering body and I was able to see all those tiny, fragile, unforgettable things with crystal clarity. It was a new experience for me.

I would create games in my head. Once I tried to separate dust particles from the tiny flying insects as they floated through the yellow beams of light. I'd watched intensely for hours. It was all I could do when I wasn't passing in and out of consciousness; my body had stopped obeying me for the first time in my life. It had been damaged—to what extent I had no idea—and I was unsure if I'd ever recover. Perhaps I'd end up like all the others, the patients....

I suppose the hospice was a dreary place, but I'd already given up on so many levels that it seemed like home to me. All the little stresses of daily life, the small stuff—washing the car, going to work, anticipating the new season of *Lost*—all seemed meaningless, a lifetime ago. It seemed I was slowly being reborn just at the hour of my death. Amen.

I couldn't be bothered with pain or pity. Especially pity. It meant nothing. Somehow I'd gained the ability during this time to rekindle a childlike capacity for pure imagination. Either I was channeling my childhood or actually developing one for the first time.

I wanted to chuckle at this thought, but didn't have the strength. It was ironic that it would be Mexico that would open my eyes, a country that years before had taken my spirit, the only woman I'd ever loved and, nearly, my life.

I was quickly becoming the antithesis of myself as I lay there preparing to die. My thoughts were answering age-old questions and offering a direct contradiction to the life of social engineering and cultural programming I'd allowed the modern world to heap upon me. It was becoming clear that, soon, all my years of cynicism would begin to fade away. I was becoming a human once again; re-humanizing, no longer concerned with who I was or what I'd done in my life. I had been a crass and offensive man, but my writing had never been so. It didn't matter that I was a good reporter, once, perhaps one of the best. Nor did it matter if my readers, my colleagues from around the world or even the D.C. politicians would ever point to me on the street and say, "There goes Terry Riley. He won the Pulitzer Prize!" No. That world had already given me up for dead. All that was left was to make peace with myself.

XXXVI

Mexico City has a completely different look at night than it does in the day. Some parts of it are quiet and sleepy, while others offer nightlife that would rival Manhattan's or Berlin's.

Kate entered the lobby of the Intercontinental Hotel and nearly slipped on the thick, polished Mexican pavers. She carried only a small weekend bag and rolled the larger suitcase as she walked quickly to the front desk. Suddenly, she was intercepted by an energetic bellman eager to help the American beauty. The bellman nodded as she walked by him, then hurried to catch her.

Slightly panicked and anxious because she spoke no Spanish, she kept heading toward the front counter while the bellman grabbed her small bag, trying to pull it from her shoulder. "What the...?" Kate stopped dead in her tracks, sliding a few inches as she did.

"*Señorita, por favor,*" the bellhop begged with a smile.

Kate yanked back, trying to keep him from taking the bag. "Hey! Let go!" she countered. "I'm quite capable of carrying this myself, thank you very much!"

"*Pero, Señorita, por favor,*" he said slightly more emphatically.

"That's it, Pal! If you don't let go I'm gonna..." Kate gave the strap one more tug and the bellman lost his grip, nearly slipping himself. Then he acquiesced to the guest.

He bowed in a forgiving way and said, "*Permiso, Señorita.*"

"Yeah, whatever!" Kate retorted as she arrived at the front desk. She was a girl on a mission.

The night manager was a lean, clean-shaven perfectionist, if not a bit of a dweeb. He was busy inputting data on his computer as Kate stepped up. He smiled and nodded in an overblown gesture of respect. "Ah yes," he said, slicking his pomaded hair. "Good evening, Señora."

"I'm looking for a Señor Terry Riley. He's staying at this hotel," Kate announced forthrightly to the clerk. "Can you ring his room for me?"

The night manager's smile quickly faded to a look of worry. "I... I... don't know this man. He is not a guest here. I cannot help you," he said, trembling as he looked over Kate's shoulder, through the lobby windows to the street. He shuddered. Outside, the black Mercedes sat ominously at the curb as two men, their faces obscured, watched his every move from a distance.

"You haven't even checked your computer to see if he's registered yet!" Kate said, surprised. That pissed her off. "Listen, I know Terry Riley's staying here, so I want you to check every name on your roster before I..."

But the manager interrupted her: "Your friend is in very great danger," he said nervously as he bowed his head so as not to be seen from outside, pretending to check the computer record. "I'm sorry, Señora, but I cannot help you any further." He then pathetically scampered into the back office to leave Kate alone and bewildered.

XXXVII

Lights illuminated the exterior of a large, white, futuristic-looking building with darkened glass and metal embedded everywhere. A sign read: *VALLE DE BRAVO DISEASE RESEARCH CENTRE. Valle de Bravo,* or "Valley of The Brave," was a resort community where many wealthy Mexicans and Europeans enjoyed their holidays. Much like Lake Tahoe or the Pocono's, Valle de Bravo was lush with trees, lakes, waterfalls and mountains to hike. It was also home to one of the world's greatest disease research facilities.

Normally, this sleepy little community would be silent in the dead of night, even at the research center. At a facility like that, you'd expect to have the odd overachieving scientist hard at work, maybe the janitorial staff, a security guard or two. But this night was different.

Men and women in red biohazard suits scurried like lab rats, loading equipment and supplies into trucks whose engines were already revving. These field-lab trucks were unique and brand new and, without the benefit of advertising, one might be mistaken for a baker's truck, even a plumber's. It was all part of the "low-key" appearance those in charge wanted.

The director, a large man in a blue biohazard suit, flipped up his breathing mask and began shouting. Words like *"Schnell!"* and

"*Rapido!*" didn't need translation as he barked out orders systematically, but in a respectful, "let's get this done" way. He was all business, all the way, yet he seemed out of place, this man who spoke German to some, English to others and Spanish to still others. No one questioned "*Herr Direktor*" or slowed their pace.

After an hour of staccato instructions, the trucks roared to life and barreled out of the sleepy little village into the clear desert night. The director checked his clipboard then turned to face the exiting vehicles with an intense glare.

XXXVIII

A campfire burned bright under the star-filled evening sky. Sancho was concentrating on the most important task at hand: devouring his supper. Ramos sat across from the boy near Father Gonzalez, sipping coffee and watching the priest stir a large cauldron with a long stick. The pot bubbled and boiled as the priest tossed in medical instruments, bandages and gowns to sterilize them for use. None of the men spoke to each other, exhausted from the day's trials of helping the dying—comforting them, holding them, removing bodies.

Just inside, I was slowly coming out of my malaise. When I finally woke, it was night. There was no real electric power to speak of; what little of it in existence was used for the antiquated medical equipment. Since the hospice had solid clay walls, candles were relatively safe inside and became the only source of indoor light. About the only thing San Cristobal had were candles—thousands of them. Maybe it was the Catholicism, maybe there had been a hippie colony around the corner back in the day; either way, the village had more than its fair share of candles. They flickered and glowed and illuminated everything with a semi-bright, eerily moving candescence. It was through the candlelight I realized where I was.

I lay still, regaining my strength, assessing how much I had left and how much I could feasibly muster up. I had decided to use mind over matter and gear up to get out of the cot, but I had to know what my surroundings were like first.

To conserve strength, I turned my head on the pillow and looked down the aisle of cots only to see several pale, eviscerated zombies that once had been human. Nearly the entire village of San Cristobal had either died or was languishing until their time. I shuddered as I saw man after man and woman after woman suffer and battle but ultimately lose their fight for life.

I turned my head the opposite direction to see a little boy. I was told later his name was Pepe. He was a favorite among the villagers because his curiosity, mischievous acts and ability to get into trouble had become legendary over his short four years of life. But now he lay dying, thin and pale, his dark eyes bulging from a face whose bones had already begun to deteriorate. The little guy stared right into my eyes, struggling to give me a smile, perhaps his last. A child's smile is the most innocent, guilt-free, blameless act on earth. His wanted no more than to communicate love for his fellow human being, even one he'd never even met.

At that moment, my heart broke. I forced a smile back to him, then turned away and began to weep quietly, burying my face in the pillow. I was so touched, so pissed, so anguished by what I had just seen, I mustered up all the strength I could. If this little guy could fight, then so could I. I slowly sat up in my bunk.

Still weary and slightly warped in the head, I grabbed the I.V. tube and yanked it from my arm. Christ! I must've been there longer than I'd thought. A tiny piece of flesh that had already begun to adhere to the tubing ripped off with the needle and tape as I pulled it out. I couldn't have cared less.

I struggled to get to my feet, grabbed my pants and shirt from the edge of the bed and slid them on without caring how I looked: miss a button here, collar inside-out there. The clay floor felt cool to my feet and instantly helped my condition. Man, I had a whopping headache.

My joints were frozen and I could barely focus on what I was seeing, but I knew the more I moved and walked, the sooner I'd feel better. At least that was the mind over matter mantra I kept repeating over and over again as I slowly proceeded.

I stumbled, heading for the hospice's front entrance. There was a glow from outside in the village square as I passed cot after cot of plague-ravaged villager. Was this my fate? How long did I have until I looked like them? I moved faster in the hope that I could beat the disease out the door before it could catch me.

As I held myself up by the archway of the door, I saw nuns in one area cooking food while others carried bandages and bedding; still others helped sterilize what was left.

"*Padre*, can I help you sterilize those instruments?" Ramos said as he finished a small plate of food.

Father Gonzalez lowered his head then stretched a false smile across his face. "Eat, my son. You have done plenty today. I do not think it matters now if anything is clean or not."

Sancho stopped eating, intrigued by what the priest had said. "Why, *Padre*?" he asked innocently.

Father Gonzalez dropped a tray of scalpels into the boiling cauldron and began to wring his hands dry with the skirt of his frock. He unrolled his cuffs, straightened his robe and walked to the fire, sitting next to Sancho like a grandfather. "Many centuries ago," he sorrowfully lamented, "this valley was green and flourished with fields and crops of every kind—legumes, vegetables… Food was abundant and plentiful."

As the sun set behind the mountains, Sancho became engrossed in the story. He gobbled more food from his plate and wiped his mouth on his shirtsleeve or forearm.

"Our Indian ancestors built an empire here that was beautiful," Father Gonzalez continued. "Magnificent. It was the center of the world. But alas, they became arrogant, losing touch with their humanity, losing love for their fellow man. They began to worship gold idols and studied the black arts. Human sacrifice became routine. Then an epidemic not unlike the one we're now experiencing spread across the valleys, laying waste to the land, wiping out all of our people."

"*Dios mio!*" Sancho said. "*Es Verdad?* Is that true, *Padre?*"

The priest nodded. "*Sí,* Sanchito. '*El Siete Plagas,*' they called it: 'The Seven Plagues.' When the Spaniards invaded Mexico nearly five hundred years ago, they brought with them the wrath of God: smallpox, typhus, measles, syphilis, influenza, drought and the worst of them—war. Some say it was the hand of God sent to remind us to love each other, not to ignore humanity. Now, every century or so, a plague returns to cleanse us of our sins."

Ramos looked at the priest with disagreement, but held his tongue out of respect.

I could hear the priest's lament as I slowly made my way to the campfire, holding onto a wooden post for support. I took small steps, a child's stride, then uttered the first words I'd spoken in I don't know how long: "'I will strike the water of the river with the staff I hold and it shall be changed to blood…'" I then appeared out of the darkness. I must have scared the crap out of them, their faces looked so shocked as they quickly turned to take me in.

"Señor Riley!" Sancho shouted in elation.

Ramos jumped to his feet and grabbed me by the shoulders. "Here, let me help you." He led me to a long, flat stone then sat me down upon it. "How do you feel? Here, sit down," he said in an unusual tone for his usually unpleasant character.

Two nuns had appeared from the shadows in the firelight; one handed me a plate of food, the other a goblet of wine. As they did, I felt something land in my hair and on my arms and realized tiny, gray snow-like flakes were descending from the sky. Could it be snowing? No, this was Mexico. I must've still been messed up in the head, yet it seemed so real to me in the desert night.

Father Gonzalez sat across from me, waiting to speak until I started eating. "Exodus, chapter seven, verse seventeen! You know your Bible well, my son," he commented, impressed by my impromptu sermon.

The smell of the freshly cooked food was so good that I couldn't control myself, and I began to shove it into my face. I realized I was ravenous. I answered the priest while chewing: "It was part of my Catholic school 'Learn or Burn' training program. You know that ol' 'the back side of a Bible is mightier than the sword' technique?" The priest chuckled. "Man, it feels like someone took a blow torch to my arm," I said, wincing in pain.

"You are very lucky, my son. Carlos drew nearly two ounces of poison from your arm. We still have no idea what kind of venom it was; it was like acid. We just know you have an angel on your shoulder. That is why you are here with us now." I gazed at the priest, mesmerized by his words.

In the States, I was a cynic of the highest degree, but here, every word he said seemed to make a lot of sense. Slowly, more and more of the dull, white flakes floated down, this time covering my plate of food. "What the hell is this stuff, *Padre?*" Shit, I just said "hell" to a priest, I thought.

Father Gonzalez turned and pointed to a hill less than a mile away. "It is ash from the pyres," he said. "We have to burn the dead to ensure containment of the virus." I nearly retched knowing my dinner plate was now covered in what were once people. The movie *Soylent Green* had a real effect on me as a kid. I immediately lost my appetite and laid the plate on the ground next to my feet. Looking up the hill, I focused on the glow of an enormous bonfire with white and gray smoke erupting and spewing forth from its center. The men doing the dirty work looked like little toy soldiers as they swung bodies in unison, tossing them as high as they could onto the fire for cremation. It was a disgusting sight.

"Do not lose faith, my son. You have survived a 'trial by fire.' God has great work planned for you, I can see that," Father Gonzalez pledged as he looked me straight in the eyes.

"With all due respect, *Padre*, if it means staying around here much longer, then forget it! Sorry, but this ain't my problem, you see!" I said callously. I felt a little duped all of a sudden. Was this the bait-and-switch team? The rebel and the priest? Ramos, the poor, misunderstood Robin Hood of the people sets me up, then pious and holy Father Gonzalez drives it home? Better men had tried.

But the priest wouldn't give up on my worthless soul that easily. He tried a different tack. "Don't be so sure, my son. Everything happens for a reason!"

I rolled my eyes. "Thanks, but I don't buy into all that 'hocus pocus' stuff. I'm what they call in America a 'lapsed Catholic,' emphasis on 'lapsed!'"

Then, slowly, from the shadows, a figure appeared. I tried to focus on it, but the other shadows from the campfire danced everywhere, creating a weird landscape. As the shadow came closer, I began to recognize it. It was Maria.

I thought I was dreaming. I blinked a few times and wiped my eyes, trying to get her image out of my head. I knew she wasn't there. She couldn't have been real. This was a ghost that had been haunting me for years. I was sick, I knew that, I just hadn't realized how bad. The figure came closer. I gasped, falling off the stone, and scrambled backwards like a crab. This place was full of ghosts.

"It's all right, Terry. It's all right," Maria whispered calmly.

My eyes widened with fright. "But you're... you're dead!" I screamed. Maria extended her arms, but I thrust my hands forward in a defensive posture to hold her spectre at bay. I began to hyperventilate, curling up in a ball like a child. I was truly terrified. All the guilt and loss I'd felt for her began to pour out of me. I cried out, "I'm sorry. I'm sorry I left you. They wouldn't let me come back. I tried. I swear, I tried. I'm so sorry!"

Suddenly, I felt her touch. Shivers raced up my spine. Maria knelt down and wrapped her arms around me like a new mother. She held me tight—tighter than anyone had ever held me. Ramos, the priest, Sancho, everyone around me, rose and walked away, giving us privacy during our bittersweet reunion.

Maria cried, "Oh, Terry. I'm here. I'm alive." The terror of guilt began to dissipate as I realized she was real. Then, even more disturbing,

I had to come to terms with the love of my life reappearing after all these years of me thinking she was dead.

"All those years I thought you'd been killed," I whined as I looked up, pulling my head up from my hands. "I've carried that with me. Not a day has gone by that I didn't think of you, how I could've saved you."

She kissed my cheek and head then said, "If you had come back for me, you'd be dead!" I tried to wriggle out of her grasp, but she wouldn't let me. I stopped struggling after a moment. "It is so good to see you again, my love," she said, stroking my forehead.

I sounded like a kid as I whimpered, "But they told me everyone in the village had been killed. How did you escape?"

With a sad smile, Maria said, "The villagers gathered the children and put them in a farm wagon we used for harvesting crops. We hid them under stalks of corn and palm leaves. I had been treating the wounded when they came and begged me to take the children before the army advanced on the village. It was an impossible task. Cortes was burning out the Zapatistas and anyone he suspected of collaborating with them, any sympathizers. In every village he killed anyone trying to flee. I had no choice, Terry. I was chosen to save those little ones."

My heart was broken. "I looked everywhere for you," I said, "for weeks, months. The State Department ordered me back to Washington before I could get back here. Cortes was executing reporters. I tried to get back, I swear!" Maria coddled me in her arms. "Why didn't you let me know you were alive?" I cried. "Why, Maria? Why?"

It was obvious she, too, was riddled with guilt and had been for some time. Maria slowly pushed me back and stared deeply into my eyes, then reached back over her shoulders to pull her Novice's veil onto her head. I was stunned. She was a nun. Her eyes began to well when she whispered, "I made a promise to God that if he would save those children from death, I would dedicate the rest of my life to him."

That wasn't the answer I wanted to hear. "But you made me a promise first!" I shouted in anger. She placed her hand on her cheek. "Terry, please don't."

I vented at her, and, unfortunately, not judicially: "Please? Please? That's what I said when I begged you to come with me that night in Chiapas, Maria... or should I say 'Sister?!'"   Slowly, she took off her veil and placed it in her lap. "I'm a Novice, Terry. I've not been ordained. I haven't taken Holy Orders yet."

My demeanor suddenly changed from angry to desperate. Was this my second chance? Was she telling me this for a reason? "Then there's still time!" I blurted out. "We could be together again, like we'd planned. Remember, Maria? Christ, the dreams we had! Not a day's gone by when I haven't seen your face everywhere, in everything. You've haunted me for years!"

She began to stroke my face then said with a serious look, "Terry, I can't leave these people now. They need me. Look around you. Can't you see what's happened here? Who would help them if I left now?"

I straightened up and shouted, "I need you! I always have. There's been a hole in my heart ever since the night I left you. Please. For God's sake, I don't think I can take losing you again."

That did it. I was serious. Serious and emotional like I'd never been before. A strange feeling consumed me, like someone was inhabiting my body, someone else's words coming out of my mouth.

XXXIX

No one ever complained about the volume of the music that blasted from the backyard of the Governor's mansion during special occasions: The vast estate was too far removed from any other hacienda for anything that went on there to bother anyone. Chavez was virtually isolated, which meant lots of privacy. But it also meant no one could hear him if he needed help.

Incandescent flood lights like those you'd see at a sports field illuminated the stepped veranda and grounds. The finely manicured lawn and gardens were visible from every angle and the trees and walkways had foot lamps so that even if you got yourself lost, you'd still be able to enjoy the scenery.

The boom of the stereo was rivaled only by the screams of people frolicking in the pool. Chavez and two young interns or housekeepers or groupies—whoever—splashed and jumped and swam around the enormous pool like children.

One woman jumped up from the bottom of the pool and climbed out, quickly drying off then scooping up a long piece of silken material to wrap around herself. She began to dance the flamenco. The second woman jumped out of the pool, with Chavez following quickly, and joined her friend. The governor dried his face and chest with a cotton beach towel then dove into a *chaise lounge* with thick, white cushions.

The two women began to undulate seductively, gyrating their hips and whirling the silk fabric as though it were a bullfighter's cloak. The first woman danced around and over and under the other; all the while, Chavez became more and more delighted with their performance.

"*Sí, Sí* my *mijas*! Oh, yes, that's it!" he shouted as he clapped to the tempo of their steps. Chavez reached for a full bottle of tequila the butler had left for him. Seeing this, the second woman quickly grabbed it up before he could reach it. She put the tip of the bottle into her mouth, bit down hard on the cork, then pulled and tugged, finally extricating it. *Pop!* Chavez nearly jumped out of his seat with excitement at the sound.

The first woman came up behind her and grabbed her chest, ripping her bathing suit top off to expose her firm, natural breasts. It was beginning to look like a choreographed act at a high-end strip club when Chavez screamed, "Oh yes!" The first woman grabbed the bottle and teasingly poured the tequila down the cleavage of her topless friend. They both leaned over and grabbed Chavez by the back of the head, pulling him into her chest to let the tequila flow. He pressed his lips against her breast plate and opened his mouth wide. Booze flowed freely into his gullet as he made a canal with his tongue. Then he swallowed. *Gulp. Gulp.* After a moment, he rolled his tongue up and down her torso, making sure he licked everywhere from her navel up to her pink aureoles and firm nipples, ignoring nary an inch.

The women jumped onto his lap, took the bottle and began to kiss and fondle each other. The music blared on. Erotic laughter filled the cool night air.

At the same moment, the French doors of the hacienda burst open. Cortes and an entourage of soldiers barreled through the foyer of the Governor's Mansion while the palace guards never twitched in an attempt to stop him. They, too, feared him, and, technically, were under his command and authority. They'd rock the boat with the governor long before confronting the general. Cortes stormed through the mansion past Chavez's guards with his jaw clenched tight and his eyes fixed on a target.

The large patio doors flung outward, but Chavez and his escorts were busy with their games. Cortes and his men marched onto the veranda and down the steps to the pool area. Seeing the debauchery, the general winced, but continued to head directly for the governor, never missing a step.

The soldiers couldn't help but get an eyeful as the governor and the scantily clad girls frolicked like a satyr and his nymphs in the forest. Each man nearly broke a smile, yet knew the risk was too great. Chavez downed another swig of tequila as the girls gave him an interactive lap dance.

"Drunk! A pathetic drunk!" Cortes screamed as he stopped at the foot of the chaise. "We have important business to attend to and you are behaving like a schoolboy in a brothel."

The two women stopped dancing immediately and cowered behind Chavez. They, too, knew this man's reputation and feared him dearly.

Unfazed, the governor slowly looked up at the infuriated officer, nearly ignoring him, and motioned for the women to leave him. But before they could, he gave them each a long kiss on the lips. This incensed Cortes. As the girls scampered past the soldiers, the men couldn't help themselves. They quickly slapped their asses and made a few catcalls. Cortes threw the soldiers a dirty look. They immediately shot upward to attention.

"I may be drunk..." Chavez said quietly as he wiped the sweat and alcohol from his face with a hand towel. Then he raised his voice: "...but I'm still governor and soon *presidente* of Mexico! Do you understand, General?"

Cortes snuffed at the comment and said, "You are nothing but a puppet. You strut around the stage like a trained parrot. Without me you would have been killed by the rebels long ago. Because of me you have the confidence and support of millions of Mexicans." The general paced around the lounge chair. "They merely hear your words, but they see my power!"

Intimidation had never worked on Chavez. Either he was cool under pressure or was so confident in his position that nothing and no one could rock him. He plopped lazily back onto the chaise after walking to a hamper and tossing in the wet towel. He reached into a wooden humidor and retrieved a long cigar, rolled it under his nose, then inhaled the aroma. He then snatched up a nearby candle and took a dramatic moment to pause when the flame rose high from the tip of the cigar. With each long drag, the tip glowed redder and hotter.

"Confidence, you say?" Chavez began. "Ha! The Mexican people love me because I am fair and benevolent and govern with a compassionate hand. They fear you like a dog that has been beaten! There is an old saying, Cortes: 'You can piss on the people's head and tell them it's raining, but they can tell the difference!' Remember that."

"You are no leader!" Cortes snapped. "These people want to be ruled; they *need* to be ruled. They do not care where their food, their power, their water comes from—they only care that it comes!" Cortes postured like Mussolini; sure he had made a profound statement.

"Stop! You are beginning to sound like a politician," Chavez laughed, "but you are not and never will be." Chavez took another drag of his cigar then gave Cortes a serious look. "What you did today to the American was stupid. Are you a fool? Mexico is in the midst of its own renaissance; it's our Enlightenment. We can no longer afford the ways that you practice—fear, intimidation, murder! From now on there will be no more '*mordida*,' no more graft, no corruption, no more pay-offs. This election has kept me too busy to oversee your activities, but I know you are up to something that is no good,"

"I am taking care of the needs of the people!" Cortes said with an insincere tone.

Chavez retorted, "'The needs of the many outweigh the needs of the few.' Yes, I'm well aware of your Marxist views, but get one thing straight! You are here only to protect my administration and the people of Mexico. If you have other ideas to that effect, I will expose your past to the War Crimes Tribunal in the Hague and anyone else who will listen without hesitation!"

Cortes seemed momentarily stunned. For the first time, the general had shown his Achilles' Heel. He lowered his eyes and sneered, "Are you threatening me?"

Chavez peered back and said, "Yes, Comrade! My friends who are loyal to the cause informed me about your days in Cuba. I know about the death squads." Chavez rose and advanced closer, backing Cortes to the edge of the clear, turquoise pool. "I also know that you lost favor with Castro and, because of your lust for power, you fled like a coward to Mexico, where you changed your identity and your look to save your pathetic ass." Chavez yelled, pointing an accusatory finger and spitting just loud enough for the soldiers to hear. He was not a stupid man. Reckless, but not stupid.

Cortes abruptly turned on his heels to face the Captain of the Guard, Alfonso Pena. Captain Pena, a young officer in his late twenties, was already a seasoned veteran in the armed services. He had always followed his general without question or hesitation, but now, hearing the governor charge Cortes with indictments his general did not deny caused Pena great reservations. Cortes didn't see the reluctance on Pena's face as he belted out another order. "*Vamanos!*" the general screamed as he stormed up the veranda and made his way back inside the mansion. His soldiers turned on a dime and followed in tight formation behind him.

Pena hung back for just a moment to bring up the rear, but gave Chavez a curious, inquisitive look. It was a look desperate for advice. Chavez could read this young man easily, but merely sighed, raising the bottle of tequila in a salute to Pena, then toasted him: "To your health, *Capitan!*" Nodding in respect, Pena followed the last soldier out.

Chavez listened to the goosesteps as they faded from his home, then shouted to his butler, "Jaime, *mas* tequila! And send me my girls!" He swirled the last bit of tequila in the first bottle, then took a long swallow, finishing it. He leaned forward and threw it hard against a clay wall. *Crash.* The glass shattered into a million shards. The governor took the cigar from the edge of the table and bit down ferociously on it.

XL

The U.S. Embassy in Mexico City was large and illuminated from various angles to allow maximum exposure, ensuring total surveillance. Although there were many windows that looked out over Revolution Boulevard, they were tinted with Mylar coating to withstand bullets and debris from a bomb blast; even more importantly, they were also protected from laser surveillance and other types of electronic eavesdropping.

You could walk up the numerous steps from the street right up to the embassy doors with little to no intervention on the part of the Marines as long as there were no crowds or rallies at the time. In case of attack or a rowdy mob, barricades would instantly shoot skyward, cutting off those who were inside from those outside, trapping and separating them from the nucleus. It was an effective, yet non-lethal, way to keep the embassy safe, controlled and protected through even the most dangerous of situations.

It was after-hours when Kate pounded on the three-inch-thick glass of the embassy's revolving doors. Barely a sound could be heard as she banged, but the Marine guards inside had already spotted her from the street and tracked her movements up each step to the door. The guards had already assessed Kate as a "non-threat" before one of them walked to the door's intercom to see what she was up to.

"We're closed, Ma'am!" the guard snapped as the external intercom crackled to life. The guard pointed to a small black button on the speaker. Kate pressed it and retorted, "Wait! I'm an American. I need to find my friend who's gone missing. He was here at the embassy yesterday and I have reason to believe he's in great danger!"

The guard at the door turned to instruct the younger guard behind the reception desk. *Clunk.* Kate heard the sound of a large bolt being released from its position. The guard pushed the revolving door in two stages for Kate to walk through. There must have been some sort of metal detector built into the sections.

When she finally entered the lobby of the embassy, the guard immediately checked her bags, frisked her then had her walk through another scanning device before allowing her to advance toward the desk. "Are you a family member of the missing person?" he said with military routine.

Kate was nervous and excited as she spoke: "I'm a co-worker, a colleague. His name is Terry Riley. We're both reporters for the *Washington Post.* He was scheduled for an interview with Ambassador Sparks yesterday, but I don't know if he ever made it." The Marine guard led her to the desk where his subordinates had already begun typing into their computer: *TERRY RILEY.*

At the same time, Philip Gutierrez was finalizing a long day of diplomacy and tact. He was walking two members of the Nigerian delegate down the long stairway in order to leave with them when he spotted Kate at the reception desk. Normally he would not have cared; it was not too late, but slightly against protocol to have visitors in at such an hour. Still, he couldn't help giving her the once-over, even at the risk of looking rude to his foreign guests.

At the bottom of the stairs, Gutierrez raised his chin to one of the guards, signaling him to open the front doors and allow the diplomats to leave. The young guard hustled over to unlock the doors and Gutierrez asked him, "Who is that woman, Sergeant?"

"She says she's looking for a friend of hers from the *Washington Post* who's missing, Sir!" the Marine said in formal response. Gutierrez apologized to his Nigerian guests and asked if they wouldn't mind leaving without him. He said a formal good-bye, complete with handshakes and bowing, then made sure the Marine locked the doors behind them before making his way back to the desk.

"There, Terry Riley! I knew he came here yesterday!" Kate shouted as she pointed at the screen. The two guards nodded.

"Yes, Mr. Riley was here. Has something happened?" Gutierrez interjected. Kate spun around and nearly grabbed his lapels in gratitude. "I'm Philip Gutierrez, Ambassador Spark's Secretary. Mr. Riley and I met yesterday." He was trying to put her at ease.

"I just flew in from Washington after receiving distressing information on a story he came down here to cover, but he hasn't been seen since he was here last," she said. "I've reason to believe his life is in jeopardy."

Gutierrez mouthed something to the guard as he tried to extract more information from Kate. "What could be so important to have you come all the way from Washington?" he probed.

Kate rallied back, "Riley's down here covering the environmental summit, but he's concentrating on Senator Dan Pritchard. There are suspicious links between the conference and the numerous drug companies Pritchard owns here in Mexico."

This was news to Gutierrez, but he kept his cool and tried to pare down her accusations. "There are a lot of American-owned companies here, especially since NAFTA was signed and ratified. Surely you can't condemn a man, even a politician, just because he owns a company in a foreign country?"

Anticipating his doubt, she fired, "I'm sure it's illegal, even here, for a company to produce cocaine and use the proceeds to get a politician elected President of the United States!"

Although he saw she was serious, he could not let her off that easily. A guard appeared with a tall glass of water and handed it to Kate. She nodded in hurried gratitude and chugged the entire glass down in three long gulps, then wiped her dripping mouth with her sleeve. No time to stand on formalities.

"Can you prove this, Miss?" Gutierrez said suspiciously.

Kate set down the empty glass on the counter and bent to reach into her large bag. "It's Kate Walker, and yes! The Justice Department has an extensive file on Pritchard. He's been under surveillance for years." She retracted a large file from her bag and handed it to him. Gutierrez opened the file and began to scan the contents:

WARNING: THE FOLLOWING ARE CLASSIFIED DOCUMENTS FROM THE U.S. JUSTICE DEPARTMENT. UNAUTHORIZED PERSONNEL VIEWING DOCUMENTS COULD BE CHARGED WITH A FELONY.

One dossier had Pritchard's name and photo with a caption that read: *SUSPECTED DRUG DEVELOPMENT OF A SUSPICIOUS NATURE. PROCEED WITH INVESTIGATION. CONSIDER FOR OPERATION CASABLANCA.*

Gutierrez absorbed as much information as he could in such a short time. He thumbed through the files extensively, reading bits and topics on nearly every page before shutting it. His brow raised slightly as he looked back to Kate. "How did you get these files?" he asked. "They *are* confidential documents, you know."

"First Amendment privilege, Mr. Secretary!" she asserted. "Look, I'm an American here looking for another American who may be in danger. You have to help me!"

Gutierrez thought for a moment then sighed. He glanced at one of the guards. The Marine abruptly left his post and went down a small flight of stairs to the basement, never to return.

"You must care an awful lot for him," Gutierrez said curiously.

"Just professional courtesy," Kate said with some discomfort. "He'd... he'd do the same for me." Kate heard a printer spit out a page.

Gutierrez grabbed it from the trolley and scanned the names on the sheet. "There was a man who was here at the same time Riley met me. His name was Doctor Carlos Ramos. I remember he was very passionate about getting him to go to his village..." Gutierrez tried to think of the name. "...San Cristobal! That was it. It's about fours from Mexico City, southwest through the desert, in a place called Valle de Luna—Valley of The Moon. Maybe he's there." Kate hurriedly gathered her things, grabbing the file from Gutierrez and stuffing it into her bag. "Thanks! It's a start," she said, racing to finish.

Gutierrez, in a moment of compassion, placed his hand on her shoulder. "Please be careful Miss Walker," he said. "That part of Mexico can be a dangerous."

XLI

The campfire had burned down to a few flickering logs and would soon be nothing but a pile of smoldering red embers. Ramos and Father Gonzalez talked quietly with Boomba and a number of men wearing black bandannas around their faces. The Zapatistas, Chiapas rebels. A few yards away, I was trying to polish off a bottle of tequila. "Don't you have any decent Irish whiskey anywhere in this godforsaken country?" I said angrily. I wasn't drunk, but I was trying hard to get there.

Maria attempted to change my dressings, but I couldn't stop fidgeting. She carefully removed the bandages around my arm, washed the wound then applied a smaller wrap that just covered my still-raw knuckles and hand, leaving the fingers exposed. She ignored my ranting, knowing it was just the pain of seeing her after all these years. She knew she had been a ghost for me, but never thought I'd suffered so.

Maria carried the soiled bandages to the boiling cauldron and dropped them in. The fire under the black-bottomed pot was bright and hot, and the water bubbled as though it were a thousand degrees. I sat back and let the image of Maria's thin, curvy frame as her tattered dress became illuminated by the fire sear into my brain. I was transfixed by her silhouette as the fire danced behind her, revealing everything the God I barely believed in now had blessed her with.

I turned a tearful eye from her to leer at Ramos, who was talking with his men. I was feeling ornery. "So you're the famous Colonel Ramos, rebel leader! You were in charge of the men who were supposed to protect Chiapas. Where were you when Cortes leveled the village and nearly killed your sister?"

Boomba and the other rebels flinched into a protective posture, but Ramos raised his hand to calm them. "You're drunk!" he shouted. Ramos lowered his head; my words had cut his pride. It seemed to be a sore spot for him.

I became relentless. "You're some piece of work, Doc," I shouted. "You got your wish: Here I am. I hope you're happy. But plan on me getting you an exclusive? I don't think I'll be alive long enough to write the fucking the story! I'm gonna end up like all the others in this shithole."

Ramos nodded to Boomba, who took his men to another corner of the village, offering me a sneer as he passed.

"Relax!" said Ramos. "For all we know, you could be immune. I've tested you three times already and you're not showing any symptoms."

I stared into space. "Relax, he says."

Ramos looked toward Sancho and said, "Look, he's not worried!" Sancho was fast asleep by the fire, snoring like a bullfrog. I watched him for a moment, envying his clear conscience as he slept—a far cry from my muddled mind.

Maria appeared with a jug of water that she placed at my feet and a goblet she handed to me. As she poured, I suddenly felt like royalty: a king being served by his queen. It was a bittersweet feeling but it didn't last long.

I hoisted the bottle of tequila to my mouth before she could hand me the water. "No thanks, I prefer your home brew!" I said in a snotty way.

Before I could take another swig, Maria grabbed the bottle out of my hand and threw it into the darkness. *Clink.* The bottle shattered into a thousand pieces. "Then you prefer a short life!" she said sternly, like a scolding mother. The gloves were off now.

I didn't know what I was saying or why, but I was hurt and I was gonna make her feel as bad as I could. "Doesn't matter much, now, does it, Sister?" I huffed sarcastically.

Maria knelt down next to me and said quietly, "It does to me."

I lost it. All the emotions that had been penned up for years came rushing out in response to her soft words and genuine concern for me. Unfortunately, I didn't break down and cry like I should have. I made the wrong move. I grabbed her and began to kiss her passionately, impulsively. She half let me, half didn't, but before she could push me away or return my kiss, Father Gonzalez interrupted: "*Ahem!*"

I released my vice-like grip on her lips and looked up to see him standing near the cauldron, watching us. He didn't seem judgmental, only slightly disturbed.

Maria was truly embarrassed. She straightened up and handed me the goblet of water, saying, "Drink this. It will purify your body."

I knew there'd be no more kissing, at least until we were alone, so I took the glass and brought it to my mouth, then hesitated. "I thought water in Mexico was full of sh... sorry—bacteria." Maria was right to stay at arm's length from me, or maybe she was keeping me at arm's length from her, I didn't know.

"This water is clean," she said as she straightened her dress. "It comes from an underground spring." She pointed to the great fountain of Saint Christopher in the center of the village. "It was discovered by our ancestors as they crossed the Badlands fleeing the Spaniards. It was an oasis of sorts. That's why this village was named San Cristobal: after Saint Christopher, the Patron Saint of Travelers." Her travelogue was beginning to take my mind off the pain in my arm as well as the pain in my heart. She reached over and touched the silver Saint Christopher's medallion around my neck. Her fingers were warm and I could feel the blood pumping through them. "It is our sacred fountain. Only the clergy drink from it now. The villagers use the other water supply." I looked around in the dark, not really understanding what she meant.

"What other water supply?" I said curiously. She moved her finger, plotting the dark horizon, eventually landing on a long, silver pipe protruding from the ground and entering one of the homes. "The AMERIMEX System," she said. "It was installed three months ago and has allowed the villagers to have fresh water flow directly into their homes." I nodded, though I couldn't believe they were just now getting running water.

Maria's soft voice began to lull me, making my eyes heavy. Seeing this, she helped me lie down on a colorful wool blanket. "Think about it, Maria," I said. "It could be a second chance for both of us."

She smiled as I mumbled, kissing my head. "Sleep now. We'll talk in the morning." She cradled my head and stroked my brow. I gave her one last look.

As if under a spell, I fell fast asleep. Maria hummed a lullaby, fixated on my silver medallion. With two fingers, she gently turned the medallion and gazed at the inscription: *TERRY, I WILL ALWAYS BE CLOSE TO YOUR HEART - LOVE, MARIA.*

XLII

The desert was black as pitch. There were no streetlamps, no signposts here; only darkness. As the field-lab trucks barreled across the Badlands toward San Cristobal, all they had as visual confirmation for the village was a tiny illumination from the campfires within its walls. Glowing specks of yellow and orange reflecting off the white stucco created a warm hue in the night. The trucks adjusted their course and made double-time toward the small enclave.

I never heard the trucks speed under the archway and scream to a halt in the center of the village. Never saw the dust cloud that preceded them as they stopped short, blinding anyone that might've suddenly awakened. The steel double doors to each truck burst open simultaneously, emitting techs in biohazard suits that ran to different positions in the village. With military precision, they began to reconnoiter, moving quickly, gathering items of clothing, foodstuffs and small animals, and placing them all into bags marked *HAZARDOUS MATERIALS*.

I felt my body lurching and thrusting to and fro. I had no choice but to awaken from my peaceful slumber. Damn, my first decent few hours of sleep in years! I thought I was still dreaming when I opened my eyes to a horde of alien-looking figures surrounding me. Two workers helped me to my feet then led me to one of the field-lab trucks. As I staggered, I could see the technicians scouring the village, searching for something. I began to feel uneasy, as if Cortes had something to do with this. I was too weak to fight.

The doors of the truck flew open and the two men hoisted me into the back. Inside, I saw Ramos sitting quietly between two suited workers, and Sancho, fast asleep, of course, and snoring loudly, between two others. "Sit down and don't say a word!" one of our captors said through his polarized face mask. I nodded and took a seat across from Ramos. The steel doors slammed behind me and were bolted down securely.

"What the hell's happening now?" I grumbled, still groggy.

"You'll know soon enough!" Ramos hissed back at me.

XLIII

The trucks arrived at a high-tech complex and backed into a loading dock area. That annoying siren—*beep, beep, beep*—made my ears pound as the driver slowly reversed. I didn't think they had to worry about children playing in the loading dock area at five A.M.!

Sancho, Ramos and I were immediately transferred down a long, white corridor that seemed to get smaller as we got closer to the end. I felt like Alice as she tumbled down the rabbit hole.

"Señor Riley, where are we?" Sancho said, wiping the sleep from his eyes.

"Quiet! Don't say a word!" one of the workers snapped.

As we made our way toward another set of security doors, a blue neon light swept the hallway. A sign read: *DECONTAMINATION CHAMBER - BIOHAZARD LEVEL III*, and a thick glass door stood between us and a darkened chamber. One of the men in a red biohazard suit swept a security card through a small metal strip. An optical infrared eye blinked. Green light. Clear.

Whoosh. The dense glass door opened. We were directed inside the chamber while the technicians remained behind in the hallway. The doors shut with the sound of a vacuum sucking, sealing the airtight chamber from the outside. The crackle of a speaker above our heads got our attention, and a monotone computer-generated voice began speaking.

"Step into the center of the chamber and remove your clothes," the computer commanded.

Feeling my old self returning, I snickered and said, "What's the magic word?" I turned to Ramos and joked, "I hope there isn't a full-body cavity search involved."

The computer instantly berated me: "Remain silent. Place clothes through the door to the right. Stand motionless and erect!"

All three of us did as we were instructed, tossing our clothes into a small steel opening that had magically appeared in the wall. A sign over it read: *HAZARDOUS MATERIAL*. The items were instantly sucked into the bin. *Whoosh*. The door closed automatically. Thousands of smart-ass comments were circling my head when a red laser light began to whirl around the chamber. It was an eerie sight until a white, snow-like substance began floating around us. Sancho whispered, "It's like Christmas!" The red light suddenly flickered off and a white neon light filled the chamber. "Viral scan complete. Decontamination process complete. Secure gowns and boots and step through door," the computer finished.

"Don't I even get a kiss?!" I shouted.

A second door opened. Ramos, Sancho and I stepped through. A large figure stood before us in a blue biohazard suit, unlike the red suits the others wore. They've taken us to their leader, I wanted to say. He removed the helmet to expose his wild hair and came toward us. He had a wicked grin on his face and a crazed look in his eye; and this guy was enormous, probably six feet and seven inches tall. He unpeeled a long Velcro strip that ran down the center of his suit and disrobed. He looked like a genius in a lab coat and sneakers. This guy was a complete whack-job, I thought.

Ramos stepped forward and said, "Manny, thank God you got my message!" Sancho and I looked at each other oddly. The Goliath embraced Ramos in a big bear hug and said in a heavy German accent,

"I'm sorry for all the cloak and dagger routine, but there are those who would do anything to get their hands on you."

I turned to Ramos, half-pissed off, half-curious, and said, "You know this guy?"

"We were roommates in medical school," Ramos said, laughing. "Manny was an exchange student from Germany. Christ! How long has it been?"

The German slapped him on the shoulders as if to squash him and said, "Too long, my friend."

Ramos introduced us: "Doctor Manfred Zobel, this is Terry Riley. He's a reporter with the *Washington Post*."

Manny lunged his giant hand out and shook mine like a rag doll. "*Mucho gusto, Señor* Riley," he said happily.

As he pulled me towards him with the handshake, I nearly tripped over my gown. "Sorry!" I said. "I'm not used to your new spring wardrobe yet."

Manny smiled, saying, "Your clothes are being tested for exposure. They will be returned to you if they're free of contaminants."

Sancho stepped up and stretched out his hand. "...And this is Sancho. He's a...? He's...?" Ramos fumbled.

Sancho interrupted, "...the third Musketeer!"

Manny shook Sancho's hand then turned back to Ramos. "My condolences," he said humbly. "Your father was a great man. A great leader." He swept his arm out to lead us into another room. "Come, let me show you what you have been missing all these years."

I took a moment to investigate my surroundings. We were in some kind of scientific laboratory—the kind you might see on the Discovery Channel or *C.S.I.*; you know, the forensic detectives series. All around the lab, centrifuges spun, separating red blood cells from the sera in each sample. High-powered, digital machinery hummed and whirred and blinked. It could have been the set of a new sci-fi thriller, but it was very real.

Sancho walked cautiously up to one of the throbbing machines that was pumping blood and fluids into a cylinder and stood in awe of the movement and workings, the likes of which he'd never seen. Accidentally, he bumped into a technician peering through a large microscope. "*Permiso!*" Sancho said. The tech merely smiled.

Manny made his way to a long steel table laid out with numerous gadgets. The tech left her post and walked to the table, into which she inserted a slide with a culture already in place. She looked into another microscope, checking the set-up. "The sample is ready for you, Doctor," she said. Manny smiled and relieved her from duty.

"Please." He motioned toward the scope. "Let us see if you remember your studies, my good friend." Ramos stepped up. "Look at this culture. Tell me, what do you see?"

Ramos peered into the eyepiece and scanned the lens. He observed a beautiful, microscopic, cellular dance. "Let's see," he said seriously, "cellular division?"

Manny's eyebrows raised. "Yes!"

Ramos continued, "Abnormally rapid multiplication?"

Manny was nearly ecstatic at his answer. "Yes! Yes! Go on."

Ramos blinked to clear his vision then went back to the optic. "The cells on the right are being attacked by the newly divided cells on the left. Were these antibodies introduced to cannibalize the existing cells?" Ramos said curiously.

Manny clapped his hands together in a thundering beat. "Bravo, my friend! Still top of your class." He then turned to me and said, "You know, Carlos could have practiced anywhere, but the politics of this country forced him to flee to the United States."

I leered toward Ramos and said, "That seems to be a habit of his."

Ramos shot me back a glare, but knew there were more important issues at hand. Sancho crept up to the microscope as we talked to look at the culture. "*Ai, no lo creo!* What are they?" he said excitedly.

"The cells on the right are carcinoma," Manny told Sancho. Ramos interjected, "Cancer cells." Manny smiled again as he picked up a thick folder of notes. "Yes. The cells on the left are cultured," he continued, "hybrids we've designed here in the lab. They destroy the cancerous cells by devouring them, inhibiting division. It's taken me over a decade to find the right DNA sequences and codes to genetically alter them."

I processed the information as best I could. "Wait a second," I jumped in, "you're telling us you've found a cure for cancer?"

Manny nodded his head, his freakish hair waving wildly. "Perhaps, my friends! Perhaps."

Manny walked to another table. He was fidgeting like a crazed genius when another lab tech approached and said, "They are ready for you, Doctor."

Manny looked up and turned to us to say, "Come, gentlemen. Now I'll show you why I brought you here."

We walked through yet another secure area—a large room with a small door and dense glass, virtually empty except for a single stainless steel table near two openings. The openings were just wide enough to insert your hands and arms into and follow the thick polymer gloves down to the fingertips. The gloves were attached to the inside of the sealed room at the edge of the table where our clothes were neatly laid. Next to the clothes sat a small wire cage. In the cage, a number of large lab rats either ran on their treadmills or went about their daily activities of eating and resting.

Manny slid his hands into the gloved holes carefully. Now he could work safely without threat of exposure. I glanced up at a sign that read: *BIOHAZARD LEVEL IV - EXTREME CONTAMINATION - DANGER - NO ENTRY WITHOUT DOUBLE-LINED BIOSAFETY SUIT.* Manny carefully picked up a long tube next to the rat cage on the table and maneuvered it over our clothes. At the tip of the pole, a green neon light flashed. "If the light flashes red, your clothes are contaminated," he said. He continued to pass the pole over the clothes, making sure not to miss a single stitch. The light turned green each time he made a pass. "Just as I thought," Manny said as he shook his head. "The light has stayed green. No contamination whatsoever." He placed the neon-tipped pole back on the table. We awaited his explanation. "The epidemic in your village could've been caused by many things. I thought at first it was cholera. Then accelerated cases looked more like the Hanta Virus. We checked for blood and proteins in the urine, separated the yellow serum from the blood then added the reagent... Nothing," he said worriedly.

"Ebola?" Ramos said, hunting for an answer.

"I had not ruled that out due to the massive hemorrhaging of the victims," Manny continued. "The greatest threat, however, would be a mutated virus that had become airborne. If it had, there would be traces of it on your clothing. But as you can see, there are none." Manny paced around in a circle with a heavy head. "So now, we must establish the 'human link,' the catalyst causing the virus to spread so rapidly." This was all Greek to me.

"Human contact? Sexual transmission? Maybe something within the food supply?" Ramos said as he searched his mind for an answer.

Manny interrupted, "There is one other!" He reached his arms back into the gloves and moved them toward the cage with the lab rats in it. Slowly, he removed the lid to the rat's water supply; the dispenser was just a glass bottle with a stainless steel nipple that allowed the rats to drink as much and as often as they wished. Opening a thin, steel box, barely visible before, Manny extracted a small syringe containing a clear liquid. He brought the syringe to the open water supply, squirted the contents of the shot into the water then replaced the lid to the dispenser.

"Water! This is a sample we took from your village water supply," Manny said as a bead of sweat emerged on his brow. Ramos, Sancho and I watched intensely as the rats immediately charged to the steel nipple, ready to indulge in the newly introduced fluid, whatever it may be. The rodents took turns sucking down as much water as they could.

It seemed nothing would happen for a moment. The rats had gone back to playing on their wheel, running around the cage and chasing each other when suddenly one rat began to stumble. Then another. And another. They all began to slowly stagger and fall to their sides; then they convulsed rigidly, as if an unknown hand was squeezing the life out of them. Finally, in the throes of death, the large lab rats hemorrhaged from every orifice. The cage became a bloody mess. It was a sickening sight.

"Jesus Christ!" I shouted as I jumped away from the glass.

Sancho, not fully understanding the implications, crossed himself nonetheless and said, "*Dios mio!*"

Manny pulled his hands back out of the gloves and through the wall with a heavy heart. "I've been testing samples like this from other villages for weeks now. It's not a virus; not a plague at all."

Ramos awaited the explanation with a look that said he already knew the answer but wanted conformation. "I don't understand," he said cautiously.

Manny walked to a large chemical chart hanging against the back wall and pointed at a lineage of chemical compositions, then stopped and lowered his head. "As a German, I've dedicated my life to studying diseases, to saving lives. I feel it is the least I can do because of the legacy of my people. I've worked to erase the curse that haunts all Germans. In any case, whatever is in the water did not get there by accident."

Ramos seemed almost relieved by Manny's answer, as though it had justified his suspicions, yet he still voiced hope in his further prodding: "Maybe something leaked into the water table from a factory or a chemical plant or something…"

Manny shook his head and said, "The ratios are too inconsistent."

I got a strange tingling in my stomach like I always did when I felt something big was happening, but I wanted to be crystal clear on the subject. "Could you translate that into English, Einstein?" I asked.

Manny smiled to break the tension, then continued, "In all the samples checked, we've found the same chemical compositions and properties, but each at a different ratio. The elements in the water are difficult to detect because our own bodies produce them."

Sancho stood in the background, unable to take his eyes off the dead rats. "Now *I'm* lost!" Ramos added.

Manny reached for a pointer and directed it at a diagram of the human body. "Steroids, Carlos!" he said. "Estrogen, and a host of other complex hormones."

I was really trying to wrap my mind around what he was saying, but I still kept falling short of the mark. "Wait a minute," I said. "You're saying that steroids and garden-variety hormones are wiping out half of Mexico?"

Manny got clinical: "In these combinations, yes! It's only logical that people are dying in such great numbers. The drugs found in your water supply were developed for birth control!" Ramos and I looked at each other in disbelief.

"In such massive doses over a short ingestion period, it could feasibly neutralize an entire populace," Manny went on to say. "The lucky ones who survived could never reproduce. The fetus would never develop; it would abort before the first trimester."

The blood ran from Ramos' face. "Population control!" he said, awestruck.

I was beginning to get the picture. "You mean they're sterilizing people?"

Manny bit his lip. "It seems so. Hemorrhaging is just one of the side effects. In other villages, we've seen dehydration, renal failure, extreme libido inhibition: symptoms resembling viral epidemia."

Even Sancho was beginning to understand what was going on. I suddenly welled up with fury. "Those sick fucks are putting something in the water supply to make sure everyone is affected?" Manny nodded regretfully. "Jesus Christ, that's systematic genocide!" I shouted, my voice carrying throughout the lab, making all the scientists cease their work.

Manny was still trying to figure one thing out. "I just don't understand why. Why would anyone want to wipe out an entire culture?"

I knew why. "Does ethnic cleansing sound familiar? Whoever's doing this wants the rebels, and anyone else who might be siding with them, eviscerated. It's like Hitler, Stalin and Mylosivec rolled into one!"

"But who?" Ramos said as he searched his thoughts, "Cortes? He isn't that smart."

That's when it hit me: "AMERIMEX! They built the system, they supply the water. Pritchard's got to be behind all this. Who else could get a hold of that much power?"

Manny brought us all back down to reality by saying, "Everyone drinking that water will either die or become sterilized if it doesn't stop soon."

The voice of reason from the last place I would have expected to hear it broke the confusion: "But why is not Maria sick, or Father Gonzalez, or the nuns?" Sancho said curiously. We all stopped for a moment. It was the most profound question yet.

"They only drink from the fountain," Ramos said.

I agreed. "That's right! Maria told me their water comes from an underground spring. That's why they haven't been affected. The villagers all drink from the new AMERIMEX system that recently got plugged into their homes."

Ramos grabbed me by the shoulders. In any other situation I would have decked him. "We've gotta get back and warn them! Manny, we need a vehicle," Ramos commanded.

Just then, Sancho jumped forward and pleaded, "Please, Doctor, let me go. I can drive *muy rapido!*" Sancho turned to me as though I didn't understand and said, "Really fast!"

XLIV

The old European-built bus was filled to capacity, and it listed and swayed from its overweight payload of passengers. It slowed to a halt, the brakes squealing like a pig, and would not enter through the village archway at San Cristobal. Red flags draped over the top of the whitewashed stucco walls read: *PELIGROSO* and *DANGER*.

Kate emerged from the bus as the driver quickly shut the door and ground the shift. The gears squeaked and whined until he landed the tranny in first gear, then punched the gas pedal, causing the overloaded bus to lurch forward, nearly peeling off its worn tires.

She had nothing to do but follow the clues to my whereabouts, and nowhere to go but inside the gates to follow them. She walked under the majestic old archway and romanticized old Mexico, the kind she'd seen in movies when she was a child. The only movement in the village was a lone technician in a red biohazard suit sweeping the ground for contamination with what looked like a metal detector. A few scrawny, starving goats baahed and bayed, but were too weak to approach her, even to beg for food. Kate made her way past the center of the village with its great fountain and headed toward the only building that looked as though someone might be inside: the hospice. As she made her way across the plaza, the large black Mercedes pulled up to the edge of the archway and waited.

XLV

It was a hot and dusty day in the Mexican desert, but that didn't stop Governor Chavez from holding one of the most important photo opportunities of his career. He and Pritchard, two politicians from different countries, were about to unveil their political flagship: the AMERIMEX Water Purification and Aqueduct Project.

Dexter Grace and the rest of Pritchard's staff flanked the senator as they were led through the plant. Meanwhile, the usual mob of international reporters clambered for shots and interviews.

It was an enormous water treatment facility, longer than a football field and larger in stature than most industrials. Although it was a newly built, modern complex, it was nonetheless densely riddled with long iron pipes for water distribution to outlying areas. Huge vats of chemicals treated the water as sweeping steel arms that looked like razor-sharp airplane propellers stirred the mixtures. Their oscillation not only ensured even distribution of the chemicals, but also kept the chlorinated substances from stagnating, thus eradicating any bacteria or impurities.

Giant returns and smaller tubes forced water and treatment fluids through every inch of the facility and out into the world with high speed from its pressurized sources. A constant stream of electricity drawing off lines throughout Mexico powered hydraulic pumps and steam build-up machines three to four stories high. Back-up generators the size of the Titanic's engines made sure that no natural disaster, earthquake or other unforeseen tragedy would ever cripple the plant, even if the rest of the country lay in utter darkness.

Chavez began mugging for the camera; reporters couldn't get enough of the flamboyant leader. He knew this was his week to get grade-A international exposure and was going to milk it for all it was worth.

"You see my friends, Mexico will no longer be considered a third-world nation," he shouted out to the reporters. "Thanks to the generosity and engineering genius of our new alliance with America, we'll soon be one of the world's leaders in, among other things, agriculture! This revolutionary water supply system is capable of purifying water from many sources."

Chavez gestured in the direction of the vats and tanks like a diva onstage for a curtain call. "Sea water pumped from Vera Cruz is desalinized. In addition, condensation and triple chlorination is used to purify water from numerous rivers and streams that were, up until now, questionably safe to drink from. The reporters anxiously waited for him to take a breath so they could ask questions, but he was on a roll. "This unique water system now services seventy villages in this valley alone, and soon, fresh water will be flowing throughout all of Mexico." He then roared in a triumphant crescendo: "The AMERIMEX Water Purification and Aqueduct System is truly a 'Hands Across the Border in Friendship' project!"

Turning to Pritchard, he winked and said, "What is the old saying, my friend?"

Pritchard stepped up on cue to deliver the punch line in his down-home country drawl: "'Don't drink the water,' Governor!"

"Ha!" Chavez began his comeback as rehearsed. "Maybe the new slogan should be, 'Do not spill a drop,' no?" Chavez laughed and others politely followed suit.

A quiet, old plant worker passed behind the reporters with a sandwich in his mouth. Chavez raced through the crowd to grab him, pulled at his sleeve and whispered something in his ear. An odd look crossed the old man's face, then he reached behind a welded section of pipe and pulled out a large monkey wrench. He handed it to the governor.

Chavez raced back through the reporters with the old man in tow and placed the wrench on an overflow release valve. As the plant worker turned the spigot on the small plug, water began to pour from the breech. Chavez cupped his hands to fill them with water, careful not to get any on his expensive suit, then lapped it up in a show of confidence. A wide grin crossed his face.

The reporters all crowded in to get a load of this outrageous act. "If it's that good, Governor, maybe you should bottle it like the French do!" one reporter jibed.

Chavez gave Pritchard an enthusiastically curious look at the suggestion. Pritchard sounded back, "Now, Son, that ain't a half-bad idea."

Chavez flicked the residual water from his hands and bade the reporters to join him. "Come, amigos, try some!"

A couple of reporters at a time stepped up to sample the water. Others began sipping, then splashing each other in playful competition. It could've easily gotten out of hand, but such spontaneous, childlike glee perfectly fit the mood of this particular tour.

In the background behind Pritchard, Chavez and the others, two men watched the tedious display in abject boredom. Dexter stepped up to Cortes and said in a lowered voice, "A real showman, your governor. He's got them drinking out of his hands."

Cortes didn't bother to turn and recognize Dexter as he retorted, "He is a true statesman. He will regain respect for Mexico and her people."

Dexter turned to stand toe-to-toe with Cortes, getting in his face. "Cut the crap, Cortes! I know what you think of Chavez. You do all the dirty work and he gets all the glory."

Cortes stayed cool even under his aggressive posturing as he said, "You would do well to govern your tongue."

Pritchard and Chavez posed for a picture, both grabbing the monkey wrench and holding it up in a show of solidarity, playing to the crowd like Abbott and Costello. Pritchard glanced over at Dexter, who returned a patronizing smile and reassuring nod then immediately snapped back at Cortes, "Is everything ready for the conference?"

Cortes looked down his nose at him and said confidently, "Everything is ready, *Señor* Grace."

Still prodding him, Dexter explained, "You know this has taken us years of political maneuvering to put together. One fuck-up from your end and we all lose. Got it?!"

Cortes took exception to Dexter's tone and quickly snapped a small, double-edged blade from his lapel. He pressed it against Dexter's stomach then took a step closer to drive his point home. "Intimidation should be left up to professionals, don't you agree?" he whispered. "All will go as planned. There will be no problems. You have my word."

Dexter didn't bat an eyelash as he answered, "Your word isn't worth a peso."

Cortes saw Chavez approaching, so he quickly stowed the blade back into his lapel. He and Dexter would now be forced to greet the politician after their no-score game of chicken. Chavez walked over and wrapped his arms around their shoulders as the reporters gathered to snap shots of the newsworthy trio. Cortes immediately covered his face from view; Dexter, however, stood confidently with a contrived smile on his face, ever the ambitious gamesman. Cortes bowed then backed away toward the entrance of the plant. As he stormed across the concrete floor, his soldiers fell in behind him from various points throughout the facility and marched out of the complex in unison behind their commander.

As the crowd of reporters followed Chavez to another site within the complex, Pritchard took an opportunity to talk to his aide. "I don't trust that guy, Dex," the senator said with a worried look on his face. "Try to avoid him. He's bad for business, if ya know what I mean."

Dexter gave Pritchard a curious look and said, "Governor Chavez, Sir?"

Pritchard exploded. "No, goddamn it! Cortes!" He tried to settle down as he continued, "Now stay on top of this. We can't afford any screw-ups this close to game time." He always used football analogies when he wanted to drive home a point. "One for the Gipper" and all that crap. "We're at the goal line, let's not fumble the damn ball."

"Yes, Sir," Dexter quickly agreed.

"Remember," Pritchard said, "it's your job to cover me, Dex."

Dexter nodded and they both looked around for any signs of inquisitive reporters. Nothing. It was Chavez they wanted. "Maybe I oughta give you a raise," Pritchard muttered. "At least you've kept that bastard Riley away from me so far."

Dexter wanted an answer to the age-old question, "What is it between you two, anyway?" so he asked it directly.

Pritchard hardly let the question bother him as he responded, "Oh, that son of a bitch thinks I was bang'n his ex-wife while they were still married."

A grin spread across Dexter's face, yet he was careful not to sound too patronizing as he asked, "What gave him that idea, Sir?"

Pritchard leaned in as though Dexter had suddenly become a drinking buddy. "Hell! She just wanted to get away from the drunk bastard and I happened to have a special place in my cabinet for her. I fit her in nicely," he bragged, "she's a smart lady—too smart for the likes of him." A sinister smile twisted his lips as he slapped Dexter hard on the shoulder. He then turned away to help Chavez keep the reporters well-fed with slick publicity fodder.

Dexter caught a glimpse of Cortes through the giant plant doors and watched as the general mobilized his men into Jeeps and other transport. After a moment, Cortes threw his hand in the air like Hitler, ordering the soldiers out of the area. A cloud of dust was all that was left in their wake.

XLVI

High in the alpine mountains, the locals of Valle de Bravo liked to get an early start on their trading, and their weekly bazaar was already in full swing by the time the morning sun had burned through the dawn haze. Under a patchwork of white canvas tarps, merchants bartered, traded and sold everything from food to trinkets to livestock, with occasional tourists paying handsomely for items they'd merely place in boxes and forget about forever once they got home.

But this day also carried with it another reason for such an early start: *El Dia De Los Muertos,* the "Day of the Dead," was approaching, and there were many preparations to be made. Like Mardi Gras, the Day of the Dead celebration was not limited to a single day; for days on end, families and tourists gathered to honor their dearly departed with elaborate parties, songs and dances—and, of course, alcohol. Lots of alcohol.

The entire town of Valle de Bravo had been decorated with bright banners and flags, and people were already getting into the spirit of the holiday by painting figurines, as well as themselves, to resemble happy skeletons. Crowds of tourists milled around the center of the town, admiring the locals' unique offerings to the dead.

Ramos, Sancho, Manny and I bolted out an exit of the Disease Research Center and headed for the parking lot near the bazaar. We headed for a shiny black four-wheel-drive pickup truck that glistened in the sun and stopped just short of it. While Sancho gawked at the vehicle like a schoolboy, Manny tossed him the keys. The boy's eyes lit up like a Christmas tree. "It's a Chevy!" he said, dumbfounded.

Manny instructed him, "Sancho, you must tell Maria and the others to boil the water before drinking it, just to be safe. Do you understand?"

The boy couldn't take his eyes off the truck, but nodded and said, "*Sí*, Doctor, I understand."

Manny continued, "Make sure all the patients drink as much clean water as they can swallow; they have to flush their systems of the impurities. Are you sure you understand everything I've told you?"

Sancho nodded again, this time turning to face him. "*Sí*, Doctor, I will not let you down," he said, saluting.

I suddenly became very proud of the little guy just then. I stepped up to shake his hand, and shake it like a man. "We owe you a lot," I said. "Especially me. You're a brave kid. Go on. Go be a hero."

With those words, he leapt forward and wrapped his arms around my waist. It nearly tore my heart out. "*Gracias, Señor* Riley! Thank you!" he said, then turned to Ramos and Manny. "Thank you all for trusting me, I will not stop until everyone is safe!"

Ramos said, "When you get to the village, get word to Boomba. He'll know what to do. Then he added, "*Mijo*, don't forget! One for all..."

A big smile took over Sancho's face as he rallied, "...and all for one!"

Sancho ran to the pickup, hopped onto the running board and jumped in the cab. He turned the ignition key and the supercharged Triton engine roared to life. Giving us a devilish grin, he gripped the steering wheel until his little knuckles turned white. I walked up to the window before he dropped it into gear.

"Here," I said as I pulled out the other half of the twenty-dollar bill I'd given him days before. "*Vaya con Dios, Amigo!*" I said. And I meant it. I knew he was going to have to race across the desert by himself through patrols and military convoys, and I knew none of that was going to stop him from saving the day if he could help it. He may have been just a wily kid when I met him, but now, I felt I was looking at a man.

Sancho peeled out of the parking lot, nearly running down a gaggle of pedestrians in the marketplace. He definitely needed some driving lessons.

"So what's the plan?" I said to Ramos.

"We're gonna take a little trip out to where they make this shit— Toluca Pharmaceuticals!" he said as we walked.

Manny shook his head cautiously and said, "You must be careful, my friends. I know this place. They supply us with research chemicals for testing. It is heavily guarded and no one that I know has ever been inside."

"You know this place? Good!" I shouted. "You're coming with us." Manny jogged across the parking lot to catch up. I was too busy thinking to hear Manny's objections. A sudden surge of confidence rushed through me. "This is gonna make a hell of a story," I said— quietly, I thought, but Ramos must've heard because he turned toward me and smiled.

Before we could strategize, something caught my eye from the bustling market below. Kate Walker? Damn, it *was* her. An old bus had stopped in the square, and Kate, looking like a tall, leggy, white fish out of water, stepped off the platform and into the crowd. Her blouse was dirty and stained with sweat and dust, and she was limping, probably from sitting on her ass too long. Whatever her condition, it was her and she was looking for me.

"Kate!" I shouted. Then I turned to Ramos and said, "Get another truck. Meet me back here in five minutes!"

Ramos and Manny gave me an odd look, but I quickly rushed down the street toward the bazaar." Riley, where the hell are you going?" Ramos shouted.

I could see Kate meandering around the market, but I was still too far away for her to hear me shout. She seemed lost as she wandered toward the nearest building—an old cathedral so large it loomed high above the village, its steeple blocking out the sun.

I ran hard and fast—so fast that I passed the large, black Mercedes without acknowledging it. Big mistake. Kate climbed the steps of the church and entered, but I wasn't far behind. I raced up the long set of steps to the large metal doors that the Spaniards had built hundreds of years before.

It took my eyes more than a moment to adjust to the drastic change from bright sunlight to near-darkness. Above me was a high, ornate ceiling surrounded by intricately carved friezes depicting scenes from ancient Roman and Mexican history, and in front of me was an enormous gold altar. That couldn't be real gold, I thought.

I quickly walked the length of the long center aisle, surprised to find the church empty. I suddenly got an eerie feeling and became slightly unnerved. I slowed toward the middle of the aisle and cautiously passed a placard that read: *DAY OF THE DEAD CELEBRATION MASS - TOMORROW 10 A.M.*

It really was a beautiful house of worship. Rows of shimmering candles reflected the gold leaf or gold paint or real gold of the altar—whatever it was, it was majestic. But this was no time to be a tourist. I had to find Kate. I yelled out judiciously, "Kate! Katie Walker!"

My own voice echoed like a choir of one. Suddenly a muffled sound came from one of the large wooden confessionals. Still cautious, I approached and saw a shadow on the terra cotta-tiled floor under the door at my feet. I hesitantly opened the confessional door. Inside knelt a penitent man, head in hands, face obscured by prayer. I was embarrassed. "God, I'm sorry!" I said to the man as I quickly closed the door.

I heard some kind of scuffling in one of the other booths, so I flung open the next door where the priest would sit. I braced myself for another surprise—and I got one. Inside the center confessional, a priest thrashed about in the seat like a marionette in the hands of a psychotic puppeteer. His throat had just been slashed from ear to ear and blood was still gushing out of him. He lunged forward into my arms then collapsed at my feet. "Holy Shit!" I screamed.

"Riley!" a woman shouted from the last booth. It was Kate's voice.

I quickly ran to the last booth and swung the door open. Inside, Kate was struggling with Mr. Jones as he tried to cover her mouth. He laughed hysterically when he saw me. My blood began to boil, but before I could lay into the hit man, a searing pain in my neck stopped me dead in my tracks. I collapsed to the floor and started to convulse in seizure.

From behind me, the penitent man from the first confessional appeared. It was Mr. Smith. I could see the stun gun in his hand still pulsating before I passed out. He'd generously applied a thousand volts of electric current to my spine. Kate could do nothing but stand there and watch, horrified and helpless.

XLVII

I was groggy, semi-conscious, still out of it as Mr. Smith carried me out of the church under his arm. I figured I must've looked drunk to the hundreds of people in the crowd since no one bothered to inquire or help. Mr. Jones walked Kate quickly to the Mercedes with a gun in her back, careful not to arouse the attention of any curious bystanders or *Federales*.

Ramos and Manny had been slowly cruising the street looking for me in an old Jeep that looked like a leftover from Guadalcanal. By this time, they had pulled up in front of the church. "Where the hell is he?" Ramos grumbled.

"Oh no!" Manny cried out. He had suddenly caught sight of Smith and Jones tossing me and Kate into the back of their black Mercedes. "Over there!"

In the backseat, Kate pulled me onto her lap. She stroked my hair as my twitching and convulsions abated. "Terry, what happened to you?" she whispered.

"It's nice to see a caring woman in this day and age, wouldn't you say, Mr. Smith?" Jones remarked to his comrade.

"Yes, I did think those days were long gone, Mr. Jones," Smith replied, sticking to the evil *Chip and Dale* routine I had already become familiar with during our previous run-in stateside.

"Don't mind us, Ms. Walker," Jones said. "Feel free to reminisce with Mr. Riley."

Kate shot him a glare and he nearly burst out laughing.

XLVIII

Celebratory banners still waved in the hot breeze, but all attendants of the publicity stunt had long since gone. Only a skeleton crew remained at the AMERIMEX Water Treatment Plant to handle the daily routine of treating the water that would be pumped to all areas of Mexico.

The black Mercedes ran over mounds of confetti and flattened balloons as it pulled off the worn blacktop and through the gates of the treatment facility. Following a few hundred yards behind, Ramos slowed the Jeep. From that distance, Ramos and Manny could see everything, but it would be difficult for the two henchmen to see them. Even if Smith or Jones had looked toward them, the Jeep would be obscured to the naked eye by the blinding brightness and the image-distorting heat waves rolling off the pavement.

Jones grabbed Kate and pulled her from the back of the car. "Hey! Watch your hands, you pervert!" she shouted as she tried to slap his face.

Jones deflected the blow and wrenched her arm behind her back with undue force. "You really should try and control your temper, young lady. It's not at all becoming," he quipped.

There was a metallic taste in my mouth and I could smell burnt hair, but I had regained most of my faculties. I decided to play opossum for a while longer to figure a way out of this mess. If I had known Ramos and Manny had followed us, I would've had a more positive attitude. Smith pulled me to my feet and pushed me forward into the complex.

Back in the Jeep, Carlos asked desperately, "Manny, do you have a gun? A weapon of any kind?"

Manny looked at Ramos with surprise and said, "Carlos, you know I'm a pacifist. No, of course not! What would I be doing with a gun?"

"Shit!" Ramos said, hitting the steering wheel with his hands.

Realizing what was at stake, Manny searched around the back of the Jeep and found a long pole with a nylon noose at the end of it. "Here! What about this?" he said.

Ramos gave him a strange look and said, "What the hell is that?"

Manny fidgeted with a small lever at the bottom of the pole, showing Carlos how the noose could tighten or loosen on demand. "It's a snake rod," he said timidly. "A rod for capturing snakes for venom analysis. I'm afraid it's not very lethal."

Ramos grabbed it as he exited the Jeep. "It'll have to do."

Manny still hadn't moved. "What about me?" he yelled. Ramos doubled back to the vehicle and flung open the passenger door to drag the enormous German out of his seat and onto his feet.

Clang. "What was that?" Ramos said as he reached behind the passenger seat. He ripped something from a metal post near the wheel well. It was a tire iron. He shoved it toward Manny and smacked it into the palm of his hand.

"I can't use this," Manny moaned. "My conscience wouldn't allow it... I'm a pacifist, for God's sake!"

"Not today!" Ramos whispered, ducking low as he bolted toward a side entrance. He jimmied the lock. *Clunk.* He swung the door open. "Come on!" he urged Manny as loudly as he dared.

Manny stared at the tire iron in his hand then ran inside after Ramos, hissing, "Wait!"

XLIX

As Smith and Jones led us through the treatment facility, the sound of our footsteps seemed to echo for miles, and it felt like we'd already covered just as much distance. Kate and I hadn't spoken, but I tried to give her visual cues when Smith and Jones weren't watching. I didn't get my point across.

On a walkway high above giant bubbling vats of water being treated and purified with thousands of pumps and pipes, they stopped and pushed us dangerously close to the railing. At the end of the vast hallway, I could see a lone plant worker sweeping up a large pile of confetti. Smith saw him, too, and began to walk his way. I felt I should scream and warn the old man so he wouldn't end up like the priest, but I couldn't risk expediting my own demise.

Smith smiled and waved as he approached the worker. "*Hola, Amigo!* Where is everyone?" he said in Spanish. "We were supposed to meet a friend here today."

The plant worker stopped sweeping and placed his hands over the broom handle. Laying his chin on them in a casual way, he said, "They are gone, *Señor*. The tour is over. Everyone has gone back to Mexico City."

Smith shook his head. I wanted to scream for the old man to run, but I didn't. I felt like such a coward. "That is a shame," Smith said, and tutted.

Jones immediately pulled out a cellular phone and coded in a series of numbers. While the two were distracted, I looked around for a *Plan B*. "Yeah, we've got Riley and one of his little friends," Jones said into the receiver, "but there's a problem: I think the German knows."

I couldn't see even one escape route or a weapon of any kind. I decided to dazzle them with bullshit, but Kate broke my concentration. "Who are these guys, Riley?" she whispered.

I took a small step backwards and she followed suit. "A couple of guys from Senator Foster's payroll" I whispered back. "After Farmgate, he must've put a contract out on me. Jesus, Kate! You're the last person I wanted to get involved with this. What are you doing here?"

She made sure Smith and Jones were occupied when she said, "I came to warn you about Pritchard. The D.O.J.'s been spooking him for years because he owns a bunch of drug companies here in Mexico. I knew if you stumbled onto it you'd get caught off guard."

I rolled my eyes and laughed. "Well, that was a self-fulfilling prophecy," I said.

Smith and Jones snapped their heads back around at us upon hearing that.

The old man was still leaning on his broomstick when Smith flipped him some cash and said, "Take the rest of the day off, Amigo."

Surprised, the old man smiled, dropped the broom where he stood and strolled out of the facility.

"You're a People Person, Mr. Smith," Jones said happily. "A real giver, that's you, Sir!" Smith turned and bowed at the compliment. "You are far too kind, Mr. Jones," he said in a fruity, elongated lilt. "Far too kind."

Okay, enough of that bullshit, I thought. "Are you two fags through licking each others colon's clean, yet?" I said, knowing full well what punishment was about to befall me.

"That's terribly insensitive and homophobic, Mr. Riley," Jones said with a straight face.

"And rather passive-aggressive, I'd say, Mr. Jones." Smith nodded in agreement as he grabbed Kate. Jones grabbed me, and they led us both across a long catwalk to the railing above a vat of filthy churn.

Suddenly, Kate locked her eyes onto two workers dumping a large barrel of white powder into the vat opposite us. The side of the barrel read: *CHLORINO TXC - TOLUCA PHARMACEUTICALS*. Her eyes grew wide as she blurted out, "Toluca Pharmaceuticals! That's it! It's Pritchard's drug company!"

Smith and Jones stopped us in the center of the catwalk, grinning at each other like a couple of schoolgirls "Oh no! Now the cat's out of the bag, as they say, Mr. Jones," Smith said sarcastically. "It seems a shame to have to kill such interesting and bright people. After all, they make such a lovely couple."

Mr. Jones looked at me and quipped, "You know, Mr. Riley, you should've become a sportswriter or columnist. The pay is much better and you wouldn't be so susceptible to messy industrial accidents."

I suddenly saw Ramos creeping along the water pipes on his belly above and behind Smith and Jones. I had to buy some time. "Wait a minute! You idiots don't work for Foster," I said. "You work for Pritchard, don't you?" It was a stretch.

Smith cupped his hands in prayer and looked skyward with joy, just missing Ramos above him. "It's days like this I truly enjoy my work, Mr. Jones.... If it's any comfort to you in your final moments, Mr. Riley, believe what you want."

But he wasn't getting off that easily. "Well, if it's not Pritchard," I said, "then who are you two swishes working for?"

"That would be a breach of confidentiality with our employer," said Jones. "I must commend you though—you came so very close."

Smith suddenly snapped his fingers at the two plant workers across the catwalk. The two workers stopped pouring powder into the vats and placed the barrel on the landing. They stood there giving us all a strange look until Smith brandished his weapon. Then they ran like hell and never looked back.

Smith turned his gun at me just as a yellow nylon noose lowered in front of his face. He didn't even have time to look up to ascertain the source of this new introduction into his field of vision before Ramos wrapped it around his neck and gave it a sharp tug. Smith was snared. Seeing his partner wriggle oddly startled Jones, who turned just in time to see Manny's huge frame descending on top of him from above. As Manny pummeled him, Jones dropped his cell phone to the ground, but had enough sense to pull his revolver. He wasn't very quick on the draw, though, giving time for Manny to come down hard on him with the tire iron. *Snap.* The echo of his arm breaking reverberated throughout the empty complex. The gun fell to the ground next to the cell phone.

"I hate guns!" Manny shouted.

Ramos, his hands still pulling at the taut rope around Smith's neck, jumped down from the pipes above, never losing his grasp. Smith choked and collapsed to the concrete in submission. Now it was my turn.

"I never thought I'd be happy to see you," I said to Ramos.

Despite the confusion of the dramatic ambush, Kate soon realized these guys were on our side. "Riley, who are these guys?"

I walked over to a pile of white powder near us and said, "Later, Kate." I scooped up a handful of chemicals and walked to Jones, who was reeling in pain.

"How's the arm, Dickhead?" I said as I dug my hand into his scalp and pulled his head back, nearly ripping out a clump of hair. I shoved the handful of powder into his mouth. He tried to scream, but I shoveled it in with all the hate and frustration I had been smothering in until the sudden reversal of our fortunes. I crammed it in deep and he began to choke on it, then I smeared the rest over his face. "What did you mean, 'I was so close?'" I screamed in his ear, nearly deafening him. "This is the shit that's contaminating the water, isn't it?" I relished the sight of him suffering. "Do you realize how many people are dying from this stuff?"

I gave him a minute to cough and spit so that he could speak. "It's just business, Mr. Riley," he said. "Nothing personal."

That was it. I wasn't going to get anywhere unless I played their game, and I knew it. I decided to do something rather unconventional. I picked up his gun from the floor and bolted a round into the chamber of the forty-five automatic. I paused for a second, hoping he'd give up more information, but the two of them sat mute.

Blam. I shot Jones in the thigh. The force threw him back against the railings. Blood spurted from his trousers as the bullet slammed through muscle and tissue and thick, blue veins.

"Riley?" Kate screamed in horror.

"*This **is** personal!*" I shouted at him.

Jones grasped his leg with his good arm and cradled the broken one against his side. He was tough, I'd give him that. "Fuck you, Riley, your dead!" he whimpered back as his breathing became labored. "You're all dead, just like your little friends in San Cristobal."

Smith tried to scramble to his feet, but Ramos still had his neck in a tight noose. "When Cortes is through with them, there won't be anything left of the village," Smith gasped as he laughed, trying to steady himself with the railing. He slowly maneuvered to Jones and compassionately helped him to his one good leg. "Come Mr. Jones," he said, "let us not be intimidated by those beneath us."

I was gearing up to really take out some frustrations on the two hit men when Manny suddenly and without warning simply freaked out. He charged Smith and Jones with his giant hands extended and rammed them both over the side of the railing. They fell fifty feet and splashed into the vat of murky liquid below. We all rushed to the edge of the railing to see them struggle, holding each other, trying to stay afloat. Slowly, like the legs of a spider creeping toward a fly caught in its web, the steel sweeper arms crossed the vat of churning chemicals. *Whap!* One of the blades swept behind Smith and Jones, slamming them in the back of the heads. It was uncertain whether they died of decapitation or drowning. Either way, they were gone for good. Kate covered her eyes in horror as their bodies quickly sank.

"Hurry!" Manny yelled, pulling our attention away from the gruesome scene. "We must go!"

L

Past the giant fountain, at the other end of the village under the shade of a wooden awning, sat Manny's new Chevy pickup. It was covered with a layer of dust and dented across the front quarter panels and hood from stones pelting it at high speeds. Sancho had made it.

There was a kind of vitality, a new spirit, in the air as the large iron pots swung over blistering fires, now no longer for sterilizing equipment and bandages, but for boiling the impurities from the contaminated water. As if in a holy ballet, the old nuns continuously brought gallons of water in bloated goat skinned bags, air-tight satchels or anything else that could support as large a volume as they could carry, and poured it into the bubbling cauldrons. The few villagers who hadn't yet been affected helped, too, stoking fires and preparing for the resurrection of their friends and neighbors from certain and excruciating death.

On the landing in front of the hospice, Maria cradled a small child, slowly making her drink from a tin cup every few minutes. She knew, now, that the child must drink to cleanse its tiny body of the AMERIMEX impurities—and it was beginning to work. The child slipped off to slumber while Maria sang an old Spanish lullaby. Her long, black hair flowed in the warm breeze, her beauty rivaled only by her gentle kindness.

Inside the hospice, Sancho was on fire. His heart filled with the pride and accomplishment that he thought he'd never see in his lifetime. He had done something good, something important. And he knew it. He held the head of a young, but pale, man and helped him to drink the freshly boiled water.

The hospice patients seemed healthier now. They moved in their beds, no longer squirming in anguish, but tossing and turning from boredom and rejuvenation. As Father Gonzalez brought in another pair of bloated bags filled with fresh water, his heart filled with joy. After finishing with a patient, the priest walked over to Sancho and placed a tired hand on the boy's shoulder.

"Sanchito. *Mijo.* We cannot thank you enough for your courage," the priest said happily. "You are the Archangel Gabriel trumpeting salvation; a true soldier for Christ."

Sancho blushed and rose from the bed. He fell to his knees, his face beginning to swell. "No, *Padre*, I'm not worthy of that," he said as he clasped his hands together in contrition. "I am a thief. I have committed crimes against God and man. That is all I've known my whole life." A river of tears poured from his eyes and his throat constricted as he choked the words out, "I want to be good, I swear, *Padre!*" Tears streamed freely down his face.

Father Gonzalez placed his left hand on Sancho's head and patted it as though he were a small child admitting a small crime. "You are too young to be so sad, my son. Do you know the story of the Good Thief?" the priest asked. "He was crucified next to Christ. He was homeless too. He had no family to love him. He was very much like you."

Sancho looked up as he purged the last of his guilt. He listened intently as Father Gonzalez continued: "He, too, asked for God's forgiveness and was welcomed into heaven." With his right hand, Father Gonzalez made the sign of the cross over the boy's head and said with compassion, "I absolve you, Christ absolves you; now you must absolve yourself."

Overcome, Sancho broke down, falling face-first to the floor, his tears now flowing more from relief than guilt. He could feel his mind healing. It was a critical moment for Sancho. At last, the one thing he had always yearned for: forgiveness.

LI

Miles from the village of San Cristobal, on a desolate stretch of flat, parched terrain, a battalion of military vehicles convoyed across the desert. The lead Jeep lurched then skidded to a halt, and the others followed suit in strict regimental fashion. After the dust cloud cleared, General Cortes stood on his seat and grabbed the roll bar to steady himself. He perused the landscape as the half-tracks, APV's and other attack vehicles aligned in perfect rows. He could see his soldiers popping their heads out of windows one after another to listen for their next orders.

"When we enter the village, you will follow my orders without question. Let no one escape!" Cortes roared.

A lone Jeep at the rear of the convoy sped to the front. It was Captain Pena. "General! This is wrong. Let us leave these people in peace. They have suffered enough," the young captain pleaded compassionately. Cortes listened as he took out a long Cuban cigar from his vest pocket. He produced a sulfur-tipped match and struck it against the side of the roll bar, his gloves creaking in the hot midday sun.

"Capitan, you are young and have a promising career ahead of you, so I will forgive your insolence this time. These villagers are Zapatista sympathizers and contaminated with plague. I have given you your orders. Follow them without question... or face my wrath." Cortes bit the end of the cigar and shouted, "*Vamanos!*"

The roar of speed preceded the military convoy like a pressure wave as they poured under the archway into the square of San Cristobal village. At once, soldiers stopped their vehicles, jumped down and fanned out across the plaza. "*Fuego!*" Cortes screamed. The soldiers opened fire, indiscriminately shooting the innocent as they scurried for cover of any kind. It became an orchestrated massacre.

Realizing what was happening, Maria quickly pulled the sleeping child to her breast and bolted into the hospice. Stray bullets flew past her head as she ran.

Inside, Sancho's peaceful moment of reflection was shattered by the sudden explosion of gunfire. He jumped to the wooden window cover and threw it open, immediately catching sight of Cortes.

Father Gonzalez instantly took charge of the situation like a true leader, yelling clear, passionate instructions to the nuns who were busy nursing the sick: "Quickly, everyone into the cellar! I will try to appeal to this madman."

Three nuns burst through the hospice door, out of breath and frantic. "*Padre*, they're burning our village," they cried.

Father Gonzalez waved them over as he pulled back a giant Mexican rug to reveal a hidden door in the floorboards. The priest knew he couldn't stop until all his people were safe. "Take everyone to the cellar and stay quiet," he said. "I will make sure he does not find you!"

Father Gonzalez was hurrying the nuns and their patients down the secret staircase when Sancho saw a glimmer of hope, a chance to stop Cortes once and for all. Quickly, he grabbed a long syringe from a surgical plate and squeezed it in his hand. He was propelled by a new emotion now: hate. His young eyes narrowed like a hawk zeroing in on its prey as he dashed out into the square and headed right to Cortes.

Maria had just handed over the child to a nun in the shelter when she looked up to see Sancho running out. "Sancho, no!" she screamed. But it was too late. Sancho had already become lost in the fray.

Meanwhile, Father Gonzalez made the sign of the cross as he looked down on the crowded cellar. He smiled as he eased down the wooden door, made sure the rug flopped back over it and secured the latch.

Sancho's mind began to feel disconnected from his body. He felt light and ethereal, running with all his strength. He could see and hear Cortes scolding random soldier after soldier, "You're not killing fast enough," or pointing out buildings and structures to be set ablaze and yelling, "Burn it! I want it all burned to the ground!" As the carnage progressively fueled Cortes' madness, Sancho drew closer and closer, finally sprinting in open field and full view of everyone.

Captain Pena caught sight of Sancho from his vantage point. With loyalty to his commander, he raised his rifle and aimed at the boy running toward the general. About to pull the trigger, he hesitated instead, then lowered his gun, thinking, Let the chips fall where the may! As Sancho drew near Cortes, he launched himself, leaping into the air and brandishing the syringe high over his head. The plan? To drive the long cardiac needle as deep into Cortes' neck as he could. But fate had planned a cruel intervention.

A young private of no particular status had, like Pena, also caught sight of Sancho. He abruptly turned from what he was doing and ran full speed to intercede on behalf of his general. It all came down to physics now: who would get there first and who would prevail. The private had already raised the butt of his gun and smashed Sancho in the face while the boy was still in midair. Yet Sancho's resolve was far greater than the young private's. As Sancho's head flew backwards from the unexpected blow, with one last gasp, he drove the syringe deep into Cortes' shoulder just below the neck. Sancho crumpled to the ground. As he lay in the dirt, writhing in pain from the blast to his face, he could feel his newly crushed orbital and facial muscles begin to swell. Blood poured from his mouth and nose and cheeks as he began to cough and moan indecipherably. Soon, blood also shot out from his ears, signaling cerebral damage, and then began to seep out everywhere.

"AAAHHH!" Cortes screamed as the searing pain from the needle spread into the dense muscles and cartilage of his scapula. Like a robot, he turned stiffly to see Sancho wriggling at his feet. The young private dropped the rifle to the ground with one hand and leaned against it with the other. He gasped from the adrenaline rush of quelling the would-be assassin. Cortes, wincing in pain, hardly acknowledged the soldier. After a moment, the private stood and attempted to extract the syringe from Cortes' shoulder.

"Stop! Stop you fool!" Cortes growled as he reached back to grip it himself. Grasping it tightly, he slowly drew the long needle out to the sound of snapping cartilage and sinew. He took a moment to examine the bloodied and gored steel spindle then threw it to the ground.

"You dare to attack me?" Cortes screamed at Sancho as he laid reeling in agony. "Kill this dog!"

The private raised his rifle, but hesitated at the sight of such a young boy already so clearly suffering. Captain Pena had approached the scene, and now the private looked to the Captain—who was, after all, his commanding officer—and said in a thoroughly confused tone, "*Capitan?*" This infuriated Cortes. The soldier was not only questioning an order from his general, but asking his captain to usurp that general's authority.

Cortes was not a patient man. He drew his own service revolver from his leather hip holster, bolted a round into the chamber then pointed it at Sancho. *Bam.* He fired once into the boy's midsection. The blast from the large-caliber revolver drove deep into Sancho and rolled through his body, tearing every organ and bone to shreds. His body surged upward as the bullet shattered his insides.

What blood was left in Sancho blew out of his mouth as he heaved. His breathing became weaker and weaker as he lay in the soft clay at the base of the fountain, bleeding to death. He stared up at the statue of Saint Christopher and the baby Jesus, who smiled down upon him. Strangely soothed, he felt his body rise as though he might float straight into the arms of the statue above him. He closed his eyes and wondered if he'd be welcomed into heaven.

The door to the hospice burst open. Thick smoke reeled across the entryway, preceding the dark figure that entered. His black, patent leather boots banged on the reducer planks as he stomped in like a snorting bull. "*Buenos dias*," Cortes sniped with a sinister smile.

LII

Still in shock, Kate held onto my hand like she needed it to live. Ramos drove hard and fast across the desert with Manny riding shotgun, his eyes keen and crazed from the latest events. I sat quietly in the backseat to make sure Kate wouldn't fall apart, but couldn't help thinking this was exactly what Kate had wanted. She'd always talked about being in the center of the action, being "in the shit!"— as she'd quote from some bad B-movie about Vietnam. I don't know, maybe this was where she belonged all the time. Problem was, Kate wouldn't even know that until she knew how she was going to deal with all this. It was her first time "in the real shit" and right now she didn't look like she was going to handle it too well. Ramos pushed the pedal down hard as we saw something in the distance.

Thick, black, sooty smoke bellowed from walls and thatched roofs of buildings as we entered San Cristobal village. The flames were twenty feet high by then and most of the structures were already razed or fully engulfed. The lucky ones—made of stone and clay and stucco—would survive. They'd be saved. The hospice was, thankfully, made of stucco.

Ramos brought the Jeep to a stop near the fountain and we jumped out quickly. We were awestruck by the sheer carnage of the attack; only the sound of wooden support poles crackling and popping as they burned broke the profound silence that surrounded us. We called out, but no one answered; then we heard soft moaning near the base of the statue.

"Over here!" Ramos yelled, running toward a dark heap that seemed to be a small body coiled in a fetal position.

"Sancho!" I gasped. His hair was matted with blood, and his face was swollen so badly that I could hardly recognize him. A gaping hole oozed blood from the center of his stomach. Ramos quickly tried to stretch him out and assess his condition. He was such a bloody mess, I couldn't tell if he were alive or dead.

Manny stepped up to aid Ramos, but all Kate and I could do was watch helplessly. "Who is that boy?" she cried. I could only shake my head as tears welled in my eyes. He'd still be okay if it hadn't been for me, I thought. God damn it! Why him?

Sancho's lips were parched and cracked from hours under the sun, but dehydration was the least of his problems. Ramos ripped a piece from his own shirt, handed it to Kate and said calmly, "Dip this into the fountain."

She took the large patch of cloth and pushed it deep into the water, bringing it back soaking and dripping. Ramos swung the wet shirt over Sancho's cracked lips and poured water over his face and mouth. "Be careful, my friend," Manny said as he diagnosed Sancho, "he has a bullet hole in his abdomen. Not too much water—just use it to wet his lips and give him a bit to rehydrate."

Somehow, Sancho was still alive. "I'm sorry," he muttered as he felt the cool water pass over his lips. He coughed, but it was a soft, weak cough—the kind usually reserved for retirement home guests on their deathbeds.

All I could do was try to comfort him. I stepped over Ramos so Sancho could see me, then knelt down to speak in his ear. "Why are you sorry, Sancho?" I said compassionately.

He took in a deep breath in order to speak again, then gasped, "I tried to stop him…"

I felt like my heart was being ripped out of my chest. "Shush! You did fine, Son, just fine."

Kate caught something out of the corner of her eye and looked up. Slow-moving figures had begun creeping around at the end of the village. From behind the hospice, patients slowly emerged from the cellar. They were alive. "Look!" Kate shouted, "Over there!" The nuns began bringing everyone up from the underground hideout one by one.

"Carlos, take care of Sancho. I will help the others," Manny said as he raced toward the burned-out hospital.

"Sancho," I whispered, "where's Maria? Where's Maria?"

He tried to open his eyes, but only one could open and look at me. It filled up with a tear as he choked out, "*El Diablo* has taken her." He didn't have to explain, I knew exactly what he meant. Sancho gasped as his eyes fluttered. Then he died.

From the front archway came a clamor of horses as they raced into the village. It was Boomba and his rebel band. Ramos and I slowly and respectfully picked Sancho's body up and set it atop the fountain's clay base. Ramos threw the bloody patch from his shirt down hard on the ground. "Damn it!" he yelled, eyes glowing red.

Boomba approached and began to dismount, one leg flying over the saddle like a rodeo cowboy, but stopped as Ramos charged him. Ramos needed to vent, and Boomba was the closet target at hand. "Where the hell were you?" Ramos roared at his friend. "Why weren't you here to stop them?"

Boomba was a strong man. In any other situation, he probably would have been macho and cocky, but when Carlos Ramos berated him, he was lucky not to shit his pants. Ramos ran up to his friend, dragged him from his horse with one hand and threw him to the ground. He poised to strike Boomba, but broke down and sobbed over him instead. Unsure of what to do in this situation, Boomba wrapped his arms around Ramos with great discomfort and held him.

After a few minutes, Manny returned with one of the nuns. She explained that Maria had been kidnapped by Cortes, but didn't know where she had been taken.

"Where is Father Gonzalez?" Manny asked. After a long pause, the old nun gave him a solemn look, shook her head and crossed herself.

"Manny, take your truck and get back to your lab," Ramos said sadly. "We're gonna need hard data on what they've been doing here." I felt like a foot soldier about to be given my tour of duty. "Riley, you and I'll go for Maria. I think I know where he'll take her."

Manny nodded and said seriously, "My friends... please be careful."

With that, Ramos drove his hand into Sancho's tattered pants pocket to retrieve the car keys and threw them to Manny, who dashed across the square to the pickup in a few, almost superhuman strides. Meanwhile, Boomba instructed his men to assist the remaining villagers and nuns. The rebels nodded in unison and set off for the task at hand.

"Maria! Come on, we've got to get to Maria," I yelled.

Kate turned to me, sensing some feeling deeper than comradery in my exhortations, and said, "Terry, who's Maria?"

Ramos ran up and interjected, "Come on, Riley, let's go!" He grabbed me and pulled me toward the Jeep.

"Hey!" Kate shouted, "I'm going with you!" Ramos jumped in the Jeep and fired it up as Kate ran up to my side. "You're not fucking leaving me here after all I've been through to try and find you!"

It was no use trying to reason with her—she was a woman: No matter what I said, she'd just do the opposite. "It's too dangerous, Kate."

She nearly blew a fuse, and yelled back over the roar of the engine, "Bullshit! It wasn't too dangerous for me to risk my ass to follow you here on my own. I'm a reporter, too, you know, and you're not leaving me here. Besides, I can help!"

Ramos gave her a blank, compassionless stare and shouted, "Get in!"

She'd never let me hear the end of it.

LIII

Sharp clomps reverberated down the long hallways of Toluca Pharmaceuticals. Cortes was anxious as he marched—apprehensive and obviously bothered. He came to a closed office door and tried to open it with one push—his usual arrogant way of making an entrance—but fumbled badly and missed the latch.

When the door finally opened, he saw Maria sitting quietly in a chair near the back corner, quietly mumbling a long prayer to herself and counting the beads on her rosary. Two soldiers stood guard on either side of her, nervously eyeing Pandora's Box, which sat silently shrouding its deadly secret on a nearby tabletop.

Captain Pena stood in a shadowy corner at the back of the room, partly out of duty and partly out of a strange protective sense for the general's current prisoner. He'd seen Cortes cross the line before; just today he had already witnessed murder and torture and crimes against humanity. He knew, also, that if he were to stand by and say nothing, he would have to answer for these acts just as surely as Cortes would, both here and in the afterlife. Pena didn't know what to do or how to do it; he just knew that he would be there for Maria's interrogation; knew he would help her through it if he could, even at the cost of his military career.

Maria remained quiet and forlorn, her eyes red from hours of crying. She didn't look up as Cortes barged in; after all, she was being held captive, a hostage, guilty of nothing. She would not be intimidated by this madman. And the general knew it.

Cortes paced from side to side in front of her, then behind her, like a cat toying with its prey. Nothing. Maria would not be moved. As he paced, he instinctively tried to rub away the pain in his shoulder while his guards eyed him curiously. This was one wound that would ache in honor of Sancho's memory for a long, long time.

Cortes turned to face Maria then took a long, deliberate drag from the soggy end of his cigar. He then blew just enough smoke in her face to make her uncomfortable. She could smell the putrid stench of tobacco mixed with his foul breath. She wanted to vomit, but didn't want to give him the satisfaction.

Captain Pena felt the urge to step up and stop everything, but couldn't muster the strength. He felt like an emotionally abused boy wanting to rebel against his father, but without the means or the tools or the courage to do so. He could only stand silent and still and invisible: Cortes had not yet seen him. The general was too preoccupied with this nun, and even he didn't know the reason.

Cortes stretched his neck and tilted his head. A series of sharp cracks punctuated the oppressive silence as he popped the cartilage in his spine—an attempt to impress Maria as much as to loosen himself up for the interrogation.

"I do not enjoy confining women—especially nuns—but I must do my job," Cortes said sternly. "You can understand that, can't you, Sister?" He stared at Maria with an evil smile. As he removed his glove, perhaps to slap her across the face, Pena suddenly appeared like a ghost from the darkness.

Years of training and paranoia had taught Cortes to handle any shock or surprise, but Pena's almost magical appearance managed to startle even him.

"General, this is wrong!" the captain said as he moved toward his commander. "She is nothing more than a bride of Christ!"

Cortes reared up at the sound of the Captain's voice. Pena could feel the hairs on the back of his neck go erect, as if they were two alpha dogs about to do battle.

"You insolent pig!" Cortes squealed. "How dare you interrupt an interrogation of a rebel sympathizer. You are relieved of duty! Dismissed! Leave here immediately!" The general slapped his hand on his hip holster to accentuate his point. Pena knew he could do no more without escalating the situation to a tragic end. He gave Maria a woeful smile, swallowed his pride and turned and marched out of the room.

Maria narrowed her eyes at Cortes in contempt. She realized the captain had overstepped his authority on her behalf, causing himself serious disciplinary action in the near future. She did not want to see anyone else injured because of this tyrant. "Your job does not include killing innocent people!" she recklessly pointed out.

Cortes smirked at her impudence and said, "San Cristobal village— your village—is the heart of the Zapatista rebel concentration. You give them aid, comfort, food and supplies, and you are thusly considered pro-Zapatista and anti-government, an enemy of the state."

Maria was not impressed by his litany of information. "They are human beings," she said. "They are Mexicans. All they wish for is freedom to live their own lives and a better Indians-rights agreement. There is no hidden agenda, no communist plot!"

"I have been tasked to protect this country," said Cortes. "That means securing Mexico from seditious factions and the scourge of disease carriers. Your village harbored both!"

"There is no disease and you know that to be true!" challenged Maria. "This was man-made. You and your people have been poisoning the water system. You've created the weapon to wipe out your own people."

Cortes began pacing the room in wider circles, creating a cushion of space between himself and his accuser. "Disease comes in many forms, as does the cure," he pontificated. "I cannot allow the weak and ignorant to continue overpopulating Mexico. In less than fifty years,

Mexico will have over 150 million people, and our natural resources are *already* being depleted, keeping us from our true destiny."

A tear welled in Maria's eye. "You leveled our village, you've slaughtered the people. There is no one left to protect."

This realization angered Cortes. "It is the powerful that survive!" he shouted.

Her fate unfolding, Maria took a new tack. Perhaps she could appeal to Cortes if he had a moral or religious conscience. "True power is the love of Christ, General," she said, speaking as though he were a student. "True power is in the hands of those who care for their fellow man—cherish it, not destroy it. Do you really think that you are above God?"

Cortes slammed his hands down on the table in front of Maria, then picked up and shook Pandora's Box. His eyes narrowed as a demonic realization took hold of his mind. "Here, I am God!" he roared, and snapped his fingers. The two guards reluctantly grabbed the nun's chair and pushed it forward toward the table. A sudden rush of terror came over Maria, but she held firmly to her convictions and began to pray once again. The soldiers turned toward each other and cast their eyes downward. They wanted nothing to do with harming a nun.

LIV

Ramos, Kate and I approached the entrance gates of Toluca Pharmaceuticals just as the sun was setting behind the far-off mountains. The factory was in a basin below the western foothills, meaning the sun set earlier here than elsewhere. Rather than hinder us, though, the early sunset bought us time to maneuver in the half-light of dusk.

Ramos pulled the Jeep off the road where laborers were loading and filling stake-bed trucks with barrels marked: *Chlorino-TXC.* The men wheeled reinforced steel dollies piled high with heavy barrels, yet moved at a snail's pace, disinterested and tired. Normally supervised by soldiers scattered everywhere, the process was overseen today by only two underlings.

From our vantage point, we could see the two guards lean against a truck, exhausted by the tedium of the operation. The older guard produced a bottle of home-brewed tequila from behind his back then looked around suspiciously to ensure the coast was clear. He uncorked the bottle with a yank from his thumb and fingers and took a long chug of the dirty rot-gut. After he could stomach no more of the first round, he handed it to his partner, who repeated the process. It didn't take long before the two were thoroughly loosened up and half the bottle was emptied. Suddenly, Captain Pena appeared. "Ahem!" The guards snapped to attention instinctively, the older one feebly trying to hide the contraband liquor behind his back. Now nervous, the two began to sweat. Drinking on duty was grounds for court martial.

"*Sí, Capitan!*" the first soldier finally responded.

Pena swept his eyes across the yard with a curious look. "Why are these trucks still here, Sergeant?"

The guards eased their stances a bit to look at what their captain was referring to. "But *Capitan*," the sergeant said nervously, "those trucks are not yet loaded."

"I… don't… care… anymore…. *Vamanos!*" Pena shouted. The order was given and the sergeant waved his hands, signaling the drivers to leave. The workers gave him an odd look, but orders were orders no matter how irrational they seemed. They ceased all loading, leaving the barrels in their places.

A great overture of small explosions shook the yard as the old diesel engines fired up and the men ground the cranky transmissions into gear. The partially loaded stake-bed trucks proceeded out of the gates and drove quickly out of the compound, right past our cover. We kept our heads down low like snipers prepared to shoot.

Pena extended an open hand to the sergeant. He now knew he was busted. Reluctantly, he handed the bottle of tequila over to Pena, who stuck the nose of the bottle into his mouth and bit down on the worn cork to pop it out with his teeth.

Pena raised the bottle to his eyes and measured the amount left. He then spit the cork to the ground. As he ran the bottle under his nose to smell the contents, the two soldiers looked nervously at each other. One sniff. And another. Pena slowly brought the tequila back to his mouth and began chugging the bottle. *Glub. Glub. Glub.* He polished off the alcohol in three swigs as the dumbfounded soldiers watched. "Ah!" Pena exhaled, "I hate what we've become, amigos. God will surely never forgive us for what we did today." With heavy hearts, the two soldiers nodded in agreement.

As darkness descended, Ramos searched the area for sizable stones that he would then collect and arrange in small piles near our hideout.

He carefully reached into the Jeep and pulled out a large, flat piece of leather. Using a pocketknife, he sliced it into three strips. With the remaining material, he fashioned three small pouches, then securely bound each strip to one pouch and knotted the strips together at the far end.

"What the hell are you doing?" I said curiously as Kate leaned over my shoulder to observe.

"It's a *bolo*, an ancient Aztec weapon," he said as he knelt to fill the satchels with the stones he'd collected.

"You're gonna try to use that against guys with guns? You know, real guns, the kind that shoot real bullets?" Ramos ignored my sarcasm and continued to construct his simple weapon. I shook my head in wonder.

"There have always been men with greater weapons than us, but my people have survived for thousands of years with nothing more than rocks and stones," he said factually.

After filling the bags with rocks and binding them together, Ramos tested the bolo's strength by whirling it over his head. As it spun faster and faster, it hummed ever more loudly, like an approaching swarm of bees. He was ready for war.

Burp. Pena chucked the empty bottle into the darkness. *Crash.* He patted the two soldiers on the shoulder then hugged each one separately. *"Adios, amigos!"* he said, nearly stumbling now from the quick infusion of alcohol to his brain. Unable to predict Pena's erratic behavior, the soldiers continued to play along, smiling, hugging, shaking hands. Pena stumbled back inside, leaving them to ponder the event.

"Ramos?!" I half-yelled, half-whispered as he suddenly bolted through the front gates and toward the two soldiers. I grabbed Kate and we followed at a close distance behind him, still under cover of darkness. At full sprint, Ramos was nearly upon the two soldiers by the time the electronic motion sensor caused the enormous exterior floodlights to burst bright.

"*Mira!*" the sergeant screamed as the soldiers quickly fumbled for their rifles. They had just bolted a round each into their chambers when

Ramos lined his sight and began to whirl the bolo fast and furiously over his head. Fortuitously, the soldiers stood so near to each other, they actually made a better, almost single target.

As the sergeant raised his weapon, flicked off the safety and drew down on his attacker, Ramos released the spinning stone-packed pouches. The bolo sailed through the air quickly; one end passing between the soldiers, the other two ends wrapping around their heads. In a split second, the three ends circled twice and met in the middle— *Bam!*—smashing the soldiers' heads together and instantaneously knocking them out. I have to say, I was impressed.

LV

Somehow, Maria's prayers could be heard throughout the warehouse. Her voice grew louder and louder and became especially frightening to the two guards near her. They squirmed with unease, wondering how such a strong, powerful sound could come from such a tiny woman.

"You still wish to mock me?" Cortes sneered.

Maria's attitude had now changed. She had accepted her fate, but was not willing to go out easily. "You must beg God's forgiveness for your cruelty!" she shouted, looking upward.

Her words had a powerful effect on Cortes. He became enraged, thinking Maria was somehow cursing him. "Silence, Witch!" he screamed as he reached over and slapped her across the face. The blow whipped her head back to one side, and she blacked out.

Now filled with the liquid courage he'd been seeking, Pena entered the room just as Cortes was striking Maria. Without thinking, he rushed to intervene. "Have you no shame, Cortes?!" Pena shouted as he locked onto the general with his gaze.

Cortes stared back in wild-eyed hysteria. He pulled the leather of his gloves taut over his fist. "She is a worthless Indian peasant and my prisoner! She has no value... and neither do you anymore!" Cortes had surely gone mad.

In one quick move, he shoved Pena aside and grabbed Maria by the hair, pulling her head back upright to strike her again. Pena lunged at Cortes, grabbing his arm and struggling to release the general's grip on Maria. He wrenched and ripped at Cortes' fingers, finally throwing him down to the ground. The two guards did not dare stop either superior, but cautiously angled toward the open door to flee.

As his general lay at his feet, Pena reached across to pick up Maria's wilted body, wrapping his arms around her to carry her to safety. But Cortes would never let that happen. As Pena slowly carried Maria to the opened door, once again Cortes drew his sidearm, aimed square at Pena's back then fired. *Blam.* Pena almost made it one step further before dropping to his knees.

Pena's last virtuous act would be to turn his body inward, cradling Maria from hitting the ground. With a single gasp, he expired. Blood poured quickly from his uniform and spread across the floor.

As Ramos, Kate and I ran down the hallway, we peered into every lighted office, searching for Maria. As we made our way toward the torture room, we literally ran smack into the two guards. Ramos and I banged into them hard, knocking all of us to the ground. There we were, four grown men clambering to regain our feet.

"Hey it's cool!" I shouted as Ramos held out his hands, showing we were unarmed and intended them no harm. The two struggled to their feet and tried to assess the situation, all the while slowly drawing the weapons from their holsters. It was a Mexican standoff, except for the fact that we didn't have guns. We were fucked!

"Wait! Wait!" I said.

They didn't seem to understand my English, or were too confused to try. They pointed their revolvers at us just as Kate interjected, "Maria? *Donde esta Maria?*"

They lowered their guns, then frantically pointed to the room they'd just fled. "*Loco! Loco!*" is all they could shout as they stood down and let us pass.

We stopped short of the entrance and peered through the crack in the open door. We watched Cortes drag Maria's limp body from Pena's, which lay dead beneath her.

"I'm granting your wish, Sister. I'm going to send you to your God!" the general shouted as he took a step to try and jam Maria's hand through the black veil of Pandora's Box.

"Maria!" Ramos screamed as he lunged into the room toward Cortes. Never, never telegraph your position, I thought—it only works in the movies. Cortes, with revolver still in hand, spun and fired. *Blam.* The bullet zinged out of the barrel and into Ramos, redirecting him, throwing his body backward in midair.

"Motherfucker!" I screamed, knowing full well I'd have to finish the job. I sprinted around the corner, giving Cortes no time to think. I jumped, leaping over Ramos, and stumbled right into Cortes. It was like I'd just offered my life to him on a platter. I'd had a deathwish in the past, but I was going to be goddamned if I was gonna let some south-of-the-border Nazi fuckhead kill me. I couldn't help but realize, though, that I had little choice in the matter now. I prepared myself for the inevitable as Cortes placed the barrel of his gun to my temple.

"You will not escape me a second time, Gringo!" Cortes shouted as he cocked the hammer. He took a step forward, but before he could squeeze the trigger, he slipped in the pool of Pena's blood, his feet falling out from under him and landing him flat on his ass. It would've been simply a hilarious sight in any other situation, but it was just the chance I needed at the time—as well as being quite a hoot.

Before I could get the better of Cortes, however, Kate suddenly appeared in the doorway holding a large fire extinguisher. She gave me a desperate look and I nodded in confidence, all the time hoping she would just turn and run away. She wrapped her fingers through the loop and yanked the pin from the red canister, then began spraying its entire contents into the room. Immediately, a cloud of thick, yellowish haze rose from the concrete floor and filled every inch of space. Not realizing that we would all be affected, I was momentarily blinded, no longer able to see Cortes. As I wiped my eyes, I could just barely make out Maria's silhouette.

Cortes managed to squeeze the trigger of his revolver as he fell, but the reports from the gun got jumbled in the rest of the commotion. The automatic pistol blasted skyward in rapid succession, the bullets ricocheting off everything and everywhere. Five, ten, fifteen—there was no way to count. *Zing* after *zing* was all that could be heard as the projectiles flew past our ears.

The gunfire was just enough to jar Maria from her unconscious state. Her eyes took a moment to focus due to the trauma to her face as well as the extinguisher mist, but she was quickly able to spot her brother's motionless body on the floor near her. Cortes was beginning to compose himself, trying to gain his footing as he maneuvered out of the slippery pool of Pena's blood. He dropped his thumb to his forty-five's release and discharged the spent magazine from the hilt. Seamlessly, he reached down to his thick, black leather belt, retrieved a spare clip and quickly reloaded. Seeing this, I scrambled toward Maria to somehow try and protect her. *Click.* Cortes pulled back the slide and bolted a round into the chamber in one lightning-fast move.

As the air began to clear, I saw Cortes, whose eyes narrowed as he smiled wide at me. Just then, Maria grabbed the black box from the table and raised it high over her head. Cortes swung around just as she came up behind him. "Maria!" I screamed. She brought the black box crashing down onto Cortes, driving his head deep inside its mysterious depths.

The blow to his head was so strong that it interlocked the wood into the fleshy excesses of his neck. Thus began a deadly dance. With only one possible action left, Cortes began to fire indiscriminately, again and again, attempting to swing his shorts in Maria's direction.

"Move!" I shouted.

First a low, faraway sound—a mumbling—came from inside the black box; then deafening screams shattered the air as Cortes met the same fate he had once so imperiously doled out to anyone he saw fit. His body began to spasm. He tried running in circles, but found no exit, no safe harbor to cushion the horrible end. His body collapsed to the floor and fluttered, then convulsed. Maria stood over him, staring at his twitching body as though in a hypnotic trance.

"Maria, get down! He may still have bullets left in his gun," I whispered loudly. She half-turned to look at me, smiled, then crumpled to the floor. A small stream of blood oozed from her chest.

LVI

The *Montes De Mixtongo* mountain range was a ruthless and uninhabitable area. I had never been there, nor even heard of it before I'd found myself driving at full speed up the narrow mountain pass, following Maria's directions. She lay in my lap across the front seat as Kate tended to Ramos in the back. You could have mistaken the four of us for young lovers just coming from a picnic except for our pain-wrenched faces and dread-filled eyes.

Bang. The Jeep launched over a fallen branch that lay across the road. "Slow down, Riley!" Kate barked, knowing I couldn't slow down lest I lose the time for saving Carlos' and Maria's lives in the process. It was speed, not comfort, that counted now.

"Okay, we're nearly at the top of the mountain, Maria," I said quietly to her as dust swirled around my face.

"Look down the mountain—do you see anyone following?" she said. I peered over a steep cliff and down its sheer walls thousands of feet. Nothing. I looked in the rearview mirror for dust plumes or any other signs of a convoy. Nothing. It seemed we were temporarily out of danger, but I sure didn't feel safe.

"Yeah, all clear!" I said as I looked into Maria's beautiful brown eyes and wiped a strand of hair from her perspiring brow.

"Turn onto the old road that leads up to the Aztec ruins," she said. "You'll see a sign just before it."

The "old road!" Well, they don't get any older than the one we were on then, but I couldn't very well argue the point with a woman who had taken a bullet meant for me. I carefully searched the rising landscape with my eyes. There. I saw a small sign, turned off onto a sliver of dirt—more a footpath than a road—and drove the last length to the top of the mountain.

It was dark now. I couldn't tell if the Jeep's lights were working, so I drove slowly into what seemed to be a minefield of ancient ruins. They rose high above us on both sides, blocking the lingering aura of the setting sun. Monolithic pyramids seemed to sprout from the earth to engulf us.

I stopped the vehicle at The Great Aztec Temple, where I could make out in the darkness long, flat steps leading to the entrance of the relic. I hopped out and ran to Maria's side, quickly scooping her up and out of the Jeep, whose lights were definitely not working. In fact, we had no working electrics of any kind, which meant there'd be no light unless I used my head.

"There are torches just inside the temple, above the valance," Maria said as she squeezed her chest to subdue the searing pain from the bullet. I entered the great temple slowly and cautiously, and reached my hand up into the darkness, feeling around with my fingers. I had no time to envision creepy crawling things attacking my hand, stinging it or tearing the flesh as I invaded their home. I felt a little like Indiana Jones testing the walls for booby traps.

I found the torches and a small pack of sulfur-tipped matches near them. It was difficult holding Maria and trying to light a large torch at the same time. It was nothing more than a long stick with a kerosene-soaked rag tied to the top—like something out of *Gilligan's Island*—but I wasn't complaining. The first torch illuminated the anteroom and I could see the hallway was narrow, built by an ancient people much smaller than us, but possessed of an architectural acumen that would rivals ours today. I found the other torches and quickly lit a path into the smaller chambers.

After carrying both Maria and Carlos into the temple, Kate and I attempted to stabilize them and assess their situations. Carlos had been shot in the upper shoulder, above the heart, and we'd have to extract the bullet. Infection and septicemia were the major concerns. Maria, on the other hand, was looking even worse. She'd taken at least one, maybe two bullets in her side and sternum, and though the wound wasn't bleeding much, vital organs had been damaged nonetheless. I was no doctor, but I knew she didn't have long without proper help.

"Riley!" Ramos said as Kate placed his head onto a leaf-covered stone pallet. "You've got to get this bullet out of me." No duh, she seemed to be thinking. The damn thing had nicked something inside him and prevented the wound from closing. He was oozing out blood faster than we could stop it.

"I can lead you through it," Maria said as she lay next to her brother. "Find a mirror and I will tell you what to do." Kate looked at me with heartbreak in her eyes. She knew Maria had just so much strength and that she'd use a lot of it helping her brother.

"Before you start," Ramos interrupted, "make two small fires outside at the edge of the cliff. Just do it!"

I didn't argue, but grabbed two torches and ran outside. I quickly yanked one of the sideview mirrors off the Jeep and wiped it down with my shirt sleeve, then I rushed to a presidio at the edge of the cliff and quickly lit two bonfires.

Kate had already prepared Ramos by cleaning the wound, but he had begun to sweat profusely from the onset of fever and was now floating in and out of consciousness. Kate had fetched fresh water from a small well in an adjacent chamber for the two to drink. She helped Maria first. "Here Maria, drink this. I found the first-aid kit near the well."

Maria sipped what little water she could and nodded to Kate when done. "We are safe. This is a holy place," she said, forcing her words. "My father brought us here when we were still children. It is a sanctuary." She turned to look at her brother's face. "Our *papi* told us if we were ever in trouble to come here."

Kate wiped Maria's forehead and smiled, saying, "Shush! Save your strength."

Maria looked into Kate's eyes and let her gaze range over the American woman's features. "You are in love with him, aren't you?" she asked.

Kate dared not disagree with her. "We're just friends, coworkers, Maria, we've... we've never," she fumbled.

Maria tapped Kate's hand softly. "He is a good man and I know you see it too. Take care of him; love him as I could not. I will always love him, but I'm no longer in his heart." Kate's eyes welled with tears as Maria spoke.

I ran the small scalpel I'd dug up from the first-aid kit through the flame a few times to sterilize it. Ramos was barely conscious now and giving me wild looks and glares. "You want to kill me, don't you, Gringo?" he yelled insanely. I had to admit, the thought of driving that scalpel deep into Ramos and watching him squirm was enticing... at least until I actually had to do it. Kate bent two forks then drove them in to open the hole in Ramos' shoulder, separating the two flaps of skin and muscle, nearly stretching them to their limit. I poured alcohol onto the wound, which elicited a series of unstoppable, shrill screams from Ramos. I knew right then why I had never become a doctor.

"Jesus Christ!" I whispered to Kate as sweat poured off my brow. "I don't know what I'm doing."

I could see Maria lurching from the pain as I tilted the mirror down for her to see. "Now probe the wound with the tip of the scalpel until you feel the bullet," she said in a small, weak voice.

"Shit!" I dug into flesh and muscle as my patient's cries of anguish filled the chamber. *Tap.* I felt something odd, something foreign. "I found it!" I shouted. It was about three inches deep into his shoulder, just up against his clavicle. I dared not dig around too much for fear of damaging anything else.

"Terry," Maria whispered, "take the long tweezers and extract the bullet. It will probably bleed quickly for a moment. Kate, heat up that knife until it's red-hot, then shove it in to cauterize the wound. After that, Terry, take the needle and thread and sew his shoulder up—the muscles first, subcutaneous skin, then the outer layer." Man, she sure was a precision nurse-turned-doctor in a crisis —one, two, three and *presto*.

We did as we were instructed and finished working on Ramos' shoulder in under an hour. Maria had been right. He bled a lot for a minute then the wound seemed to close. "It's no work of art, but he's alive," I said, asking absolution in my backhanded way. Just then, a shadow passed over me, making me start. "Who's there?!" I shouted, grabbing the scalpel to protect the other three.

"It's okay!" a voice said from the darkness, "We're friends of Ramos." Out of the darkness, Boomba and his men appeared. "We've brought supplies," a female voice said as both men and women quickly gathered around us to help. Kate and I were gratefully relieved of any further surgical duties as the others took over to save their friends.

LVII

Kate sat upright across from me on a bed of leaves in one of the chambers. We watched each other as the flames of a makeshift fire flickered, and I began to look at her in a different way. I had never really noticed her before: her sensitive side, her beautiful side, her caring side, which had been so active through all this recent turmoil. Kate now seemed like a woman I'd never known before.

"Do you still love her?" she said with a serious timbre in her voice.

I dropped my head to take inventory of my feelings. "Maria and I fell in love during a crisis," I began, "a war. It was a dangerous time, and what we had was risky and volatile and short-lived. I realize that now, but I've spent years racking myself with guilt over her supposed death. That kind of guilt would affect anyone." I could tell she thought I was avoiding her question, though, so I just came clean: "Yes, I still love her. I'll always love her."

Just then, a woman entered the chamber, interrupting us. She had made some food; she knew we would be hungry. She was young and beautiful, but couldn't speak English. She handed us two plates and cupped her fingers, motioning for us to eat. I smiled and gladly began to do just that.

Throughout the night, I heard strange sounds in the high jungle. A full moon illuminated everything inside and out of the temple, even the chambers themselves, with an eerie light in which shadows playfully danced around. A strong wind would occasionally blow through the ruin, sending a chill through my bones. I couldn't sleep, so I kept checking on Maria each hour or so, walking over the sleeping bodies of Boomba and the others to get to where she lay.

From where she was, she could see her brother by just opening her eyes and turning her head. Even though he tossed and turned, Maria seemed sure he'd make it through. I knelt down to talk quietly with her. "Carlos is stable now," she whispered to me as I dabbed her mouth with a moist cloth. "You should be proud of yourself for what you did."

"You were always trying to save the world," I said, smiling. "I just wish you could have saved us."

Maria took my hand and stroked it gently. She was pale now from loss of blood and weakness, but she still managed to open those beautiful eyes that could cut right through me. "Do you remember once you told me that love alone wasn't strong enough to save the world?" she asked.

I was a bit embarrassed that she was outing my poor taste in commentary so late in the game. I evaded the question by saying, "You should know better than to listen to me."

She struggled to smile as she continued, "Finish the work you started, my love. Take care of Kate. I think she means more to you than you realize."

My eyes began to swell with tears. I didn't really know how to address the emotions I was feeling, so I said, "Maria, you're going to be okay. Just hold on. We'll be together again, I know we will." I could hear the desperation in my own voice.

"I will haunt you no longer, my love," she said, then took one final gasp of air as she reached up to kiss me. I quickly pulled her the rest of the way to my lips as she blew her last breath into my mouth. I wouldn't release my grip on her lifeless body for what seemed like hours.

LVIII

It was unusually quiet at the Disease Research Center. Everyone had gone home hours before; even the tech rats that lived on caffeine and Big Gulps had left early to prepare for the upcoming holiday. No one was roaming the halls or putting the finishing touches onto some genetic project. It was simply still. Nobody, not even a security guard, was anywhere to be found.

Manny marched down the corridor singularly focused on his lab door and fumbling with his keys. He seemed to be filled with an unusual amount of confidence and strength. The sign above the red optical eye over which Manny flashed his pass read: *LEVEL IV - CAUTION - PRESSURIZED DOORS - AIRBORNE BACTERIA - DANGER*. The optical eye changed to green and a *clunk* could be heard as the steel bolt automatically slid free of its locked position.

Manny entered the LEVEL IV lab through the sealed anteroom and quickly changed into his blue biosuit. He proceeded to open the inner doors with the precision of an automaton then secured his helmet, connecting the hoses and checking the oxygen regulator. Now, protected from any microscopic bacteria or virus, he could safely enter the steel vault.

The sound of his own labored breathing pounded in his ears as he coded in a series of numbers on a digital security pad. A swish of pressurized air escaped as the sealed door to the narrow vault sprang open. He was nervous—very nervous—but he was on a mission, and he wasn't stopping for anything or anybody.

Manny cautiously made his way to the stainless steel cabinets and his hand led him to the exact drawer he was looking for. "*Scheisse!*" he cursed to himself. The drawer had already been opened and the contents— files and papers and research—were strewn all over the floor, scattered everywhere. Files that read *TOXICOLOGY* and *BLOOD SAMPLES*, among others, were empty, useless without their original documents.

Manny's labored breathing was so heavy that he didn't hear a sound as the vault door behind him slowly opened. He was so busy trying to gather any useful information, he never noticed anyone approaching. The interloper wore a red biosuit and helmet with a reflective, tinted visor that looked like something Neil Armstrong had worn on the moon. Entering the vault with deliberate stealth, the figure slowly produced a fire ax from behind his back and raised it overhead. Just as the ax was about to come crashing down onto his skull, Manny suddenly caught the intruder's reflection in the polished steel of the cabinets. It didn't matter, though—it was too late.

Like a demon in red plastic, the figure swung the ax down with amazing force, attempting to split Manny's helmet in two to drive the blade through his head. Instead, the ax glanced off the back of the shiny, insulated helmet and sliced Manny's oxygen tube, immediately ending his supply of fresh, clean air.

Manny's eyes widened through his clear visor as he fell to the ground gasping. A loud hiss escaped from the supply hose that was no longer connected to his helmet as the precious purified air that ensured his safety from bacteria and viral bugs seeped quickly away. There was nothing left but the contaminated air in the vault to breathe.

The assassin dropped the ax to the vault floor and stood over Manny, producing a small vial from an inside pocket of his biosuit. The vial read: *LEVEL IV - VIRUS*. As soon as he had carefully uncorked the vial, red strobe lights and sirens blared. A sign in the vault flashed as a monotone computer-generated voice said, "Contamination has occurred. Now implementing oxygen-free environment!" It then repeated the warning over and over again.

The large steel vault door began to slowly close as the assassin dropped the vial at Manny's feet. He slinked out around the door just as it clicked shut. Manny's muffled cries for help went unheeded as he watched his fate being sealed. *Clunk.* The long steel bolt slid back into the lock position. Then… silence.

LIX

When the sun crossed the horizon at dawn, I found myself gazing over an endless sea of Aztec and Mayan ruins whose peaks pierced the jungle canopy for miles. Howler Monkeys squawked. Tropical birds cawed. Every imaginable sound I'd ever heard on Animal Planet was competing for a place in this misty, exotic world.

A procession of mourners poured out of the great temple. In their center they bore aloft a makeshift litter that cradled Maria. Her body was draped in a thin white shroud that covered her from head to toe. I was at the foot of the steps with Kate next to me, ready to walk with the wake. I half expected to see a second litter being carried out with Ramos atop, but his fever had broken early in the morning and, with the help of his lieutenants, he was now slowly bringing up the rear of Maria's procession. He held up his wounded arm, tightly bound with a clean linen dressing.

The Zapatistas encircled a small area to protect Maria's corpse, and began mourning in earnest. Tears flowed to the accompaniment of various whimpers and cries of agony. These were a passionate people not easily given to sorrow, yet this outpouring of emotion came easily on this day. After all, they were weeping for their Maria, patron saint of the sick and injured. She was truly a saint in their eyes, and I realized just then that she was always meant to be their Maria, not mine.

"We shall take Maria to our village and honor her there," Boomba said, "and we will get Carlos to the hospice." I nodded to Boomba as the others helped Ramos onto a horse and used a rope to secure him for the trek down the mountain. "Carlos has told us that you are going to Mexico City to confront the leaders of our plight." I nodded again. "We will be there too!" Boomba finished. We shook hands as he mounted his horse and shouted, "*Vaya con Dios, amigos!*"

LX

If you could have seen the Jeep from the mountaintop we had just left, all you would've been able to make out was a comet-like streak of dirt and dust trailing in the wake as I barreled across the desert floor. Boomba and his troop had split off from us, and Kate and I badly needed gasoline and supplies to make our own way. The coast seemed clear: Cortes was dead, Smith and Jones were out of the picture, and I believed any other party who might be after us could only speculate as to our current location. As far as I could discern, we were safe... at least for the moment. Man, I could really use a drink, I thought.

I saw a look of anger and determination on my face as I glanced every few seconds in the rearview mirror to make sure we weren't being followed. I had the throttle at full bore and was getting the hang of driving fast and reckless.

"Why didn't you ever mention Maria before?" Kate suddenly asked, breaking my automotive reverie.

"It was a long time ago," I retorted curtly, not wanting to get into an ancient history lesson. It was just too early for that. Kate and I had never been on the same timeline, so why start now?

"I'm sorry, I didn't mean...," she demurred.

I ran my fingers through my hair slowly, grimacing in emotional pain and feeling like a heel. "No! No! It's okay," I said, girding myself for the inevitable "opening up." I continued, "Maria was like no woman I'd ever known. I met her when I was covering the Chiapas Massacres about five years ago. We had a short, passionate fling. I thought it was love, but I guess it was just obsession."

I looked across the horizon and slammed the gear shift into fifth. "But the guilt of my leaving her to die at the hands of that monster Cortes... I never could forgive myself, you know?" Kate let me tell it in my own time.

To keep a low profile, I drove near a riverbed at the edge of the foothills. As we came upon a bend in the river, I slowed the Jeep and stopped before it overheated. I'd been pushing it too hard and couldn't risk having a breakdown in the middle of the Badlands. It was a good time to rest. I pulled the vehicle under some shade trees and grabbed a basket packed with provisions. "Come on!" I said as I exited.

We marched over a small knoll to a place where the river was calm and shallow, then sat down amid a small grove of trees on the bank. This must have been a favorite spot for the locals because there were a number of children splashing and playing in the river while their mothers washed clothes on the opposite side. No one even bothered to look up at the strange gringos who had just arrived. They just went on with their daily routines.

I suddenly got an urge to stand up and tear off my shirt. I made tracks into the river. "Riley?" Kate shouted as I dove in.

Man, that was a soothing bath. Under the placid surface of the river, the cool water seemed to magically cleanse away all the problems and the pain from my body and mind. When I emerged, my head bobbed up and down as I tried to gain my footing in the chilly mud floor of the shoal. I caught Kate stretching her neck to see if I was all right, then sitting back down with relief. She dug into the basket to see what food was there. I didn't wave her in or shout something trite like, "The water's great!" I just relaxed and floated on my back, occasionally submerging myself, each time feeling lighter and lighter.

After a while, I swam over to where the children were playing and joined in. I splashed a few of them, picked some up and threw them into the deeper parts of the river, gave them piggy-back rides—anything to keep my mind off the events of the past few days. Occasionally, I'd look back at Kate to see her smile, but quickly turn her head, pretending she hadn't noticed.

She finally made her way to the water's edge and began to give herself a sponge bath, careful to expose only a shoulder here and an ankle there. As I gazed upon her, I realized I'd never seen her in a sexual way before that moment, and I liked it. But now I didn't know if my new feelings for Kate were simply a knee-jerk reaction to Maria's death—grief confusing my emotions and all that—or actual feelings caused by Kate—the woman, not the annoying up-and-coming reporter.

"I'm starting to see where the reporter ends and the man begins," Kate said as I stood over her, dripping wet. She was looking up, but had to cover her eyes from the intense sun. She reached over and handed me a small towel to dry off with. I couldn't help but fantasize that we were on a romantic picnic somewhere in an exotic country, just the two of us. I was starting to feel like this was an appetizer before the main course: sex.

She sat there with her legs curled under her and quietly dished some food onto a plate in the formal manner of a newly-graduated *Geisha* serving her first official meal. As she handed me the plate, I knew I had to get my mind out of the gutter to focus on the task at hand. Change the subject, change the subject, I directed myself.

"Ramos will be fine," I said out of the blue. "His wounds will heal." I hated chit chat.

"Yeah, *he'll* be fine," she said, "but it's you I'm worried about. You carry so many secrets inside." She was angling at something, and I didn't have the strength to fight her.

"It wasn't all Maria, you know" I said sheepishly, "the drinking, the self-loathing, the reason I've been so self-destructive."

Kate was brilliant. She said nothing. She just slowly and quietly chewed her food, drawing me in deeper and deeper. It was overpowering, the cunning she used to extract every ounce of information from me without saying a word. A lot of women have that ability. All right, enough with the pressure, I thought. I'll tell you the whole story:

"A few years ago, a source turned me onto some irregularities in the Department of Agriculture. Massive amounts of grain were being exported to Russia long after the wall had come down, but nobody was mentioning it." Kate took the small towel and began drying my back. It must've been some unconscious way of saying, "Yeah, I'm listening" without having to come right out and say it.

"See," I continued, "Mexico was simultaneously getting an influx of arms for their military machine, so I linked the two and began to follow the trail." Kate kept rubbing and rubbing my back even though it was already dry. She was lulling me into a false sense of security and it was working: I couldn't shut my mouth. "It was the old 'bait-and-switch'—you know, 'Grain for Guns,'—and it led right up the steps of Capitol Hill."

She said inquisitively, "Pritchard?"

I shook my head and said, "Foster! Senator Steven Foster. He chaired the Organized Crime Subcommittee, which was supposed to investigate drug trafficking and narco-dollar laundering." Kate continued to rub me, crossing over to my sides, then my lower back—you get the picture. "Years were spent compiling information on the mob by this subcommittee, but their findings were never published," I said, remembering the facts slowly. "Senator Foster gave the Senate Oversight Commission some bullshit stories then threw them a couple of low-level drug traffickers as scapegoats. For his diligence, Congress appointed him Diplomatic Liaison to Russia." Kate was totally enveloped in the story by now, but I was careful to watch the time. I couldn't afford to lose sight of the goal.

"What nobody knew was that Foster was on the mob's payroll. He'd recruited union wiseguys to scam undocumented grain supplies and sell them to the Russians for a huge profit. He made so much money, he had to launder it just to make room in his house."

Kate interjected, "But how could he have gotten away with it?"

I turned to face her and said, "Since he now had diplomatic immunity, neither the Feds nor Interpol—nobody—was gonna be able to catch the transfers. But he still had a problem: how to convert millions and millions in cash through dummy corporations without eventually getting caught."

Kate's eyes widened with revelation. "Farmgate!" she exclaimed.

"Yep," I said. "It took me over a year to uncover the whole story; how deep it really went. When I finally did, it made the headlines around the world."

"You say that as if it were a bad thing," Kate commented. "You should be proud of yourself for exposing such a corrupt bastard! He was a crook of the worst kind. A trusted politician!"

I picked up a flat stone lying at my feet, took aim and side-armed it into the river. It skipped along the top of the water five or six times then dropped to the bottom. "Kate, you've been a reporter long enough to realize that every headline comes at a price, as they used to say."

She looked at me, utterly confused, and said, "What do you mean?"

I lay back into the sand, crossed my hands behind my head and stared into the vast blue sky. "I didn't see him coming. All I saw were the security guards running down the hallway behind him. It was surreal," I said as I described my dream, my living nightmare. "I looked up and there he was standing over me. He was holding something in one hand then pulled out a pistol with the other."

Kate prodded me, "Okay, go on..."

I closed my eyes to remember the event in detail. "I was a goner. I knew it in a split second. There he was, Senator Foster, the man whose life I'd just ruined, with a gun pointed straight at my face."

"Jesus!" Kate interrupted.

"He tossed something at me and it landed in my lap. He waved the gun for me to pick it up. It was a picture of him with his family: a wife, two daughters, two sons. When I looked up again, he'd put the gun in his mouth and pulled the trigger. He blew his brains out all over me that day. I've never been able to get that image out of my mind."

LXI

The streets of Mexico City were always filled with millions of people on this day; celebrants dressed in colorful Halloween-type costumes. They marched in parades, had impromptu parties on the sidewalks and danced in the mercado on this official holiday that capped off the long celebration of the Day of the Dead—one of Mexico's most important and most revered holidays.

A procession of limousines dropped off a seemingly endless series of international dignitaries at the foot of the Mexican Senate building while crowds of camera-snapping tourists mingled with revelers in costume. Security wasn't the highest priority here, not due to lack of manpower or lack of concern, but because of the fact that any restriction of this holiday—that is, any action taken by anyone either officially or casually to impede the natural unfolding of any holy day's events—might spark an already agitated populous into rioting.

In proud evidence everywhere were colorful banners and graffiti in support of the Zapatistas. Rebels, this day, could easily walk the streets of the city with impunity, and thousands of people chose outlaw garb as their costumes *du jour*. It would have been impossible for the government to stop every suspicious looking person, so Chavez instructed the authorities to do nothing at all. It was the wise move.

Kate and I scurried through the crowd, making our way to the Mexican Senate. I had no plan, no idea about how we were going to get in. All my identification—press passes, clothes, everything—had been confiscated or burned by Cortes.

As we approached the city center, I climbed up a light post to get a better view. We were less than a hundred yards from the steps of the Senate and nearly home free. Then I saw the checkpoints. Mexico City police, *Federales* and special units scattered across the street, trying to blend in with the locals. Thank God I'd seen enough of them to know when they were looking for something or someone. I feared they were looking for me.

About the same time, Pritchard, Dexter and the rest of the staff arrived by limo. The senator emerged from the towncar with a look on his face that said, *It's a nice day for politics!* He smiled and cajoled as he gave and got salutations from his fans and groupies within earshot.

What I hadn't seen at the time, standing just below a large banner that read *WELCOME INTERNATIONAL DIGNITARIES TO THE WORLD CONFERENCE ON THE ENVIRONMENT*, were two United States Federal Agents. If the Feds were here, something was up. They were dressed in suits, but not too nice as to stand out in a crowd; truly incognito. They stood at the top of the steps before the entrance to the Mexican Senate.

The lead, Special Agent Polk, was lean, with slightly graying temples. He pressed an earpiece into place and spoke quietly into a tiny microphone wired up under his sleeve and down to his cuff. He brought his arm up to his face as if to cough and said, "The eagle has landed!"

I knew that inside the Senate, heads of state from around the world were converging in the large auditorium, getting ready to assess the world environmental crisis and to point fingers at the worst environmental treaty violators. Exchanges would be heated and, although lax outside, security inside would probably be tight as a drum. I knew I had to do something to get inside and stay inside safely until I could do what I needed to do.

"Damn it!" I huffed. "Where the hell is Manny with those documents?" I jumped down from the lamp post and grabbed Kate by the arm. "This is where we were gonna meet, right?" Kate nodded. "He's late and we've got to get in there before they seal the doors for a closed session! What the hell are we going to do?" Kate just shrugged.

A vendor pedaled a cart overflowing with traditional costumes slowly past us. Hats and piñatas dangled from a wooden rack that also held capes and face paint along with jovial skeleton masks. Everything imaginable filled the cart's basin.

"*Buenos dias, Señora!*" the vendor said as he tipped his hat to Kate. I was about to lead Kate through the gauntlet when I saw three *Federales* walking toward us through the crowd—searching. I had an idea.

"*Señor!*" I yelled to the vendor before he turned the corner.

LXII

Kate and I were nearly at the side entrance of the Senate when we turned to admire each other dressed in full Day of the Dead regalia. We looked like freaks: I wore a grotesque mask and black cape and carried a sickle, while Kate could only be described as Mary Poppins on acid. I couldn't help but laugh hysterically.

"Come on, Riley," Kate snapped, "we're going to be late." I raised my mask to show Kate the tears streaming down my face. I couldn't remember the last time I'd laughed so hard, and it just kept pouring out. I was paralyzed.

"Maybe we oughta go to the U.S. Embassy, or catch a plane back home, let the Feds handle this one," she said nervously. "I'm not going to make the same mistake again. This is what it takes to be a reporter. I'd forgotten that for a long time, but now I'm going to do the right thing."

I stretched out my hand and said, "Do you have your press pass on you?"

She dug through her purse. "Yep! And I brought these..." She handed me the pass along with a pen, notepad and a microcassette recorder.

"I'll take the pass and the recorder, but I still have my secret weapon!" I said as I proudly displayed my gold pen.

"Where did you hide that?" she inquired.

"Don't ask!" I retorted. "All right," I said, suddenly serious, "they're not looking for you, so you need to get close to Pritchard and stay on him. I'll find Manny and somehow get the documents to the ambassador's secretary, Gutierrez; he'll be able to get them out of the country through diplomatic channels." I grabbed Kate by the shoulders and held her firmly. "Just promise me that whatever happens, you'll finish the story, all right?"

Kate smiled and clutched my hands, then said, "That's one thing you can bet your ass on!"

I suddenly felt a surge of renewed confidence, the likes of which I hadn't experienced in years. I impulsively pulled her to me for a deep, passionate kiss. When I let go, Kate nearly dropped to the ground, her eyes still closed, still taking in the kiss. I charged up the final steps of the Senate, leaving her to find her own way.

"Hey! How am I going to get in?" I heard Kate shout behind me.

I had successfully passed outer security and entered through the revolving doors just as guards were about to lock the delegates in and the public out. I still had my mask up off my face when I entered, not realizing the two federal agents had already drawn a bead on me. Out of the corner of my eye, I saw them raising their sleeves to their mouths, but I was under the impression it meant nothing to me at that point. I quickly threw my mask back on and queued up in line as the last of the reporters entered.

Four guards at the X-ray machine monitored purses and laptop bags and such as they passed through on the conveyor belt. They didn't seem terribly interested in doing their job well; perhaps they felt no real threat of domestic terrorism or international dignitary kidnapping. They seemed more concerned with getting people in and out through their station and ending their day as soon as humanly possible.

I had just stepped up behind the last reporter to go through the machine when I quickly flashed Kate's press pass, my thumb conveniently placed over her photo. With my other hand I slowly pulled my mask off to show my face, hoping the guards wouldn't try to match it with the press pass. I had just faked them out and was hurrying through the detector when suddenly a loud series of beeps stopped me in my tracks. Not now, I thought.

One of the guards casually walked over to frisk me. It felt like he was picking my pockets when he pulled out my notepad and threw it in a wooden box sitting on the edge of the conveyor belt. The microcassette followed next, and finally, my gold pen. He dropped them all in the box, scanned me again with a hand-held radar device that looked more like a policeman's baton than a security wand and sent me on my way.

I gathered up my items, which were sitting next to a pile of more questionable contraband: pot pipes, switch blades, even a roll of duct tape. *Duct tape?* I scooped up the roll with my other things and raced down the hall toward the auditorium.

LXIII

The entire lecture hall was pitch black until a single beam of light burst forth from a window high above the audience. A film began. It showed a series of ecological disasters happening throughout the world over the past ten decades, since the beginning of twentieth century. You could only make out the tops of hats and overblown hairdos along the flickering projector light's trajectory to the enormous screen.

"Man has become the greatest threat to the environment and if we don't change our ways, there will be dark days ahead!" the narrator warned. Blah, blah, blah. I didn't have time for sentimental conjecture. I had bigger fish to fry.

As the film ended, the house lights came up and Chavez suddenly appeared at the podium, smiling to all the diplomats and dignitaries in his usual, pandering style. "You don't have to look far to see the strides Mexico has made to help our environment," he began. "Air pollution levels are at their lowest in three decades. We have introduced electric and clean-burning fuel-powered mass transportation and imposed heavy fines to ensure tighter factory controls." He paused to take a breath. "We've developed desert land that is now fertile with both native vegetation and agriculture..."

From the top of the auditorium steps, I watched as Chavez continued to make the first of what he envisioned to be many historical speeches. I had to admit, he sounded good, but I was more concerned with getting my microcassette tape recorder to work. I checked the batteries. Good. I checked the tape. Good. I rewound it to the start so I'd have ninety minutes to burn if need be. I pushed the red record button and quietly whispered, "Test... test." It played back at just the volume and clarity I'd wanted.

At the same time, Dexter Grace was scanning the audience. It might have been habit or just sheer boredom, but he was looking for something. *Bing.* He found it. Me. His eyes narrowed as he watched me fiddling with my shirt sleeves twenty rows behind him.

Ironically, there were other eyes that were following Dexter's moves: those of Philip Gutierrez, in attendance as part of his official responsibilities. He keyed in on Dexter with a pair of powerful opera glasses, and turned to see what Dexter was looking at.

I was fumbling with my shirt sleeve, smoothing out the wrinkles and trying to get the rest of the dirt off my cuffs, when I felt the sharp pain of my arm being yanked behind me. "Ouch!" I cried as I was spirited out of the auditorium by an unseen presence. Maybe it was one of the security guards that had found out I was using an illegal press pass, maybe it was one of Cortes' men I hadn't counted on following me. All I knew was that the tremendous pain I felt made me think my arm was about to snap clean off. Then a new sensation of cold steel jamming into my ribs arrested my attention. I was getting pretty sick and fucking tired of being pushed around. To be frank, I was beginning to equate Mexico with nothing but pain and misery.

I turned my head to glance over my shoulder and saw two men in suits dragging me backward down a semi-darkened hallway. They were big, store-bought type guys. Dexter suddenly appeared walking in front of me—or should I say behind me? Either way, I could see him.

"You are a tremendous pain in the ass! You know that, Riley?" Dexter said as he set the pace. All my legs could do was shuffle backwards to keep up.

"Do you always have this much trouble getting a date, Dexter?!" I laughed sarcastically. Why not? What did I have to lose? It was just another beating. I was getting used to it.

As we turned a corner, we passed a corridor that connected the foyer to the rest of the building. Kate was there, trying to gain entrance by beguiling the security guards. When asked to show her press identification, she merely fumbled through her purse, knocking things over in the process and holding up the line of people behind her.

I watched as she flirtatiously apologized, yet kept anyone from passing around her until the guards let her through. It worked. She frustrated them so much they let her pass without a pass!

Just before I was dragged out of view, she caught a glimpse of me being manhandled down the hallway. I opened my eyes wide, trying to signal her, but Dexter blocked my view. I couldn't see if she'd understood me or not.

LXIV

The solid wood door flew open and I flew with it. The two guards tossed me like day-old bread across the room so that I hit the back wall. It was a senatorial suite, complete with a bay window over the Senate floor, thick velvet curtains and an electronics board with all sorts of toys on it. Unlike most of the small rooms and torture chambers I had visited recently in Mexico, this was nice. It must have been Pritchard's to use while he was here. I thought, hey, if I was going to get it again, I couldn't think of a nicer place to take a beating.

Dexter snapped at the two men, "Well? Search him, you idiots!" Man, I bet this clown had friends all over the place. He was a real "Mister Happy." He stepped up behind the men as they padded me down. They could've done a more thorough job, but Dexter had pissed them off just enough to hurry through their task without much care. My secret was still safe.

Dexter leaned over one of the men to get in my face as he finished. "This is between you and me now!" he growled.

I stood there like a mime doing jumping jacks, my arms spread wide in the air and my feet a yard apart. I should have seriously considered a new line of work right then and there, but this asshole had gotten under my skin.

The two thugs dug through my pockets and tossed my notepad, my gold pen—everything they could dig up–onto the bare table. "I'm sick of this shit!" I huffed. "Why doesn't Pritchard fight his own goddamn battles? He's a big boy." Dexter seemed unaffected by my comment. He was a cold, hard customer at game time. He merely turned to the table and thumbed through my belongings, inspecting the articles for anything unusual.

Suddenly, he reached for my gold pen. I was hoping he wouldn't notice that. He picked it up and waved it in my face. "You should've chosen a more powerful weapon," he quipped.

I straightened up from being accosted and replied, "It's mightier than the sword, in case you haven't heard."

Dexter took another step closer. I really think he enjoyed these gay repartees. "Not if your head is on the chopping block!" he said, laughing. "Well, as they say, 'To the victor go the spoils!'" He shoved my favorite gold pen into his front shirt pocket, then nodded to one of his goons. *Bam.* The appointed goon punched me square in the solar plexus. I doubled over in pain then took a knee for support. As I gasped for air, I suddenly looked up to see an electronics board with a number of toggle switches on it. *Intercom In, Intercom Out, Security*—you name it—this thing could order you a pizza from Libya. I pondered the *Intercom Out* switch...

I crawled up the wall in a spasm of pain, not faking it by any means but exaggerating my movements, and flipped all the toggles I could, blocking my machinations with my body. "You better start looking for a new ass to kiss, 'cause I've got your boss Pritchard by the balls!" I said, and coughed.

Dexter Grace looked at his fingernails as though assessing his need for a manicure. "The last threats of a desperate man," he yawned. He looked at his two men, who snickered on queue. "I know about the chemicals in the water," I said, beginning to gesture with my hands. "I can see the headlines now: 'PRESIDENTIAL HOPEFUL CAUGHT IN DEADLY CONSPIRACY!' Or how's this one, Asshole?— 'PRITCHARD LINKED TO MEXICO'S MASS MURDERS!'"

Dexter nodded to one of the men, who produced a file and tossed it onto the table. The contents spread everywhere.

"Well, I don't think you're going to get too far without proof," Dexter said with matter-of-fact confidence. He walked to the table and picked up a couple of pages of scientific data, then let them fall to the floor. "I took the liberty of relieving your German friend, the good doctor, of his Hippocratic duties... Oh, and his life as well!" He tossed a security pass onto the papers. It read: *DR. MANFRED ZOBEL.* Dexter folded his arms in contempt.

That was it! I bolted for him, screaming, "You motherfuck...!" *Bam.* The other slugger delivered a punishing blow to my rib cage. I crumpled to the ground panting, trying to catch my breath. This was bad. Not only was the one person who could prove everything now dead, but Dexter had the documents and was going to destroy them to protect Pritchard. This was the kind of conspiracy that made Watergate a footnote in history books.

As I lay on the floor trying to get my strength to rise, I saw shadows appear under the bottom crack of the door. Dexter paced in front of me, but luckily never took notice. I wanted to call out, but I had no idea who would come through the door. Before I could shout something, Dexter decided to compliment me by saying, "I must admit, I admire your tenacity. After all, Mr. Smith and Mr. Jones were pros, not easily duped by the likes of you. I may have underestimated your talents." He knew about the hitmen, I thought. How?

I felt like bleeding on his shoes—That would show him!—as I crouched on the floor in agony. "You! You did this? Why?"

Dexter flipped his hand back like the flaming queen he really was and said dramatically, "If you have to ask, then you know nothing of politics!" He paced around my crippled body, shouting, "Money, you idiot! It's always about the money! Can't make a decent living as a senatorial aide and you sure as hell can't make one working for the E.P.A."

I watched the shadows get closer to the door and stop as Dexter rambled on: "Luckily, after Pritchard hired me, he sent me here to oversee the AMERIMEX operations. I had complete autonomy over all the facilities. The only problem was, I needed someone to keep things under control, if you know what I mean."

I sat up a bit, then slowly grabbed the edge of the table and pulled myself up to say, "*Cortes!*" I spasmed as the pain of shouting shot up my side.

"Why not?" was Dexter's rejoinder. "He was perfect. Greedy. Sadistic. Genocidal. Hated wholeheartedly by the indigenous people here. Believe me, it didn't take much to recruit the likes of him." Dexter chuckled.

"Then what about Pritchard?" I queried.

"What about him?" Again with the theatrics: "He's just a skirt-chasing idiot more concerned with banging the help than public policy. He doesn't have a clue what we've been doing down here."

My head was hurting from trying to connect all the dots. This whole complex murdering machine had been created by Dexter Grace? God does play cruel jokes on the world, I thought.

"Now I've got orders from every third-world nation on the map for my little population control device," he continued. "They love it in China and India—and let's not forget our Eastern European buddies! I'll be retiring on my own island earning prime plus twenty while that dumb-fuck Pritchard is facing a grand jury inquiry."

I now had new respect for the term "evil." I pleaded with him: "Jesus Christ, Dex, even you can't be that cold! These are human beings, for Christ's sake!"

"Well, there are just too many of them!" he yipped, flitting about the room like Tinkerbell while attempting to justify his insidious plan. "Hey, it's hardly been a secret: Mexico's had a 'volunteer birth control program' for decades. I've just accelerated the process a bit. Look on the bright side: It gives our poor, struggling environment a fighting chance!"

The office door suddenly burst open and I could hear a reverb monitor screech outside. Pritchard entered first, with Chavez directly behind him. And they were pissed. Pritchard marched up to Dexter and screamed, "An idiot, am I? Well let me tell you something, Boy! You're in a whole shitload of trouble!"

Dexter seemed unfazed as he said, "You know, it's rude to stand outside doorways and listen to other people's conversations! Didn't your mother ever teach you that?" He laughed hysterically as he and his guards drew pistols from their jackets almost in unison.

"This is perfect!" Dexter shrieked. "All you've done is moved up my timetable." Dexter's men covered Pritchard and Chavez with their pistols. Good, I thought. They had forgotten about me for the moment.

"I think my report will read as follows," Dexter orated: "*Terry Riley, outspoken critic of Senator Pritchard, had become an obsessed stalker of the high-ranking politician and followed him to Mexico City. In a confused state, Riley shot the senator and his political ally, Mexican Governor Roberto Chavez. Hearing the shots, I entered the senatorial suite with guards just as Riley perpetrated the brutal crime. Having no other option, the guards shot the assailant, Mr. Riley, to death.*" Dexter then walked up to Pritchard, waving his gun in his face and said, "Ironic, don't you think, this being the Day of the Dead?"

LXV

Kate frantically searched the complex for any sign of help—anyone she might know or anyone at all who had power enough to stop whoever was about to commit a crime on my person. Peering through the floor-to-ceiling windows, she could see a large crowd gathering on the steps of the Senate. Everyone was looking up at something, but she couldn't see what. As she hurried by a window, Boomba suddenly rushed the window with hundreds of his people in tow. He was seconds too late to get her attention.

Sweat began to bead on Kate's forehead as she ran down the long circular hallways, each door either entering an empty suite or some pocket broom closet. *Presidential Suite*, one read, *Governor's Suite*, another. Still more numerous were doors to private bathrooms or just faux doors leading to nothing but electrical panels or security keyboards. She tried not to panic, to focus on her journalist's no-nonsense know-how. "Be methodical," she said to herself.

She had nearly run around the entire building when she saw Gutierrez flanked by a number of men in both dress suits and casual clothes. "Secretary Gutierrez!" Kate shouted, waving her hands in the air as she ran towards him. "I found him! I found Terry Riley, but there were these men dragging him away and I couldn't..."

Gutierrez grabbed her as she ran right into him. "We know, Kate," he said. "Ms. Walker, you stay behind the last man here, understand?" he then whispered as they made their way down the hall to where I was. The agents fanned out, taking forward or flanking positions, careful to step lightly and remain far enough from the doorway so as not to announce their presence.

One agent threw up his hand and made a fist. Everyone stopped. He quickly opened it, spreading his fingers wide, and the others agents took their positions in unison, drawing their weapons simultaneously.

Gutierrez looked overhead and side to side. He drew a small box in the air with both his index fingers, and the other agents nodded.

"What does that mean?" Kate asked quietly.

The young agent assigned to her answered back, "It's not the ideal scenario, Ma'am. We're in close quarters." She nodded her head then pulled back behind a small pillar as the agents prepared to raid the suite.

Suddenly, Kate remembered something and dug into her pants pocket. It was the cell phone I'd retrieved off Jones at the Amerimex plant. She knew that whoever was holding me hostage in that office was probably tied to the two assassins, and it gave her an idea.

She tapped the agent in front of her to get Gutierrez's attention. He did. Gutierrez froze the assault momentarily and scrambled back to Kate. "I've got an idea to distract them before you go in," she said in a commanding fashion. "Get your men ready."

Gutierrez nodded and hurried back to the others, whispering instructions to one agent, who sent it down the line. "Wait for my signal," was the last thing Gutierrez said as Kate punched the keypad on the cell phone.

LXVI

The tension was thick and hot in the senatorial suite, with Dexter poised to kill Pritchard, giving me and Chavez an iron-clad alibi in the process.

"Why, you ungrateful little bastard!" Pritchard bellowed.

Dexter gave his head a half-turn to look straight at one of his men and said calmly, "Shoot this redneck!"

As Dexter's henchman raised his gun to Pritchard's chest, Chavez jumped in to try and plead with him. "Stop! That is an order!" he shouted. The man hesitated just long enough for Chavez to think he'd had an effect. Suddenly, the cell phone in Dexter's vest pocket went off. *Ring!* It cut the silence like a bullet, startling everybody. Everybody but me, that is.

I saw my chance and I took it. With one step forward and with a quick move like I'd seen Ramos pull off, I kicked the gun out of the man's hand just as he fired. Chavez, who was standing in front of Pritchard, fell backwards, and the two of them both fell to the ground. Shit, now they've both been shot, I worried. The instant my foot hit the ground, I threw a right hook into the second henchman's throat, traumatizing his windpipe. He grasped his neck and gagged for air.

A bullet zinged past my ear as the other shooter picked up his weapon and drew down on me. But the shot had come from over my shoulder. It found its target, sending Dexter's thug flying against the back wall to crumple like a rag doll.

Federal agents poured into the suite and the melee began. They quickly took charge of the situation by standing over both men with weapons ready, just waiting for either of them to make that one stupid move that would prove the *coup de grac*e of the whole mess. Dexter was thrown to the ground and wrestled for his gun by four agents who didn't get a single speck of dirt on their perfectly tailored suits. After a moment, I was able to catch my breath.

As soon as the suite was secured, Gutierrez entered with Kate. The agents lifted Dexter to his feet, bending his arms back behind him for maximum control, as I made my way over to Pritchard and Chavez.

"You okay, Senator?" I said, this time actually meaning it. "Any holes?"

He was obviously shaken, but grasped me by my shoulder and said, "Son of a bitch, Riley, you saved my butt!"

Lying near us, Chavez began to moan. He'd taken a bullet in the bicep just as I kicked the gun; it had blown right through his muscle. It was bleeding like hell, but the artery was untouched.

"Bobby, you okay?" Pritchard yelled in his old friend's ear.

"I was shot in the arm, not in the ear!" Chavez cried back with painful laughter. "I'm okay. At least I think so!" It seemed like an odd reaction to me. A guy gets shot, just a hair from having his head blown off, and now he's laughing?

"What's so funny, Governor?" I said, pressing on his shoulder to stop the bleeding. I was getting pretty good at triage by now. Chavez looked up and smiled, saying, "This will get the sympathy vote and skyrocket my popularity percentage!"

Gutierrez and the federal agents flanked Dexter and the others as they marched through the lobby doors of the Senate. It was then I realized everyone inside the auditorium and outside on the streets had heard Dexter's entire confession. Every dignitary, every diplomat, every Mexican within earshot of the building on that most revered of holidays had heard it. Crowds had gathered as Boomba and hundreds of others lined the steps, waiting for us to come out. It looked like a volatile situation that could spark up and have people rioting in an instant. The crowd parted into two halves as we began to walk through it. I saw Boomba in the front near us, then, as he moved aside, I saw Ramos. He was smiling.

"You did it, Riley! Now the world will have to listen." Ramos beamed.

Suddenly, the crowd of people threw up their hands and cheered, "*Viva Mexico!*"

The federal agents led me and Kate to an unmarked car. Just as I was about to get in, I stopped. "Wait!" I yelled to the agents who were holding Dexter. I ran over and stared him down in front of everyone.

For a man of few words, the little prick just couldn't keep his mouth shut. "You've got nothing Riley! You're a hack! I've got Plausible Deniability on my side. I'll walk, you'll see. I'll never do a day in jail!" He sounded like a spoiled child throwing a tantrum. Who was he trying to convince, anyway?

He could have been right, but I was nonetheless going to get one last jab in—literally. I hauled off and smashed him in the stomach with a hard right. Only his captors kept him from dropping to the ground. The agents just smiled and looked the other way.

While Dexter remained doubled over from the blow, I snatched my gold pen from his front pocket and said, "Remember what you said, Asshole, 'To the victor go the spoils!'"

LXVII

A stretch limousine with diplomatic plates pulled up to the curb at the terminal of the Mexico City Airport. It was long and black and looked like it had been cleaned every day since it had come off the assembly line. The driver jumped from the front and opened the back door quickly, tipping his hat in the process. Kate exited first, then Gutierrez, and I followed behind. We stood outside the bustling terminal, hoping to avoid having to queue up in line.

Gutierrez extended his hand, took mine then placed his other hand on top in a firm grip. "You've done this country and your own a great service," he said seriously. "Your friends did not die in vain! I've just gotten word that Governor Chavez has agreed to sit down with the Zapatistas in Chiapas to enact a new Indian Rights amendment. You have my word we're taking all the appropriate steps to stop the killing and bring those responsible to justice."

I gave him a playful glare and said, "And you have my word we'll be checking your work!"

We all laughed, but it was a sad laugh. I knew we had done something good. A "mitzvah," the Jews call it. A good deed. Would it really amount to anything? Wasn't this kind of stuff going on everywhere around the world? In the grand scheme of things, did it really amount to a hill of beans? I didn't know.

"Miss Walker, what will you do now?" Gutierrez said as he shook Kate's hand with great respect.

She looked to me and said, "Well, we have a story to write!" I gave her an arch, questioning look, but broke into a smile just as Gutierrez stepped back into his limousine.

Behind ours, another limo pulled up. Pritchard hopped out and his staff rushed to flank him. He could hardly contain his enthusiasm as he ran up to us. An excited crowd of reporters waiting to ambush Pritchard inside the terminal was held back by security behind the glass doors.

"Terry, I've got a big hole to fill in my cabinet now," Pritchard said happily. "Ya ever think about write'n elsewhere, I could use a good P.R. man! Interested?"

I turned to Kate. She widened her eyes and bit her lip as if to say, "Don't do it."

"No thanks," I said. "Don't take this the wrong way, but nothing's changed between us. I still think you're crooked, and someday I'll prove it."

Pritchard just laughed like a good ol' country boy and slapped me on the back. "Friend or foe," he said, "you did save my life, and Dan Pritchard doesn't leave a debt unpaid!"

I couldn't believe this guy. What a cheesemeister. "Save it!" I laughed. "You've got a lot of explaining to do to Congress, and the media's gonna have a field day with this story. No spin doctor on earth will be able to keep that kind of heat off you!"

Undeterred, Pritchard just smiled as wide as a country mile and said, "Well, thank the good Lord the American public has a short attention span!" He turned, and his staff turned with him to head inside the terminal. The second before the doors opened to unleash the fray, he turned back to me and shouted, "You shoulda seen that son of a bitch Chavez. He nearly jumped off the operating table when the new opinion polls were released. He's a shoo-in for *Presidente* now!"

Reporters poured out of the terminal doors as they opened, surrounding Pritchard, swarming him, begging answers to the latest drama. He smiled diplomatically and cut through the deluge, answering each and every question with just enough spin to not answer any of them.

I just shook my head, half in disgust and half in admiration of a man like that being able to hold such a high office.

"*Señor* Riley?" a messenger called to me from the terminal. I nodded as he ran up and handed me a package. "This is for you!" I reached into my pocket, but before I could tip him, he was gone.

I opened the small box to see a folded pink piece of paper. "What's this?" I said to Kate curiously. I picked the paper out of the box, unfolded it and read the note: *You wouldn't want to leave Mexico without this!* It was the custody form that had inextricably linked Ramos to me while I was in Mexico. I read further: *Consider it a souvenir. It's a bail receipt, anyway, not a custody form. You were free to leave Mexico anytime you wanted. But we're glad you stayed. Vaya con Dios, Amigo!*

LXVIII

High above the Yucatan Peninsula and heading out over the Caribbean Sea, I was enjoying the first-class cabin and all its accommodations. I leaned back into the soft, crushed leather seat and sipped coffee as Kate typed away on her laptop next to me. I'd lost my taste for alcohol along with other vices on this trip. I took a deep breath and sighed out the stress. I kicked off my shoes, stretched my legs then gave Kate the once-over with my peripheral vision, thinking, I might hang with this girl for a while.

A few rows up, Pritchard leaned into the aisle, looking back at me. He raised a brimming flute of champagne, winked and gave me a "thumbs-up." Man, this guy was working way too hard to bury the past. I took out my gold pen and tapped it on the reporter's notepad that was sitting on the tray table next to my single-serving meal.

I had an itch and began scratching my arm. It was really bugging the hell out of me so I unbuttoned my sleeve and rolled it up to my elbow. "Ouch!" I whimpered as I peeled the duct tape off my forearm. I had forgotten all about my secret weapon: the microcassette recorder. I had adhered it to my arm under my sleeve in order to get everything on tape. That was one of the smartest things I'd ever done. Dexter wasn't getting out of this one, and I was going to make sure that it would be my retirement policy.

Pulling out a small wire near the handset, I shoved the clear plastic earpiece into my ear, rewound the tape and pushed the play button. I smiled with immense satisfaction as everything that Dexter had said in that senate suite played back to me as clear as a bell. Man, my only worry at that point was that the plane would go down.

LXIX

I lay on my couch with my feet up, sleeping for the first time since I could remember. The *Post* had decided to spring for a lot of amenities, but none more important than a couple of maids and a cleaning crew. Even though my apartment looked like new again, however, I was more concerned with finishing the erotic dream I was having.

I had left the plasma on Fox News, which was broadcasting my story every half-hour, while simultaneously scrolling the story at the bottom of the screen. I had seen all the coverage already—hell, I had lived through it. There was no need to rehash it over and over again. I was getting my first quality shut-eye and wasn't going to let anything interrupt it.

Had I been more alert, or paranoid like I was in the old days, I would have awakened to see the shadowy figure creep in through my apartment door. The stranger slowly followed the hallway into the living room where I was sleeping. I couldn't sense another's presence; my instincts had dulled since Mexico and it wasn't until I felt something land on my head that I was remotely concerned.

Thwap. Thwap. Slowly, I awoke to hear a snapping noise. I opened one eye and looked up to see the *Washington Post* headline: *THE EIGHTH PLAGUE—MEXICO'S DEADLY SECRET.*

The paper neared my face as a finger came from around the side and pointed to the byline: *by Terry Riley & Kate Walker.* I reached up to lower the paper as Kate appeared above me. She smiled freely, with a look of love in her eyes. "You gave me a byline, Sweetie?" she cooed.

I took the paper from her and folded it neatly, saying, "You can't be a rookie all your life. Now the real work begins!"

She snatched the paper out of my hands, threw it to the floor and jumped on top of me. I had to hand it to her, the girl knew how to kiss. I didn't need a road map, either. I picked her up and carried her into my bedroom, then slammed the door behind me with one good back-kick.

EPILOGUE

Ding. The thick double doors of the elevator opened quickly as the muted sound of the bell announced the penthouse floor's latest arrival. Senator Pritchard stepped into the dimly lit hallway, turned, then marched down the length of the corridor toward the suite at the end.

He approached two oak doors that ran from floor to ceiling and didn't slow down as he pushed through them, bursting into the room confidently, without hesitation. In the half-light, he made out an oval conference table of polished mahogany and teak, large enough to seat forty or fifty large men, yet subtle, not ostentatious.

High-back leather chairs spaced a foot or so apart from each other encircled the table. Every seat was filled, Pritchard could see by the light of the single low-voltage lamp that hung above each one. Cigar and cigarette smoke was so dense in the enormous room that every person's face was obscured, only to be discerned if they leaned forward toward the center of the table, perhaps to reach for one of the ashtrays that crowded the surface.

A single chair sat empty at the head of the table. Pritchard walked directly to it. An obscured figure of a man grabbed both sides of the chair and pulled it back just as Pritchard walked up. He waited for

Pritchard to stop and begin to sit before pushing the chair gracefully in to meet the senator's relaxing rear end at just the right moment.

Out of the darkness to the right of Pritchard, a long cigar slowly appeared. It had already been trimmed and was nearly brought to Pritchard's mouth before he grabbed it and put it between his teeth. A flame was produced out of the darkness from the other side and Pritchard rolled the fat, tightly packed Cohiba over and over until the tip glowed red. Pritchard nodded then waved the man away. His cigar smoke lofted upward with that of the others', adding to the impenetrable atmosphere.

Pritchard began to speak to the many faceless cohorts and subjugates at the table, yet this time, his voice had no trace of an accent, no good ol' boy, shit-kickin', down-home character to it. He now spoke in a clean, eerie, almost sterile, neutral American voice.

"Gentlemen, I know you are all concerned with the events that have recently transpired in Mexico, but I assure you everything is under control," Pritchard announced calmly.

At the opposite end of the table, a man half-appeared under the light and coldly replied, "You know we don't like publicity, Senator. How can you guarantee our investments have not been compromised?" It was an ominous, booming voice that commanded respect, like that of a god or the Wizard of Oz.

Pritchard merely leaned back in his leather chair, unconcerned. He took a long drag off his cigar, held it in his lungs for a moment then blew the thick smoke skyward.

Taking a deep breath, he continued, "General Cortes has been tried and convicted of mass genocide, posthumously, of course, and Dexter Grace, my former aide, is about to have a tragic and untimely accident on his way to the Grand Jury arraignment. He was the last link!" Signaling one of his silent, shadowy assistants to dim the lights, Pritchard pushed a button on the table before him that parted the wall behind him to reveal a large screen. "Now let me show you what we'll be making available to those who are interested in our services," the senator said as the lights went low and the screen lit up with his latest P.R. promo:

Above the tree line, high on a snowy mountain peak, a cold stream of water flows down to the valley below. The mountains, trees and nature here are beautiful, and the air is clean. White water rapids flow into babbling brooks and streams that meander into a large reservoir and finally to the water's ultimate destination: a treatment facility that is constantly busy purifying it for mass consumption...

Pritchard's voice reverberates over the image:

"Our final analysis shows the formula to be perfected...."

Water flows into pipes that lead into a major metropolitan area. Through the city. Into households. And finally through kitchen faucets and taps.

A large lake sits near a school and a community playground. Children play there, swinging on swing sets, splashing in the cool water.

Pritchard's voiceover continues:

"We're now ready for worldwide distribution...."

A small Mexican boy takes a drink from a public water fountain, slurping up as much as he can before taking a breath. After drinking as much water as he can swallow, he runs back to a baseball diamond where a little league baseball game is in progress.

The diamond is adjacent to beautifully groomed lawns, public parks, neighborhood homes, mountains. It's the city of Los Angeles, where the Hollywood Sign looms high above its inhabitants...

The sound of Pritchard's ominous and sterile voice, now live again, sliced cleanly and swiftly into his cronies' greedy heads as the lights went back up and the image of the metropolitan city faded to black.

"As of this morning," he announced with tidy smugness, "the *Times* has me leading in the polls by a thirteen-percent margin, and as soon as I'm sworn in as President, you can consider the whole little Mexican fiasco officially dead and buried!"

About the Author:

Kyle Fitzharris worked intelligence under Non Official Cover (NOC) in Central America and Mexico, at one point leading a task force of eight federal agencies. His efforts helped to indict international conspirators responsible for drug smuggling, money laundering, murder-for-hire, and terrorist funding. He currently resides in Westlake Village, California.

Printed in the United States
135950LV00004B/3/P